PENGUIN BOOKS

HEY, COWBOY, WANNA GET LUCKY?

Baxter Black, whose eleven volumes of self-published cowboy poetry are a phenomenon, is a regular commentator on National Public Radio and writes a weekly column, "On the Edge of Common Sense," which currently appears in over one hundred publications. This is his first novel.

Other Books by Baxter Black

The Cowboy and His Dog
A Rider, A Roper, and a Heck'uva Windmill Man
On the Edge of Common Sense, The Best So Far
Doc, While Yer Here
Coyote Cowboy Poetry
Buckaroo History
Croutons on a Cow Pie
The Buckskin Mare
Cowboy Standard Time
Croutons on a Cow Pie, Volume II
Dunny and the Duck

Hey, Cowboy, Wanna Get Lucky?

Baxter Black

PENGUIN BOOKS

PENGUIN BOOKS
Published by the Penguin Group
Penguin Books USA Inc., 375 Hudson Street, New York, New York 10014, U.S.A.
Penguin Books Ltd, 27 Wrights Lane, London W8 5TZ, England
Penguin Books Australia Ltd, Ringwood, Victoria, Australia
Penguin Books Canada Ltd, 10 Alcorn Avenue, Toronto, Ontario, Canada M4V 3B2
Penguin Books (N.Z.) Ltd, 182–190 Wairau Road, Auckland 10, New Zealand

Penguin Books Ltd, Registered Offices: Harmondsworth, Middlesex, England

First published in the United States of America by Crown Publishers, Inc., 1994
Reprinted by arrangement with Crown Publishers, Inc.
Published in Penguin Books 1995

1 3 5 7 9 10 8 6 4 2

PUBLISHER'S NOTE
This is a work of fiction. Names, characters, places, and incidents either are the product of the author's imagination or are used fictitiously, and any resemblance to actual persons, living or dead, events, or locales is entirely coincidental.

THE LIBRARY OF CONGRESS HAS CATALOGUED THE HARDCOVER AS FOLLOWS:
Black, Baxter,
Hey, Cowboy, wanna get lucky?/Baxter Black. — 1st ed.
p. cm.
1. Cowboys—West (U.S.)—Fiction. 2. Rodeos—West (U.S.)—Fiction. I. Title.
PS3552.L288H4 1994
813′.54—dc20 93-40603
ISBN 0-517-59377-7 (hc.)
ISBN 0 14 02.5093 X (pbk.)

Printed in the United States of America
Set in Century Expanded

Dedicated to Harley May,
World Champion Steer Wrestler of 1952, 1956 and 1965, and
president of the Rodeo Cowboys Association 1957–1960.

When Baxter asked Harley how today's rodeo
cowboys differed from rodeo cowboys in his day,
Harley replied wistfully,
"Nobody robs a bank anymore."

LEGACY OF THE RODEO MAN

There's a hundred years of history and a hundred before that
All gathered in the thinkin' goin' on beneath his hat.
And back behind his eyeballs and pumpin' through his veins
Is the ghost of every cowboy that ever held the reins.

Every coil in his lasso's been thrown a million times
His quiet concentration's been distilled through ancient minds.
It's evolution workin' when the silver scratches hide
And a ghostly cowboy chorus fills his head and says, "Let's ride."

The famous and the rowdy, the savage and the sane
The bluebloods and the hotbloods and the corriente strain
All knew his mother's mothers or was his daddy's kin
'Til he's nearly purely cowboy, born to ride and bred to win.

He's got Buffalo Bill Cody and Goodnight's jigger boss
And all the brave blue soldiers that General Custer lost
The ghost of Pancho Villa, Sittin' Bull and Jessie James
All gathered by his campfire keepin' score and takin' names.

There's every Royal Mountie that ever got his man
And every day-work cowboy that ever made a hand
Each man that's rode before him, yup, every mother's son
Is in his corner, rootin', when he nods to make his run.

Freckles Brown might pull his bull rope, Casey Tibbs might jerk the flank,
Bill Pickett might be hazin' when he starts to turn the crank
Plus Remington and Russell lookin' down his buckhorn sight
All watchin' through the window of this cowboy's eyes tonight.

And standin' in the catch pen or in chute number nine
Is the offspring of a mountain that's come down from olden time
A volcano waitin' quiet, 'til they climb upon his back
Rumblin' like the engine of a freight train on the track.

A cross between a she bear and a bad four wheel drive
With the fury of an eagle when it makes a power dive
A snake who's lost its caution or a badger gone berserk
He's a screamin', stompin', clawin', rabid, mad dog piece o' work.

From the rollers in his nostrils to the foam upon his lips
From the hooves as hard as granite to the horns with dagger tips
From the flat black starin' shark's eye that's the mirror of his soul

Shines the challenge to each cowboy like the devil callin' roll.

In the seconds that tick slowly 'til he climbs upon his back
Each rider faces down the fear that makes his mouth go slack
And cuts his guts to ribbons and gives his tongue a coat
He swallows back the panic gorge that's risin' in his throat.

The smell of hot blue copper fills the air around his head
Then a single, solid, shiver shakes away the doubt and dread
The cold flame burns within him 'til his skin's as cold as ice
And the dues he paid to get here are worth every sacrifice

All the miles spent sleepy drivin', all the money down the drain
All the "if I's" and the "nearly's," all the bandages and pain
All the female tears left dryin', all the fever and the fight
Are just a small downpayment on the ride he makes tonight.

And his pardner in this madness that the cowboys call a game
Is a ton of buckin' thunder bent on provin' why he came
But the cowboy never wavers he intends to do his best
And of that widow maker he expects of him no less.

There's a solemn silent moment that every rider knows
When time stops on a heartbeat like the earth itself was froze
Then all the ancient instinct fills the space between his ears
'Til the whispers of his phantoms are the only thing he hears

When you get down to the cuttin' and the leather touches hide

And there's nothin' left to think about, he nods and says,
"Outside!"
Then frozen for an instant against the open gate
Is hist'ry turned to flesh and blood, a warrior incarnate.

And while they pose like statues in that flicker of an eye
There's somethin' almost sacred, you can see it if you try.
It's guts and love and glory—one mortal's chance at fame
His legacy is rodeo and cowboy is his name.

"Turn 'im out."

Hey, Cowboy, Wanna Get Lucky?

This is the tale of two rodeo cowboys named Lick and Cody. The story might just as well have been about two baseball players named Duke and Pee Wee, two country singers named George and Tammy, or the pros from Dover. But I, the author, am most familiar with the sport of rodeo and have been to the towns and cities where rodeo cowboys ply their trade.

In their quest to qualify for the National Finals (the Superbowl of rodeo), thus furnishing a plot, Lick and Cody expose themselves to considerable adventure and philosophical examination.

To those of you who follow rodeo: you will recognize the scenery and the characters, both quad- and bi-pedal. If this book is your first trip "back of the chutes," I offer this brief introductory explanation of the sport. Rodeo is divided into timed events (roping, bulldogging and barrel racing) and roughstock events (bareback bronc riding, saddle bronc riding and bull riding).

Our two cowboys compete in the roughstock events, specializing in the bull riding. The bulls and broncs are as varied in their personality and athletic ability as the cowboys who try to ride them. It is also important to remember that as hard as the bull and the rider compete against each other, neither would have a job without the other. It is a weird sort of partnership fraught with mutual antagonism and mutual respect.

Professional rodeo has evolved as a sport. Today the National Finals takes place in Las Vegas, Nevada. The amount of money won by contestants has grown significantly over the years. Although there are still many "characters" competing, the contestants are regarded as professional athletes.

From 1965 to 1984, the National Finals Rodeo was held in Oklahoma City. It was a golden time when rodeo was populated with colorful, flamboyant, hard ridin', hard playin' riders of the purple sage. My story is set near the end of this time period when the contestants, though professionals, were still thought of as cowboys.

As to the telling of this tale, it is the prerogative of an author to interrupt a story's narrative now and then. True, the good authors never exercise this cheesy little device, but they often wish they had. All they need is nerve.

I interrupt when I feel a rescue is necessary. A rescue of you, or Lick and Cody, or myself. I like to think one of us gets a welcome respite this way.

I invite you to ride along with me. I promise you a modest smattering of sex, violence, intrigue and the occasional philosophical observation.

We shall experience, in addition to a walk on the wacko and wild side of rodeo, these universal phenomena:

The significance of the slow dance
The misconception that it is easy to be irresponsible
Equal opportunity highwaymen
Fear
The existence of second string guardian angels
Doubt
Camels, cowboys, pool players, buckaroos and bigots
The color purple
Love
Interspecies marriage as an option
And moonlight

1

June 24
Lehi, Utah

The gate blew open like the lid comin' off a boxcar full'a dynamite! Like a lateral from the Bionic Man! Like straddlin' the *Hindenberg* and strikin' a match!

It's hard to believe a creature that weighed eighteen hundred and fifty pounds could duck and dive like a point guard for the Boston Celtics. His feet left tracks the size of a human face and pounded quarter moons into the dirt. As he spun in front of the chute, he kicked so high a freeze-frame showed him standin' on his head! He demanded attention like a runaway truck on a 7 percent grade! He was big and sleek and fast and all business!

Then he faked to the left and set-shot his rider from the three-point line! Cody Wing, bull rider, hit the ground like a bag of loose salt! His lights went out. It was dark inside his brain. Little paramedic neurons groped for the fuse box. Finally tiny pinholes brightened and began to flicker on the backside of his eyelids. Far off a noise tinkled at the edge of his hearing.

His eyelid fluttered, then opened. His pupil slid into sight. The sounds of concern began to piece themselves into recognizable words:

". . . ambulance. Good thinking . . ."

"Look, he's comin' around!"

"Cody, can you hear me? Are you all right?"

Miming a tropical fish, Cody replied, "Spand . . . stpand . . . sisspand . . ."

"Spam?"

"Sisstand . . ."

"Stand? What is it, Cody? Talk slow!"

"Yer sisstanding on my hand!"

"Oh! Yeah, sorry. Here, see if you can git up."

Lick gently hefted Cody to his feet. "I think he's okay, boys. I'll take care of him."

"A no-score for Cody Wing! All that cowboy gets is your applause!" The announcer summed up Cody's rodeo career.

The two walked back behind the buckin' chutes. Lick supported his partner as they slogged through the heavy arena dirt. The bull riding continued and the crowd roared on. Lick gathered up the tools of their trade and they headed for the pickup.

"My head hurts," observed Cody, palpating his temples like a ripe avocado.

"No wonder. Looked like he conked you good. You were out for awhile. You okay?"

"Dizzy is all, but I reckon I'll git over it. Did I make the buzzer?"

"Not quite. Close though," answered Lick.

"What now?" asked Cody.

"The dance, I guess."

Cody and Lick were traveling companions, confidants, soul brothers and close as a pair of dice in a crapshooter's hand. They both wrote "rodeo cowboy" under "Occupation" on their tax returns. They made good traveling partners despite their obvious differences. For starters they resembled each other the way a broken gate resembles a bowling ball. Cody was certainly the handsomer of the two. At 6'0", he was tall for a roughstock rider. Had he led a normal life he would have weighed 185. As it was, he was fifteen pounds underweight. He had light brown hair, was clean-cut and clean-shaven. Lick, at 5'9", weighed a solid 160. He wore a size nine boot, had black shaggy hair and a thick black mustache. You only knew he was smiling by his eyes. He carried the coloring of his Spanish grandfather.

They parked outside the Lehi Legion Hall. Smokey and the Orem Ramblers were bangin' through their version of "Good Hearted Woman." The thumping bass carried out into the street.

Cody and Lick milled around in the parking lot for twenty minutes, trying to devise some clever way to sneak into the dance. The lady at the door finally came over and explained to them that if they were contestants, they could get in free. They had to leave their beer outside.

Like two hoot owls, they entered the henhouse.

Cody stood to the side and Lick dove into the fray. Cody waited. A lion on the edge of the savannah. What was not apparent to the King of the Jungle was that the gazelles had already set out their decoys. They watched from their cowboy blind as Cody sniffed the air. It wouldn't take long.

Small town rodeos have small town dances. They are attended by small town girls. Small town girls like to be around chivalrous knights of the rope and the range. Snuff-dippin' dragon fighters engaged in that primitive ritual of impressing the female of the species. The smaller the town, the further a knight can be from the Round Table. Cody was a congressman's salary away from the National Finals!

He circled and stepped up to Kim. Kim was ready. One should never assume that small town girls are naive. They have watched the courtship protocol among dogs, dairy cows and ruffed grouse. They have seen a wrecker back up to a disabled Ford Fairlane. They've been trolling all their lives. They know how to set a hook.

"Like to dance?" asked Cody.

"Umm . . ." Kim said, waiting to hear what the next song would be. She knew a fast dance would put her at a disadvantage in employing her powers. A slow one, on the other hand, would allow her to evaluate the prey's potential.

So much depends on the first turn around the floor. It is on this initial exploratory coupling that the evolutionary instincts passed up through eons of amino acid bonding, virus replicating, fish spawning, dinosaur bugling, orangutan flashing, Neanderthal snorting and ragweed pollination all come to a blinding seductive pinnacle . . . THE SLOW DANCE!

The Ramblers launched into "Please Release Me."

Kim breathed a sigh of relief. Cody put his right arm around her waist, assuming the Arthur Murray stance. She quickly canceled the three-inch rule. She lay her head on his shoulder.

"Man, you sure . . ." He started to say "smell good" but thought better of it and finished ". . . dance well." Of course she smelled good! She did it on purpose! Her perfume was strong enough to drive a hyena off a bucket of baboon livers! Her perfume was overpowering. It was deliberate, and necessary in the case of cowboys. Delicate fragrances don't hold up well in competition with horse sweat and two-day-old beer.

Cody squeezed her a little tighter. "Good band," he said as he established contact with the positive and negative poles of her estrogen battery.

"Yes," she replied, and began charging.

They danced three more dances, then walked outside. It was cool after the steamy, rambunctious dance floor.

"So," she asked, "were you up tonight?"

"Yup. Didn't do too well."

"You weren't that guy that got knocked out, were you?"

"That's me, Cody Wing, fall guy."

Cody had started this rodeo season with less enthusiasm than any of the years before. His roots, which went deep, were startin' to pull. He was thinkin' of home more often. He was only twenty-eight, but he'd been on the road nearly ten years and never come close to qualifying for the National Finals. This year held no greater promise.

"Where ya go from here?" she asked.

"Blackfoot. I'm up Friday night. Say, would you like a beer?"

"No. Thanks, I don't drink. LDS, ya know, Mormon," she explained. "But I wouldn't mind another dance, though."

They reentered the melee, danced a couple more dances, then walked back outside. Cody kissed her. She kissed him back. They must have found some common ground because they were soon sitting in the front seat of Cody's pickup steaming up the windows.

Just as the heavy petting was about to cross that line between a misdemeanor and a felony, Lick opened the door with a jerk! He jumped in on the passenger side!

"Cody, we gotta go! Howdy, ma'am. I mean right now!" He looked back over his shoulder. "Start the truck! Go!"

Cody cranked the engine and jammed it into gear, whacking Kim's knee! She groaned. "Sorry," he said.

Just as Cody popped the clutch, his door jerked open! A hand reached in and grabbed his collar! Lick reached across Kim and tried to straighten the steering wheel. Not easy, since Cody was holding on to it with a deadman's grip while the attacker was trying to pull him through the open door!

Lick climbed over Kim and got one arm around Cody's waist and the other around his neck. His tug-of-war opponent was now braced against the outside of the door frame with his boots and pulling Cody's arm out of its socket! He leaned back like a crewman on a sloop!

The pickup was chugging through the gravel parking lot in low gear.

"Drive!" commanded Lick to Kim, who now lay under him with one foot on the floor and the other doubled up against the passenger door.

She reached up blindly and grasped the wheel.

"Right! To the right!" he barked.

Kim got her other hand to the wheel and pulled down with all her might. The truck made a slow tow barge correction clockwise. It was enough to miss a horse trailer but she couldn't hold it against the combined weight of Cody and his two-hundred-pound appendage. They jerked it back to the left!

Lick had locked his leg around the gearshift and was trying to stick his thumb in the attacker's eye. Unable to reach it without losing his hold on Cody, he threw a week's accumulation of junk food wrappers he found on the dash at the clinging primate. The pickup continued its slow grind up on the Legion Hall lawn.

They circled the flagpole and headed back toward the building.

Kim felt somethin' roll across the floorboard and hit her foot. She grabbed at it. Clutching it in both hands, she got the top off a plastic quart container of motor oil.

From her vantage point, she could only feel and hear the scuffle. Lick was takin' pokes at the orangutan with his free right hand. Kim jammed the quart of oil up between Lick and Cody and tipped it over the back of Cody's head.

It ran down his neck, his shirt and his close company. Lick got a mouthful. It covered the bad guy's hands and went up his sleeves. His grip slipped. He slid to Cody's elbow. The pickup hit the curb and the antagonist looked briefly as a possum would look just before you hit him with a car. He disappeared like a smoke jumper.

Something that sounded like a full beer can hit the roof of their camper shell.

They got Cody loaded and his door shut. The pickup swerved out of the parking lot and through the quiet neighborhood surrounding it. Five blocks away they pulled over. The cab smelled like a drag race.

They debouched onto the sidewalk a block from Main Street.

Oil covered their faces and hair and shirts. It was wicking itself to every porous nook and cranny.

"Any chance we could clean up at your place?" Lick asked Kim politely.

She studied them. They reminded her of a picture she'd seen in *National Geographic* of two sea gulls washed ashore after an oil spill.

"None," she said, and walked off down the sidewalk.

Cody look at Lick in the glow of a street lamp.

"Jeez," asked Cody, "what happened to your hat?"

"I was tryin' to help this lady tuck in her shirttail when this big bruiser walked up behind me and pulled my hat down over my eyes! 'Bout cut off my ear! I turned around and took a swing at him, 'course I was blind, and hit this woman's arm who was dancin' by an' her hand come out and whacked that big sucker flat across the face. Well, he ducked down, just as I was comin' up pullin' off my hat, and I caught him full fist in the nose! Sounded awful! Sorta like a can bein' crinkled. He was bleedin' all over and blowin' froth . . . by then his sixteen brothers had showed up and—" Lick sighed and wiped a drop of 10W30 off his chin. "Anyway, here I am."

2

Friday Night, June 25
Blackfoot, Idaho

Cody was up in the bareback riding tonight. Lick was helpin' him set his riggin'. Lick listened as the loudspeaker played the final strains of "Barebackers Get Ready," a.k.a. our national anthem. As the crowd's cheering waned, the announcer took up the baton. "Ladies and gentlemen, thank you and be seated! Those of us here in the booth, behind the chutes and in the arena welcome you to one of America's oldest traditions! The wildest, woolliest, fastest, greatest show on earth! Professional rodeo!

"Sit on the edge of your seats for the next two hours and hang and rattle with the best cowboys! The prettiest cowgirls! And the toughest stock from the purple mountains' majesty to the shores of Tripoli!" (He spoke only in exclamation points!)

"In the spirit of Buffalo Bill Cody, Casey Tibbs and John Wayne ... [not to mention Elmer Gantry, Winston Churchill and P. T. Barnum]!" The announcer paused dramatically. He lowered his voice. "Dear Lord, we ask that you watch over these daring young men and women as they pit themselves in clean competition and reverent sportsmanship against some of your finest workmanship. May their hearts rise to the challenge and may they go home safely. Amen.

"Ladies and gentlemen, little buckaroos and cowgirls, anytime you see anything you like, put your hands together, stomp your feet and yahoo! Speaking of which, how 'bout one more big round of applause for the rodeo board, all the riding clubs, princesses and queens in the grand entry tonight! Weren't they great! Great job, men! My hat's off to you!"

This man was slicker than silk pajamas on a snake! He was rodeo's answer to exploding cake and fluorescent paint! To the ultimate game show host! To the Vatican in party hats! He was young, clever, witty, handsome and smooth. The raspberry-flavored Chap Stick melted off a buckle bunny's lips when she spoke his name . . . Emerald Dune, Rodeo Announcer!

Emerald had style, pizzazz, money, adoration, a long-suffering wife in Santa Fe, a photographic memory and a persistent case of gnawed-to-the-quick fingernails. Emerald was an evangelist. He would have been a superb disc jockey, vacuum cleaner salesman, Baptist preacher, con man, politician or panhandler, but he was a spectacular rodeo announcer!

However, all of Emerald's hypnotic mesmerizing was going over Cody's head. He was in his own small world "psychin' up." He was total concentration, oblivious to the pageantry and preaching.

Emerald would put down the microphone in two hours, three hundred dollars richer. The stock contractor would feed and bed his livestock, then go have a nice combination plate at the Hong Kong Cafe and Bowling Alley. The crowd would drive through the traffic, homeward bound, satisfied that they had spent their eight dollars wisely.

Cody might spend the night in Intensive Care with a concussion or a ruptured spleen. He might wake up tomorrow with a cast on his arm or his back in traction. There was also a fair-to-middlin' chance that due to a lost entry fee, his bankroll would be fifty dollars lighter by ten P.M.!

Inside Cody's body anticipation was stirring the adrenaline. The nerve synapses fire, reload and fire again like the two of clubs clothespinned to a bicycle spoke! The little pili muscles hiding in the follicles have a gang erection and the hairs on the back of his neck snap smartly to attention! Skin prickles, nose tickles, spurs jingle, toes tingle!

Lickity helped Cody down on his bronc. They pounded, mashed and pulled his gloved, rosined left hand through the suitcase handle on the bareback riggin'.

"Out of chute number four, a veteran professional cowboy from Ten Sleep, Wyoming . . . Cody Wing, on the Maid Brothers' fine buckin' horse Velvet Try Me! Folks, put your hands together for this top cowboy. You're gonna love . . ."

Cody dropped down on Velvet Try Me. She was developing a fine reputation as a pounder of would-be bareback riders. Lick was standing on the decking behind the chute. He had a loose grip on the back of Cody's belt. It was Cody's umbilicus to Earth. A safety line in case the horse did something in the chute that wasn't standard operating procedure. Like tryin' to climb over the top or goin' down on her knees and shakin' like a wet dog! Next to Lick, one of the chute hands was holding the tail of the flank strap.

Cody scooted up on the riggin', raised his boot heels above the mare's shoulders, screwed down his hat and spit out his chew. He went through his mental checklist: Rare back, point yer toes, squeeze the handle. He nodded his head. The gate swung open.

Velvet Try Me rainbowed out of chute number four! Cody marked her out and hung the steel to'er like the push rods on a locomotive! Try Me jumped the track! She slid, slipped and rolled around inside her skin! She punched holes in the arena dirt!

Cody rocked, she fired! She bucked, he pulled! Balance is critical in bareback ridin'. Not much more than a face card worth of contact exists between horse and rider. With your feet up in the air swingin' free, and you rared back so far your head can touch the horse's rump, it's a precarious perch!

It takes balance. Balance and power.

Power is essential in bareback riding. The hand's grip in the riggin'. Only the arm to keep your seat under your hand. The shoulder absorbing the jerk. Meeting a bareback rider is like shaking hands with a marble statue.

Velvet Try Me was testing Cody's salt.

Somewhere in the last two seconds of the eight-second ride, Cody reached his limit. Everything in his firebox . . . experience, intuition, talent and training . . . were at full throttle and blowin' blue smoke! The enraptured crowd was sitting on Cody's shoulder makin' the ride with him. It was then, over the din of twenty-five hundred rabid fans, that Cody reached down inside himself. He whispered, "Yer mine . . ."

The hair stood up on the crowd's collective neck. The buckin' horse went down!

From the grandstand it looked like Cody's head hit the ground! His legs pistoned! The horse exploded! She climbed outta the hole with Cody stuck to'er like a remora on a shark's back!

Cody was makin' a ride! You couldn't have cut him loose with a laser torch! The whistle blew. The crowd went wild!

Cody quit spurrin' and Try Me broke into a hard gallop. They were racing around the arena counterclockwise. Gallant Fox heading into the stretch.

The pickup men were riding like demons to catch the pair! One finally managed to get close enough to tempt Cody. Cody loosed his grip in the riggin' and leaned to the left to grab the pickup man's waist.

Velvet Try Me still had a trick up her sleeve. At the moment she felt Cody's balance shift, the instant he was committed, she slammed on the brakes and sidestepped to starboard! The pickup man and his horse shot on by. Cody saw the rump glide out from under his nose. He poised for a split second, extended in midair, then flew crablike into the dirt!

He spit dirt and rose to thunderous applause!

Cody tipped his hat, like it was just another day's work. But if you'd touched him at that moment it would have been like layin' your hand on an electric motor. He was hummin'!

Cody had ridden Try Me with all he had left . . . will. Will, want to, grit, gumption, whatever it is that allows housewives to lift cars off babies and Samsons to pull down temples.

The crowd waited nervously for the score to be posted. They were nervous because of a loose brick in the facade of rodeo rules which says: hard-to-ride horses don't always score the highest. Most in the grandstands that night would have been disgruntled but not surprised if Cody's ride had scored out of the money. Style often counts more than difficulty.

But rodeo is not like making a centerpiece out of angel hair and glitter. We're talkin' about a horse that can buck you off and a cowboy that claims she can't. That's how rodeo began and tonight the judges didn't forget it.

Cody had reached the buckin' chutes when Emerald Dune announced the score. Cody and his pardner, Velvet Try Me, scored an 82 . . . good enough for top money that night.

They deserved it.

3

Saturday Night, June 26
Blackfoot, Idaho

The following night, the last performance of the rodeo, our boys' luck continued. Lick drew a good bull and rode him to second place. Cody's score on Try Me had stood up to the competition and split top money. At most rodeos an 82 score would have been enough to win some money, though the roughstock events scoring system is subjective. Vague guidelines in "how they buck": hard, smooth or quick, etc., and "how they rode": spurring action, grace and timing, etc., are used by the two judges. These two judges stand on the arena floor, one on each side of the chute. There are a few nonnegotiable rules, including marking the horse out, not touching the animal with the free hand, proper attire (hat, long-sleeve shirt and boots), and the eight-second time limit. But no one counts the number of spur strokes, bull spins, bucks or yahoos!

These two judges are each allowed to give up to 25 points for the animal's performance and up to 25 points for the cowboy's effort. So it is theoretically possible to get a 100 mark. In real life, however, any score in the 80s is considered very good, but there are rodeos where a 70s score will win.

The score depends on the stock, the cowboys, the competition, the arena, the weather and the judges' dispositions on any given night. However, it would be fair to say that rodeo judges are chintzy with their precious numbers regardless of their mood, as witnessed by the fact that in all the history of professional rodeo, the number of perfect scores could be counted on a cloven hoof.

Lick and Cody, along with a platoon of cowboys, potato pickers and miners, went into town after the show to celebrate.

"By gosh, Lickity, you really done good tonight!" Cody smiled over his third beer. He truly relished his friend's success. "An eighty-five! Terrific!"

"Ya didn't do bad yer ownself," said Lick. "Tough horse. I don't believe the average feller would'a stayed on!" Cody modestly pooh-poohed the compliment, though he was deeply pleased.

"Yeah," Lick continued, lifting his glass of beer and studying the neon reflection in the bubbles. "I got to the inside on the first spin and he jes' kept goin'. Sure was smooth. Pinkeye gave me the book on him and he did just what he said he would."

"Good job, Lick! And you, too, Cody," congratulated LoBall McKinney. "Lemme buy you cowboys another!"

This waddie bonhommie was takin' place at the Don't Lie to Her, Just Take the Fifth Amendment Bar.

"Lookie there, Lick. Isn't that . . . ?" Cody hesitated. Lick, who was jovially drunk, looked over his shoulder. Headin' toward him like a torpedo in a ten-foot stock tank was what, by any other name, would still be a bombshell!

Whoa! Baxter, here! Baxter Black, author of this careening collection of words. As you can see, we're only into the third chapter and our two heroes are about to tangle with the opposite sex . . . again. Didn't I promise you sex, violence and intrigue? But I hasten to assure you—it is not gratuitous. When you cowboy for a livin' and you're a normal thirty-year-old male, rodeo and women figure heavily in your daily meditation.

Arco Peacock had poured her 130 pounds into a size six dress! It was shiny red and seemed to run out of material three-fourths of the way up! She held a master's degree in plant genetics, but that would not have been your first guess if clothing had been your only guide. Even she conceded she dressed, as songwriter Chris Wall would say, "just a tad on the trashy side"! However, she was without guile and her good nature was genuine.

Lick took in her blond mane, dazzling smile and almost invisible shoulder straps. He swiveled on the bar stool to greet her.

"Bob! It's good to see ya!" She beamed as she brushed by Lick to greet the man at the bar standing behind Cody.

Lick blushed to himself. Cody, embarrassed for his friend, attempted comfort by saying, "Well, you haven't seen her for a while. Maybe she's not wearing her contacts."

As if on cue Arco touched Cody's elbow. "Cody? Is that you? And Lick! You lil' sweetheart! I saw you ride tonight! Great!" Arco slid around to stand beside Lick, unconsciously placing herself center stage for a bar full of admiring cowboys.

I say **unconsciously,** ***friends, because I have known people like Arco. Maybe*** **instinctively** ***is an even better choice of words. It may have been simply part of her autonomic nervous system, like postprandial digestion or mydriasis on a dark night. Knowing where to position yourself in a flower bed has a direct bearing on the possibility of pollination. Which is just to say that Arco Peacock innately knew where the spotlight would fall.***

Her dress was factory-issue Corvette red. It idled in contrast to her pale white back and legs. She was also the only woman within a quarter mile wearing a dress. She moved, shifted and nickered as naturally as a three-year-old filly with a little pasture exposure!

"Aw, Lick. It's good to see you again."

"You, too, Arco. It's been a while." He remembered her in stocking feet bringing him a glass of OJ. He, sitting at her breakfast table in the morning sun. They were both wonderfully relaxed. It was a Sunday, he remembered, last fall.

"Sorry you couldn't make it to my little party."

"Yeah, well, by the time I picked up my mail, it was too late," he explained.

"Truth is, Lick, I was hopin' you'd made it back this spring. I know you're on the road and all, but I really enjoyed your company."

"Me, too. But I jus' got busy. I think that was the last time I read the funnies out loud. And you made those great big cinnamon rolls. We ate the whole pan! Sure was a great day!"

"Oh, Lick . . ." She touched his face with her hand. "I . . . it's so good to see you!"

"Would you like a beer? We might go to breakfast later if yer up for it."

"No. No, I can't," she said quickly. "I've made other plans." Their small talk dwindled, and she excused herself, leaving a flickering, palpable electricity in the air.

Cody was talking rodeo with a couple boys at a nearby table. Lick ran his fingers up and down the frosty beer glass and studied the mirror behind the bar. In its reflection he saw Arco reappear from the ladies' room and walk to another table. LoBall came up to Lick. They started visiting and time flew to last call.

At one P.M., Cody, Lick and LoBall stood by the curb in front of The Fifth Amendment. They were feelin' frisky.

"When was the last time you climbed a mountain?"

"Whataya talkin' about, Lick?" asked LoBall.

Lick pointed above the bar. There was a second story. An old sign climbed the vertical face from the bar porch and extended two feet above the roof ledge.

"Gimme a boost," directed Lick as he reached for the porch brace. LoBall lent his shoulders and Lick clambered up. The vertical sign was perpendicular to the brick face and was supported by a rusty angle-iron frame. Lick started his climb as the gathering crowd in the street cheered him on!

"I better help him, LoBall," said Cody, and followed Sir Edmund Screw Loose!

They scaled the roof ledge to tumultuous applause and disappeared. Up on the roof it was peaceful and quiet. The sky was clear and the stars were showering their blessing on the relaxed revelers. They sat, dangling their legs over the edge.

"Arco sure looked good, didn't she, Lick?"

"Boy, I'll say. We had a good visit. I thought we might've hit it off again but she had other plans."

"Too bad. Say, have you heard from Anaconda Kathy lately?"

"No. We kinda had it out in March. She said she either wanted something permanent or nothin' at all."

"You were seein' her off and on when we started travelin' together. That's been over two years," observed Cody.

"I know. I don't blame her. I think keepin' me in the cavvy was interferin' with her gettin' involved with anybody else. But anyway . . . it's for the best."

"She loved you, ya know!"

"Yeah, well, I can't help it," Lick said impatiently.

Cody felt a little twinge. Anaconda Kathy was his favorite of all Lick's girlfriends. A good, ranch-raised girl who could ride but wasn't horsey. She and Cody had hit it off. They had had several long talks. Usually about Lick. Cody defended him and tried not to encourage her too much, but she had stars in her eyes. Cody figured she probably had seen the light and decided she couldn't wait any longer. That, and the hurt. He'd seen it in her eyes. The ache of unreturned love.

"Well, she's better off," sighed Cody.

"You can say that about all of 'em!" laughed Lick.

"We sure cut a fat hog this weekend, pardner," mused Cody.

"We had it comin'," said Lick.

"You both come on down!" A voice from below broke their reverie. Two powerful flashlight beams shined up from the narrow alley below them. It separated the bar from Farmer's Feed and Seed warehouse, next door.

Lick stood up on the ledge, did a Tarzan yell, pounded his chest and leaped out into space!

* * *

The drunk tank is a wretched place. Suffice it to say, our two tarnished Sherpas sobered up instantly as the cell door slid shut with a migraine-splitting bang!

Cody was grody. Lick got sick.

There is one good thing about a drunk tank. It is an excellent place to put a drunk. No one appreciates a drunk as much as another drunk. It's like putting two horse people together at the same table;

no one has to feel guilty about ignoring them as long as they've got each other. In a drunk tank there is no such thing as a fashionable drunk.

Monday Morning, June 28
Bingham County Courthouse

"How do you plead?"

Lick mentally reviewed his options:

1. *Innocent as a newborn babe.*
2. No lo contendre. *(No, wait, he was a Mexican bantamweight from Los Angeles.)*
3. *On my hands and knees.*
4. *Guilty as sin.*
5. *Your Honor, my body was taken over by extraterrestrial beings disguised as Japanese businessmen bearing business cards intent on sabotaging the Farmer's Feed and Seed warehouse.*
6. *I was blinded like Saul, forsook my rabble-rousing ways and took one giant step for mankind.*

"To what?" asked the hyperventilated Lick.

"Disturbing the peace, destruction of private property."

"Uh, Yer Honor, would you explain what happens if I plead guilty or innocent or whatever."

"Sure. Innocent, we appoint you a lawyer and set bail. Guilty, you can be fined and/or sentenced to time in the county jail."

"How much?"

"Time or money?"

"Both."

"Maximum fine, five hundred dollars. Maximum jail, thirty days."

"Guilty, I guess."

"The defendant pleads guilty and is fined two hundred and fifty dollars, plus three days' work at the Farmer's Feed and Seed. Sentence to begin immediately. Pay the clerk. Next case."

"Cody Wing," said the baliff, "charged with disturbing the peace and destruction of private property."

"How do you plead?"

"Well, Yer Honor, I was just tryin' to keep an eye on Lick, there, and I guess I didn't do a real good job."

"Son, I want to ask you a question. Bill, I mean the arresting officer, said you watched your friend jump off the roof of the Fifth Amendment Bar and crash through the greenhouse roof of Farmer's Feed and Seed next door. Not exactly a brilliant move in itself, but then you jumped after him and put a second hole in Harvey Loomis's roof! That doesn't show a whole lot of good sense. What the hell— Strike that! What the hell— Strike it! Aw, hell, what the hell did you do that for?"

"I guess I wanted to make sure he wuddn't hurt."

"Good thinking. How do you plead?"

"Guilty."

"Sentenced to three days working for Farmer's Feed and Seed plus court cost. Next case."

Monday, Tuesday and Wednesday were spent loading feed, restacking pallets, pulling weeds, digging trenches, shoveling elevator pits, sweeping floors, washing windows, and sneezing. Actually, other than for the hard labor, it wasn't so bad. Harvey Loomis thought the whole episode was sort of funny. Insurance covered the cost of the two green sheets of corrugated plastic and replaced the potted Japanese black pine they deboughed on impact. Cody and Lick rebagged the Cow Power fertilizer they'd punctured by landing spurs first. Harvey even took the boys home for supper Wednesday after work.

They left town that Wednesday night, June 30, smelling like Cow Power and fermented grain.

4

Thursday, July 1

The boys took the scenic route from Blackfoot to Cody, Wyoming. They cruised through the cool pines of four national forests and two national parks. It was an easy day. They were both up tomorrow at the big Cody, Wyoming rodeo.

As they drove north, abreast of the Tetons, Lick finally lost his patience.

"Dang it, Cody! I'm tired of examining my love life! Can't you talk about anythin' else!"

"Well, ya don't hafta git mad! All I said was Anaconda Kathy—"

"Anaconda Kathy, Arco, Chadron, the Women's Army Corps! I'm just tired of it, that's all. Can't we talk about your love life for a change? You've about wore the subject out! I'm just not in the mood to settle down. You want me to git married again? Is that what you want?

"Maybe you already got one picked out! Who? Arco? Wouldn't we be a pair! We'd look like a Snap-On Tool calendar; she'd be the girl with the boom box in her sweater and I'd be the hubcap hammer!"

"I think she's pretty nice, if you ask me," answered Cody indignantly. "She's a lot smarter than she acts like. Hell, she's a college graduate! Got a good job. And I'll bet she'd be as true as a skunk's mate."

"A skunk's mate!" said Lick. "I don't believe it!"

"You know," explained Cody, "when you run over a skunk, the other one hangs around, pining . . ."

"I know! I know!" said Lick, "and usually gets run over, too!"

"Ah, Lick, I just think you oughta pay a little more attention. There's a lot of good ol' gals slippin' right through your hands and I don't think you even know it."

"Look, Cody, I'm not interested. Sometimes a feller knows when he's better off and I dang sure know I am. That's the difference 'tween you and me. I never had it so good, and I know it!"

"So what about Chadron?" continued Cody.

"Give it a rest, Cody. I've come a long way to git here and I'm not about to change."

* * *

Lick *had* come a long way.

His daddy was a fair-do-well cattle trader, horse trainer, drug salesman, uranium miner and day-work cowboy who could hang Sheetrock. Lick's folks had lived several places while Lick was growing up, mostly in the high plains of Kansas, Texas and New Mexico. Presently they were living in Hereford, Texas, where Papa was cowboying in a feedlot and riding colts for an extra C-note a month.

Lick was the oldest of three brothers: Lick, Clay and Tye. Papa taught the boys how to shoe a horse, sack a colt, doctor a steer, build a tight five-wire fence, plait a set of rawhide reins complete with buttons, spot a sick calf, know the value of steroids when tradin' horses and hang Sheetrock. Everything a man needs to know to spend the rest of his life self-unemployed.

Mama's maiden name was Chavez. Her mother had been a Jannsen who married Elojio Chavez from Las Vegas, New Mexico. Elojio, Lick's grandpa, was proud of the fact that he could trace his family back two hundred years in New Mexico history. Lick had the dark hair and eyes of his Spanish ancestors. Both his brothers were lighter complected and taller than Lick. They had real jobs.

Lick's paternal grandparents had come from Texas and Oklahoma.

During Lick's growing up, his folks never really owned anything. They rented or lived in company houses and always got by. Papa was a hand and never was out of work long. Mama was a genius at keeping a healthy, happy home on an irregular income.

Lick grew up lookin' for a way out. . . .

As luck would have it, they pulled into the Bronze Boot in Cody, Wyoming, just as the action was starting. The Bronze Boot was packed with cowboys, rodeo fans and wild Wyoming women!

Lick got liquored up by ten, mothered up by eleven, and hustled by twelve! Uva Dell was a snake, in the Adam and Eve sense of the word! She had long black hair, showin' a few lines and wearin' Wrangler leotards! Five foot two and thin as a Nevada mustang, she could fold a dollar bill to the size of a postage stamp with her tongue and slice cheese with her nose!

Son of a scrofulous cad! I knew that woman! Settle down, Bax. Well, it's just that anybody who's ever stuck his hand in a snarling dog's cage to see if he bites can figger out what's comin'! Lick is about to commit a common act of lunacy and even if we were there we would not be able to stop him. It is that indefensible phenomenon that allows a man to climb into a strange car with a strange woman in a strange town and drive off! With no idea as to destination, ETA or return ticket!

"How much further?" asked Lick. "I thought you said it was just outta town."

"It is, cowboy. Just up the road a piece."

Lick looked at her. Her features appeared almost craggy in the green glow of the dash lights. She wasn't a big woman but she certainly looked like she could take care of herself.

"Nice pickup," he remarked.

"Here it is," she said as she wheeled off the highway onto a gravel road. They drove another mile, then Uva Dell pulled into the country equivalent of a cul-de-sac. She switched off the lights. Lick scooted over next to her.

"Let's go for a little walk in the moonlight," she suggested.

They wandered directly to the back of the pickup. She dropped the tailgate and Lick sat on the edge dangling his feet.

"Mighty pretty out here," he said as she rubbed his knees. It was pretty. The Wyoming landscape, the starry night and the overwhelming silence.

He lay back and stared up at the stars. "By gosh, Uva Dell, this sure is nice. Yer place nearby?"

"Close enough, but you're not in a hurry are you?"

"Nope. I'm sure not. I wouldn't mind soakin' up a little of the peaceful."

"Lemme take your boots off," she offered.

He allowed her to pull 'em off. She set them in the pickup bed. Then she desocked him.

"That feel better, cowboy?"

"Just right, Uva Dell."

"Are you still hot?" she asked.

"Humm," he said slyly. "Yeah, I am . . . just a bit."

"You get yourself comfortable. I gotta get somethin' outta the front."

Lick did as he was told. Then lay back. He heard her rattle around in the cab, the door shut and she said, "Close your eyes."

He heard her step around to the back of the pickup.

"What is it you do for a livin'?" he asked dreamily.

"I'm a highwayman."

"A what?" asked Lick, eyes still closed.

"A highwayman," she repeated. His brain registered the distinct sound of a revolver being cocked. "And I rob cowboys."

He sat straight up!

"What!"

"Stick 'em up!" Lick was staring down the barrel of the biggest pistol he'd ever seen! If you've ever stuck your head in a well casing, you know how he felt! She held the cannon rock steady. He made a mental note of that fact.

"Slide off that tailgate. I'm serious about those hands. Git 'em high."

Lick scooched to the edge and dropped to the gravel. He winced.

"Now move over a little." He did. She rifled the pockets of his jeans that lay in the bed of the truck. She transferred the bills from his pocket to hers.

"You got a wallet?" she asked pleasantly.

"Uva Dell, this seems like a dumb question to ask, but is this a joke?"

She dropped the barrel of the pistol in the flick of an eye and pulled the trigger! The inside of Lick's bare legs stung from the flying rock and sand! She raised the barrel level to his nose and cocked it.

"I reckon not," he said, his ears ringing like a stuck siren.

"I reckon not," she said, smiling.

"Actually, I do have a wallet but it's in the pickup. My pickup, I mean."

"Oh, well," she said, "I never did do it for the money. I'm gonna have to go now but I can't leave you like this."

"Thank goodness," sighed Lick. He started to reach for his pants.

"Don't move!"

He snapped smartly to his goal post imitation.

"Take off the rest of your clothes."

"Uva Dell, I'm really not in the mood," he complained.

"I believe you misunderstood my intentions," she replied.

"You wouldn't really shoot me, would ya?"

"No. I wouldn't wanna kill you but I'd sure put a bullet through your foot. Only problem is, this pistol is so big it usually takes the ankle with it. 'Least, that's been my experience."

"You mean you've shot people before?" he asked, peeling off his shirt.

"Only in the foot. Off with the shorts, too. Throw 'em in the back of the pickup." She slammed the tailgate up. "All right, walk over there by that hump."

Lick minced across the rocky turnaround.

She started the pickup, backed around and captured him in the brights. "Nice buns!" she shouted, then let out a war whoop, fired her pistol in the air and spewed gravel as the truck fishtailed toward the road!

Lick watched the taillights disappear. The sound of the growling engine eventually faded into the night.

Friends, this might be a safe place for some gentle reflection. Where a man might reevaluate the priorities in his life. A moment to examine the Yin and Yang of the yo-yo of Existence. Where does* Homo sapien *truly fit on this old mud ball we call Earth? How would he fare were he reduced to his natural state and left alone in the wilderness?

And furthermore, how would Robin Hood deal with Maid Marian turned maniac bandit and foot shooter? It is the ultimate equality. Feminism assimilated to the point where you can't tell the good guys from the bad. Interesting, isn't it, that the instigator of this final solution was not social conscience, divorce lawyers or natural selection. It was Samuel Colt's invention, the revolving cylinder single-action handgun.

Uva Dell's behavior would certainly upset some modern sociologist's chauvinistic preconceptions. Unless, of course, that sociologist was conversant with Wyoming's history of women's suffrage and had spent some time studying Wyoming women in their natural habitat.

As Lick said to himself alone under the stars, "Well pick my nose with a fork-ed stick! That never happened before!"

Dawn found him back on the blacktop. A yard light burned weakly half a mile up the road, kissing the night good-bye. As Lick drew closer to the ranch headquarters, he was able to see the layout of the buildings and corrals in the spreading sunrise. He spotted what appeared to be a chicken house. He circled through the pasture and snuck up on the chicken house. He peered through the chicken wire window. The hens were fast asleep while their bodies were busy accumulating calcium and troweling it into a shell. Lick was looking for a garment to cover his goose-bumped body.

Belfry, cowdog in charge of ranch security, lay by the sheep wire fence in front of the ranch house curled against the morning chill. He opened one eye. He spied a big pink intruder crossing the lane from the chicken house to the horse barn. The hair stood between Belfry's shoulder blades!

Now, dogs take their guarding seriously. However, it does not make great demands on their courage to bark and growl menacingly at the school bus or an occasional molasses salesman. Yet it's part of the job, boring though it may seem to those of us whose jobs include such daily excitements as writing a memo, reading a memo or filing a memo.

Belfry shivered, curled tighter and blinked his eye in the wild hope that the mysterious invader was just a figment of his imagination. No! There it was creeping into the horse barn!

Belfry reviewed his options from the Official Cowdog Ranch Security Handbook:

1. *Close his eyes and pretend to be asleep.*
2. *Sneak around and get a closer look.*
3. *Bark and wake up Wilbur's old lady.*
4. *Attack.*

He chose the easy way out: number 3. At the first yap Lick zipped into the tack room and came flying back out wrapped in a turquoise saddle blanket! The high-stepping cowboy cleared the barbwire fence into the pasture and rolled into a ditch! He lay there panting.

"Yap, yap, yap, bark, woof, woof!"

"What is it, Belfry?"

"Yap, yap, bark, bark, bark!"

"Okay, okay. Let me get my glasses."

"Yap, yap, woof, bow wow!"

"What is it, Ethel?"

"Don't know, Wilbur. Prob'ly nothin'."

"Woof, woof, bark and yap!"

"Okay, okay, shut up, Belfry!"

"Bark, bark, woof, woof, woof!"

"Shaddup, you sunuvabitch."

"Yap, yap, yap!"

Wham, wham, whap!

"Whimper, whimper, whine."

Belfry rolled over on his back and grinned ingratiatingly.

"Okay. Good dog. Go back to sleep."

Pat, pat, pat.

"Sigh."

Lick stayed frozen another five minutes, then crept back toward the main road.

It is not easy to thumb a ride at six o'clock in the morning dressed in a turquoise horse blanket. Fortunately, he was stranded in Wyoming, where such behavior is commonplace. He was picked up by an aged ex-prospector who mistook him for a soul brother coming back from a revival in Meeteetse. The ancient 1950 GMC pickup slowed, then stopped. He was taking two small shoats and a week-old Holstein calf to a girlfriend north of Cody. They were crowded in the front seat between a cardboard box of transmission gears and a gunnysack full of aluminum cans. Lick climbed in the back between two bales of hay and a block of salt. There was no room for him in the inn.

On the way through town, Lick unloaded on First Street and walked out to the rodeo grounds. The contestant area was filled with travel trailers. It was 7:30 A.M., not much stirring. He was weaving his way from pickup to camper to horse trailer, looking for Cody's pickup. He was also trying to avoid attracting attention.

"Hey, LoBall, come take a look at this!"

"Who is it?"

"Bill! Wake up!"

"Somebody go git Franco and Charlie!"

"Monty, git yer butt out here! Yer not gonna believe this!"

Somebody started honking his horn. Soon other horns joined in and the entire entourage of rodeo overnighters were piling out of their campers to watch the spectacle.

"Who is it?"

"Dunno. Who is it?"

"Where?"

"Over there."

"I think it's Lick."

"Who?"

"Lick!"

"Hey, Lick, is that you?"

"It is! It's Lick!"

Lick clutched his blanket tighter to his bosom. He led an ever growing number of pie-eyed piperettes through the contestant parking area like a disinterested bitch in heat.

Cody opened the back of the camper to insistent pounding. He looked out at He Who Squats in the Goatheads and then at the throng surrounding his vehicle.

"What the hell! Lick?"

"Let me in."

"Sure, sure."

Lick crawled over the tailgate.

"Look! He's nekkid!"

A woman screamed . . . inside the camper! The piercing shriek coursed through Lick's tympanic bullae directly to the microchip in the cerebral cortex labeled EMERGENCY ONLY! Epinephrine was released at the appropriate synapses and his body straightened out like a frog in biology lab! He hit his head on the aluminum camper top! He grabbed his head with his left hand, caught the saddle blanket on a galvanized screw on the tack box, stumbled and braced his fall with his right hand!

The turquoise blanket disappeared as if a magician had jerked a tablecloth out from under an eight-piece table setting!

"This is Sheila. Sheila, this is Lick!"

"Howdy, ma'am."

She screamed again.

5

July 2
Cody, Wyoming

By three o'clock the afternoon following the escapade with Mademoiselle Uva Dell, Cody and Lick were behind the bucking chutes at the Cody, Wyoming rodeo grounds. They were rosining their bull ropes, tying on spurs and distractedly visiting with other riders.

Most of the competitors here today would be up in Livingston, Montana, and again in Red Lodge, Montana, this weekend. This included Lick and Cody, as well. The three towns planned their rodeos to coincide.

Lick was still thickheaded and dry-eyed from lack of sleep, not to mention a little sore from his forced march. The bull he had drawn today was new to him and the other cowboys. Nobody had any information on him. All the stock contractor's pickup man could tell Lick was that he was gentle. He would eat grain out of your hand.

Cody's draw was well known. The "book" on him was that he was a good honest bucker and a money bull if things worked right.

Lick finally threw up and felt a little better. He was able to help Cody get down on his bull, which came in the first chuteload to buck out. Cody got it together and scored a 76, which put him in third place at the time.

Lick's bull came in with the second chuteload. He was a big, beefy yellow Charolais with two floppy horns. He stood quietly in the chute as Cody and Lick set Lick's rope. While Cody was reaching underneath the bull's belly to catch the tail of the bull rope he noticed a familiar brand on the bull's right hip.

"Well I'll be durn!" Cody remarked, "Lick, this ol' bull's got Chubby Duckworth's brand on him. Does he have an underbit on both ears? Sure does! Duckworth's got a gypo deal up south of Sheridan. Runs quite a few cows and never pays over four hundred dollars for a bull. No wonder nobody's seen this bugger before. Chubby's been breedin' cows with him and musta needed some cash so he sold off a herd sire! I don't know nuthin' 'bout him, but if he's anything like Chubby, I wouldn't trust him!"

Great, thought Lick. *Just what I need after spending the night stark naked on the Serengeti of Wyoming.* "Pull it," he said. "I'm next."

Lick was ready by the time the arena director laced his jerk rope through the chute gate. Lick nodded furiously! The gate swung open! Lick could no longer hear the crowd or see anything outside his orbit. The bull's first move was to tense and take a deep breath. The result was a tightening of the rope that bit into Lick's gloved hand! Lick didn't have time to smile, but it felt good. It brought him back to his own reality. The way a familiar hammer feels to a framer. Riding bulls was what he was good at. It was the center of his universe, his bottom line, the caffeine in his primordial coffee.

Most rodeo bulls show little finesse. They rely on quickness and overwhelming power. When you realize they could easily demolish a cinder block building or a five-strand barbwire fence, it is remarkable that every cowboy is not reduced to kindling by the conclusion of each ride!

Big Yellow came out with a respectable first jump. Then he turned back and bucked straight along the chute gates at the end of the arena! Cowboys sitting on the gates and standing in front of them scattered like handbills in a hurricane!

Big Yellow got so close that he was intermittently rubbing Lick's left leg along the boards! Not so obvious that the judges would notice but enough to interfere with Lick's action. Lick was supposed to be concentrating but it was difficult with Big Yellow swooping in and out whacking his knee against the rough-cut two-by-eights.

During the next dive to the outside, Lick picked up his inside leg and drove his spur into the bull's shoulder! The bull swung to the right and bucked straight out toward the center of the arena! The eight-second whistle blew! Lick stopped spurring and the bull stopped bucking. He stood still with Lick sitting astride him. Lick rapidly uncoiled the rope from his hand and waited a moment for Big Yellow to move again, knowing it was safer to bail off a moving bull than a standing one. At least you'd be goin' opposite directions when you hit the ground. The bull continued to stand. The crowd started laughing! Finally Lick slid off and raced a few steps back toward the chutes! Big Yellow stood there a few seconds then quietly followed Lick's exit, sniffing at the ground, looking up at the crowd and good-naturedly appearing to enjoy his part in the show. The crowd loved it! Lick thought it was humorous, too. But the judges had no sense of humor and marked Lick a measly 56.

Cody eventually placed fourth and won a third in Red Lodge. Lick rode all three of his bulls that weekend but was out of the money every time. The boys spent a couple days in Ten Sleep with Cody's folks and Big Yellow was fourteen hundred pounds of hamburger by Tuesday!

6

Wednesday, July 7
Nampa, Idaho

Go west, young man," Horace Greeley said to his incompetent son-in-law in an effort to get him away from the table.

Lick and Cody, well rested and healed after two days of Mama Wing's cooking, also heeded Horace's command. West across Wyoming to Nampa, Idaho.

Idaho. I speak of that great state with the fondness that Willie Shoemaker speaks of Churchill Downs. I spent ten years of my life working for a big cow outfit up there.

Southwestern Idaho, like eastern Oregon and northern Nevada, is cowboy country. Not pickup drivin', CB talkin', team ropin', Marlboro smokin', beboppin' baseball cap cowboys. I mean real cowboys!

I had come up from New Mexico, where I was raised. Cowboys in the Southwest were not flashy. We enjoyed bein' cowboys but we were Spartan in our plumage.

I rode into Idaho and found myself in the Wild West! They reveled in being cowboys! They wallowed in it! Shoot, they call themselves buckaroos!

Ridin' a deep-seat centerfire saddle with a horn like a cedar post! Tapaderos, rommals, rawhide reins, bosals, horsehair McCarties, reatas and big, cover-the-country horses!

Hightop boots tucked in, riding heels, jingle bobs, rowels like

spinners on a '58 Olds, chinks, silver buckles, silk scarves and big high-crown black hats. When gazing on one of these sagebrush centaurs you do not confuse him with an insurance salesman from Spokane!

In all fairness, these buckaroos are no better at cowboyin' than my compadres in New Mexico or Texas. But it's possible they enjoy it more. Doesn't a blue jay have more fun bein' a bird than a sparrow does? Dressin' in a Batman suit on Halloween doesn't make you Robin's godfather or entitle you to Superman's home phone number, but if you can do a journeyman's job of ropin' and ridin' and you wanna dress like a Remington painting, more power to ya!

Now, you cannot necessarily assume just 'cause a feller's got on a black hat and he's broke that he's a cowboy! But, as any boondockin' bird-watcher will tell you, if you're lookin' for a certain kind of bird, you've got to look in the right places! These buckaroos do not normally frequent highly populated areas. They are seldom spotted in Baskin-Robbins, a Marriott lobby, or the First Presbyterian Church.

Since cowboyin' is a seven-day-a-week job, you're liable to see them anytime. For those of you who wish to begin "buckaroo watchin'," familiarize yourself with the bars, pool halls and tack shops in places like Grasmere, Mountain City, Denio, Wagon Tire, McDermitt, Three Creek, Tuscarora, Jordan Valley and Reynolds Creek. Just hang out with your binoculars around your neck and your notebook in your hand. You'll know it the minute you see one.

Lick and Cody were in downtown Nampa, at Bits' Saddle and Canvas, swapping war stories with the owners. A few other cowboys were getting tack and riggins resewed or riveted. The brothers who owned the place, Four and Six, always did a healthy business during Snake River Stampede week. They were the best for miles around, and preferred to work on workin' cowboy tack, but backyard horse people and trail ride cowboys contributed their share to the cash register.

"Man!" said Cody. "Twelve hundred dollars for a saddle! How do these buckaroos, drawin' six hundred a month, afford one of these?"

"I don't know, but they do. Sold one yestiddy to a guy cowboyin' on South Mountain fer ol' Tex. Paid cash."

"Are ya up tonight?" Four asked.

"Nope. My pardner is, though. I'm up Friday in the bareback."

"Four Bits! How you doin'?" Four turned to the newcomer.

"Good, Jack. Whatta ya up to?"

"I thought this might be a good place to do an interview with some of the cowboys in town for the rodeo. Sorta get the feel of the show. How about these two?" The radioman turned to Cody.

"Hi, I'm Jack Dale, K2HO Radio." Jack looked like the perennial anchorman. Genial and bright with a modulated voice and hair you could see through. "Maybe you could help us with a little spot to promote the rodeo?" He offered his hand to Cody.

"Sure. Cody Wing." Jack shook his hand warmly.

"How about you?" Jack asked the man behind Cody.

"Be glad to. Do I look okay?"

Cody looked around. It was Ned. Ned? Not Ned!

Nobody liked Ned. It was understandable, of course, so no one gave it much thought. Ned is one of those names that's hard to grow up with. Certainly there are many Neds down through history who have distinguished the name: Ned the Great, Ned the Lion-hearted, Ned the Conqueror, Ned the Red, to name a few. But no modern screen star has chosen the name Ned. There is no Ned Valentino, Ned Gable or Ned Eastwood.

This Ned was a calf roper. His father was a roper turned banker and his mother taught school. They loved him enough to subsidize his roping, for the time being.

But Ned had a way about him that irritated people! It wasn't that he wasn't intelligent, he was; but he wasn't smart. He was intellectual, but not bright; educated, but shallow; literate, but ponderous; enlightened, but not witty; sentimental, but tactless; calculating, but unimaginative. All in all, he was a clod.

He exemplified the difference between risqué and obscene.

His hair was thick and greasy. He had bad breath. He couldn't say "Sasquatch" without spitting on his listener. He cleaned his fingernails, picked his nose, broke wind, or scratched his crotch at indelicate times.

Once he asked Lick why he never had any luck with women.

"Ned," said Lick, "they think you're the kind of person who'd wait under a fire escape for three hours, on the chance you might get to look up their dress!"

"Hum," pondered Ned. "I never thought of that."

"What's your name?" asked Jack.

"Ned." Ned had begun to sweat.

"Are you two partners?"

"No! No," answered Cody.

"I just want to turn on this tape recorder and ask you a few questions. Easy, no big deal, and if it's good, we'll run it this week. Okay?"

"Do we have to sign anything? I mean, for royalties and things?" asked Ned.

"Royalties?" Jack almost laughed, until he realized the question was sincere.

"Yes. I've read some AFTRA brochures in my spare time, and often seventy-five dollars is paid for speaking parts. I'm not sure how the FCC looks on radio interviews, but, speaking for myself and my friend"—Ned put his arm around Cody, Cody shrank—"we'd certainly consider it. Wouldn't we, Cody?" He smiled and breathed in Cody's face. Two freckles and a blackhead shriveled like napalmed mushrooms!

"This would just be a sort of man-in-the-street-type interview. Usually no money is paid," explained Jack.

"Certainly, we can see your point, but you must understand that celebrities, movie stars, or rodeo stars have to be careful about allowing visual or auditorial reproductions of themselves or part of themselves to be used by the media to sell advertising space. I'm sure we can—"

"Shut up, Ned," said Cody.

"I'm just tryin'—"

"Shut up!"

"But—"

Cody looked at Ned. Ned shut up.

"Okay, it's on. Just act natural." Jack held up the small cassette recorder. "This is Jack Dale, K2HO Radio, live, down here at Bits' Saddle and Canvas in downtown Nampa. The Treasure Valley has rodeo fever! Several of the contestants entered in the big Snake River Stampede, to be held Tuesday through Saturday, July thirteenth through the seventeenth, are in here picking up supplies. I've been talking to a couple of cowboys, Cody Wing and Ned, uh . . . ?" Jack looked toward Ned for the answer. No answer. Ned was in the ozone. ". . . and Ned.

"Cody, what's your event?"

"Bareback and bulls."

"Ned. Ned, what's your event?"

"I am entered in the calf roping event." Ned enunciated each syllable carefully.

"What would you say is the difference between the riding events and the roping events?"

"Ropers and doggers," explained Cody, "have to haul their horses and it costs more to rodeo. Roughstock riders just haul themselves and their gear. 'Course they get hurt more often."

"There's more colored people and white trash in the bucking events, but we have our share of Mexicans in the roping," added Ned, loosening up a little.

"What?" said the astonished interviewer.

"You know, more Negroid types and riffraff from the lower class," Ned said expansively. "They tend to go into bull riding. Low investment and I've read their skulls are thicker."

There was a pause. Cody turned to Ned. "Did you go to school to learn all this stuff, Ned? Or does it percolate through the sewer pipes in your brain and condense like droplets on your tongue?"

"Well, you're a good example," retorted Ned. "I happen to know you're not a college graduate." He caught Jack's eye to emphasize the point.

Jack, who had earned his high school diploma in the navy, did not acknowledge Ned's evidence. His tape recorder continued to roll along.

Suddenly a big canvas duffle bag popped over Ned's head and

was pulled down to his boot tops! The drawstring jerked tight around his knees and Ned fell over like a limp sausage. Two cowboys nodded to Cody and dragged the package out of the store. It bumped over the doorjamb and disappeared down the sidewalk. Jack and Cody watched it go.

Jack looked at Cody. "Gosh, is he one of you guys?"

Cody sighed. "Did ya ever have a dog that kept messin' on the carpet? He's your dog and you love him, but sometimes you just want to cut out his liver and feed him to the coyotes."

7

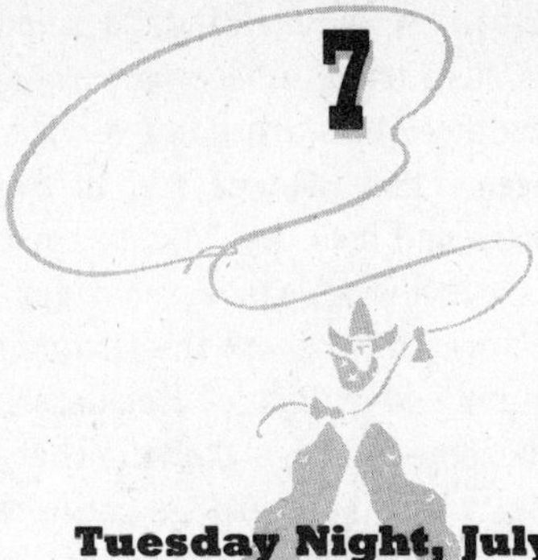

Tuesday Night, July 13
Nampa, Idaho

That night, the first performance of the Snake River Stampede went smoothly. They were down to the final event, the bull riding. The crowd could sense the excitement in the announcer's voice:

"Ladies and gentlemen. You are in for a treat tonight! Two-time world champion bull rider, Manly Ott, from Kit Carson, cool, costly, colorful Colorado, has drawn bull number ten-twenty, unridden in four years! He has thrown hundreds of cowboys, never fought a draw, the pride of Bobby Monday's string, the devil's nightmare, Kamikaze!"

Cody and Lick stood on the chute gate. Every mother lovin' rodeo cowboy, would-be bull rider, and in-the-know spectator sat in rapt anticipation. Manly, like Lick, Cody and others of their samurai persuasion, had tried to ride Kamikaze. Some, several times; all unsuccessfully.

If Manly conquered ol' 1020, he would more than likely win the whole shootin' match, but most of the smart money was on the bull!

Manly was a champion. He made a good living riding bulls. He was short and stocky with an outgoing personality and a baby face. Not everyone liked Manly's cocky attitude, but they respected him. He was actually putting something in a savings account!

Bull riders are a strange lot. It takes a man with all his lichens on the south side to climb on the back of a leather-covered, two-ton, recoiling artillery field cannon, tie his hand to the breech lock and have someone push it over a cliff!

They ride without protection. No padding, no helmets, no fifteen-yard penalty protecting them from unnecessary roughness. And no help save the clowns. Rodeo clowns dress in oversize cutoffs, gaudy scarves and painted faces. These clowns are, in fact, bullfighters. They usually work in pairs and it is their job to separate bull rider and beast at the ride's conclusion. Once the rider is down they put themselves in harm's way and divert the revenging behemoth's attention away from the bull rider. Brave? Reckless? A death wish?

Why would anyone become a rodeo clown? That query can be answered only by asking, why do some dogs chase cars?

Most bull riders are young, in their twenties. In their hearts and minds, they are indestructible. By thirty, a man can feel his vulnerability. He can't see the end of the tunnel, but he knows it has one! Ten years of bull riding takes a fearsome physical toll on a man's body. It makes one yearn for a gentler, safer occupation like that of a professional kickoff-return specialist.

And what about that basic lifesaving instinct, fear? It is always there but it is overcome or reckoned with in a million different ways. It is a private emotion. The fear experienced by Peter when the cock crowed the third time; the sinkin' feeling ol' Chris Columbus had after seventeen days of slack-sail calm a thousand miles from Lisbon; the high, faraway voice of panic in the ear of a nineteen-year-old marine pinned down on Tarawa Beach; it's all the same. It makes your bladder loosen, your skin prickle! It puts your heart in your throat and bile on the back of your tongue!

But it is overcome. Threats, love, duty, pride, and Valium. Concentration, will, the power of positive thinking. Lunacy, therapy and partial lobotomy: all methods employed to face our fears.

Manly was ready. But how about Kamikaze? What was he thinking? In all fairness . . . whoever named the Dumb Friends League has dang sure punched a few cows! Cows can't think, as in "think tank." Organizing a three-day meeting of Motor Vehicle Department managers would not be their bag. An algebraic equation leaves them cold. A bachelor of science degree is beyond their comprehension. They do things by instinct, like giving milk or growing hair. They learn by repetition the way rainwater hunts a groove in a hillside. Action-Reaction.

They naturally shy away from endeavors that require a specific answer. The most cows could hope to achieve in the modern world would be a master's degree in psychology.

Kamikaze was no different. He knew that cowboys tried to ride him. He knew he didn't like it. If the rider got hurt, it was nothing to him. He didn't comprehend consequences. He was incapable of feeling guilt. He had the attention span of a Bartlett pear. He could associate the bucking chute and the arena with the ride. He could concentrate on disengaging the rider and venting his spleen, but once the conflict was over, he dismissed it.

However, Kamikaze could mull things over in a narrow, bovine sort of way.

He remembered Manly Ott. Kamikaze recognized those cowboys who had tried to ride him. Manly had come back to the pens before the rodeo, leaned over the fence and stared at him for several minutes. Kamikaze had ignored him, although he could feel the cowboy's brain waves boring into his hide. Manly's aura was as recognizable to Kamikaze as his driver's license photo would be to you or me. The more Manly concentrated, the stronger Kamikaze could feel his presence. *Him again,* mused the bull. *Learn slow.*

Manly slipped down over Kamikaze in chute number three. He kept his head well back from the playful two-foot horns that curved up and out like an evangelist's arms during the invitation. Kamikaze was a "chute fighter" to boot. He employed these diversionary tactics to break the concentration of his next victim.

One of the reasons Kamikaze was hard to ride was that he followed no set bucking pattern. Most bulls had a routine that was observed and remembered by the fraternity of bull riders. Whether he spun to the right, spun to the left, bucked straight out or whatever: it was called the bull's "book"—as in "What's the book on this bull?"

Kamikaze's book changed storylines each time, but at least the ending was consistent: buck off the cowboy and try to kill him!

Manly had watched Kamikaze buck many times and tried to ride him three times in the last two years. If anybody could ride 1020, Manly Ott could. He was the best the Professional Rodeo Cowboys of America could put up. Everybody watching knew that. A quiet fell over the tense crowd.

Manly dropped down on the big smooth back, scooted up on his left hand secured behind the hump, and nodded his head. Before the gate was fully opened, Kamikaze exploded through the opening, deliberately cracking Manly's right knee into the post! Sensing Manly's slight imbalance, he wheeled to the left, throwing the rider's leg farther back along his right side and off his rope just slightly. He felt Manly pull himself back into the eye of the hurricane by brute strength! Kamikaze could feel Manly's body and leg coming back into position. When the momentum had just about brought him back, Kamikaze made his next move to the right! Manly's leg carried right on by the ideal spot and slid perceptibly onto the right shoulder. Off balance again, leaning slightly to the right, Manly dropped his head into the range of the lethal horns. Although it couldn't be seen from the fence, Manly felt the huge muscles underneath him flex and move him, against his will, an inch farther into the deadly arc! At the conclusion of the second jump, Kamikaze's front feet hit ground first, hurtling the passenger forward, like the driver in a front-end collision! Reaching back with his big blunt horn, the diameter of a good-sized corral pole, he tapped Manly on the cheek, fracturing his mandible and third right premolar!

Manly's grip released and he came off the right rear quarter. He landed flat on his back. Looking up, he saw one huge cloven hoof, two loosely swinging balls and a final hoof pass over his head, from left to right.

The next thing he knew, the clowns were pushing him up on the fence, out of danger.

Kamikaze ran out of the arena. He stopped long enough to have the flank strap removed and wandered back toward the hay rack.

Two jumps. Not bad, noted the bull. He would spend a peaceful evening under the stars nibbling on Canyon County alfalfa and resting.

Manly Ott would spend four hours on a surgery table under an orthopedist and an oral surgeon at Mercy Hospital.

* * *

"Ready?" asked Cody.

"Yup," said Lick.

Normally, Lick would not have paid much attention to the bull riders who went before him. He was concentrating on his own ride. But whenever Kamikaze bucked out, he watched. Everybody watched! The bull Lick had drawn tonight was a pretty good draw. A spinning bull, but not a real whirling dervish. He figured it would take plenty of spinning action to get a very good score.

Now, those of you readers who have never ridden a bull should appreciate that all the action takes place in eight seconds. Eight short seconds. In eight seconds, a man can walk from his Barcalounger to the refrigerator; a car can drive through Patricia, Texas; a 727 can cross the Mississippi River at milepost 204 north of Alton, Illinois; and a solar hiccup can shoot a sunbeam a million three hundred thousand miles into space!

However, it does seem considerably longer if you are a participant! I can vouch for that since I, myself, rode bulls, till my brains came in.

Lick was down in the chute, hand in the rope and nodding his head. Time starts when the bull crosses that invisible line into the arena.

One thousand and one, one thousand and two, one thousand and three, one thousand and four, one thousand and five, one thousand and six, one thousand and seven, one thousand and eight. Whistle! Just that fast.

Lick's mind is on autopilot. Feel, react. The muscles don't even bother to check in with the gray matter. The neurons on the board of directors have already laid out a game plan and unless some new situation arises that demands their attention, they are content to let the muscles handle it. This is natural, of course. That's why a good banjo player can pick out "Lonesome Road Blues" and talk to the bass man at the same time. The mind does the talkin', the fingers do the walkin'. The same applies to bookkeepers on adding machines, jugglers on high wires and radio evangelists quoting Scripture.

The drawback to this useful phenomenon that allows your body to perform a task while your mind is occupied elsewhere is just that! The more accustomed you are to doing something, the less you have to think about doing it. Your brain doesn't have to concentrate and that can be a costly error in the bull riding event. Hence, bull riders and bronc riders in particular make an intense effort to keep their minds on the ride: to concentrate.

Lick concentrated. He rode his bull.

When the whistle blew he released his grip and was tossed six feet in the air. He landed free and clear.

That was the good part.

Unfortunately, he scored a 65, which was out of the money. The bull didn't spin as much as Lick had hoped. Ah, well, the luck of the draw.

Lick had made plans to fly in a private plane with three other cowboys to the rodeo in Salinas, California. He would compete there Wednesday and Thursday, fly back to Nampa on Friday to watch Cody ride.

At 10:45 that night, he and his compadres lifted off the Nampa runway into a starry sky and headed southwest.

8

Tuesday Night Late, July 13
Nampa, Idaho

Cody had neither the money nor the inclination to join Lick on his trip to Salinas. He would wait in Nampa for Lick's return. While Lick was beginning to doze to the hypnotizing hum of the twin engine Aztec, Cody found himself three miles up Nampa-Caldwell Boulevard in the spidery confines and extraterrestrial neon glow of Pingle's Cowboy Bar. He had danced a few, met and adopted Smila Snees. Smila was a pear-shaped maiden with big brown eyes. She stood by Cody as his quarter stood in line to shoot a little eight ball.

"You need another beer 'fore my game, darlin'?" he asked her.

"No, thank you. How about you?" she countered, carefully choosing her words to avoid her conspicuous lisp.

"Yeah, here's a five. Go git another Velvet and Seven if ya don't mind."

One fourth of the boys in the dance hall were professional rodeo cowboys in town for the show. The rest were local cowboys, ropers, boot salesmen, farmers' sons and would-be truck drivers.

Cody shoved his quarter down the throat of the green-backed turtle with sixteen balls. He racked 'em up. Cody was a marginal speller, a fair guitar picker, an average bull rider and a C+ lover, but that blue chalker could shoot pool! He was even a better snooker player, which made him lethal in rotation, cutthroat and eight ball. When he sighted down a long green shot, it was like a proctologist taking aim on a pachyderm.

That night he played a lot for quarters. The challengers just kept placing them edge to edge along the baize lawn. Tonight he played a little sloppy, deliberately, but never relinquished the table. Finally, one of the local shooters spotted him and offered to play him for five. Cody let him win two out of three, then raised the bet to twenty a game. He won the next three, and was fifty-five dollars to the good.

Smila decided to have a couple glasses of white wine, with ice, which loosened her tongue.

"Thath great, Cody! Thith ith tho ekthyting!"

"I'll play ya, Cody." A bear paw squeezed his shoulder. Cody knew without turning around who was offering the challenge: Big Handy Loon.

They didn't call him Big Handy for nothin'! He was 6'4", 260, wore a 7⅝ Resistol and could palm a forty-pound medicine ball! His reddish blond hair was crew-cut over his cauliflower ears and his unibrow ran from temple to temple. There was no warmth in his smile, no humor in his laughter.

"I wuz jis' quittin', Big Handy."

"Yer luck run out, little feller? Guess he'd rather not play me. Just the local bums." Big Handy addressed Grenadine Sheffliff and winked conspiratorially. Grenadine squeezed his nineteen-inch bicep and smiled. She had long legs, long purple fingernails, long black hair and a long brisket! She wore clothing that diverted an onlooker's gaze from her less desirable characteristics to her assets: designer jeans, knee-high leather boots, five diamond rings, and a sequined, but tasteful, halter top. A two-ounce gold pendant bounced back and forth between her Acapulco cleavage like a one-armed salmon going up a Columbia fish ladder! She attracted considerable attention.

Cody had good reason not to play Big Handy. Big Handy was a compulsive winner. He hated to lose! His temper was legend. Stories of broken windows, tables, bottles and bones were well known to every professional rodeo circuit follower.

"Tell ya what, Cody, ol' son, you and I will play for a measly twenty bucks a game, and the loser buys the ladies a round. How could a fine gentleman like you refuse to buy two such fine-lookin' ladies a drink?"

"I'd rather not," said Cody.

"Ooooh, c'mon, Cody! You can do it! Bethydth, ith tho muth fun wathin' you thoot!"

"Good, lil' darlin'," encouraged Big Handy. "You give 'im a little squeeze for good luck and I'll rack 'em. Don't say good-bye to this quarter, sweet thing, it's just an investment."

Big Handy slipped the coin in the slot.

Cody and Big Handy each played up to their potential. Cody ran the table off the break three games in a row. Big Handy touched the cue ball with his stick five times, sunk two balls and scratched twice. He became increasingly frustrated and his temperature rose one tenth of a degree each time Smila thanked him profusely for the round.

"Oh, thank you, Big Handy. Thith ith tho nith of you. Maybe you'll get to thoot the neckth time.

"Thoot the thripth off 'em, Cody!"

* * *

Closing time put an end to Big Handy's financial drain.

"Let's get up a card game," suggested Big Handy with an edge to his voice.

"Jeez, Handy, I'd really rather—"

"You got a hunnerd and twenny dollars of mine, little man." His eyes were glittering.

"Who else wants to play?" He looked at the crowd standing around the table. "Smitty? Bobby? Pork Chop?"

* * *

Back at Big Handy's motel room, the boys set up. They spread a blanket over a square table and the five of them played. By three o'clock in the morning, Big Handy was ahead thirty-five dollars, Cody was down fifty, and nobody else was hurtin'. They played dealer's choice, dollar ante, ten-dollar limit and three bumps.

"I'm 'bout ready to call it a night." Cody yawned. Smila squeezed his leg.

"One more hand. Okay?" Big Handy offered. Everybody nodded.

"Jacks or back." Big Handy shuffled and dealt everyone five cards, facedown. "Bobby, can you open? Pork Chop? Cody?"

"Yup, I'll open for ten," answered Cody.

Smitty stayed.

"Your ten and ten." Everybody involuntarily looked at Big Handy.

"Twenny to you, Bobby."

"Fold. See you guys later, I'm hittin' the sack."

"I'm in," proffered Pork Chop.

"Call," said Cody.

Smitty threw his cards into the pot and left the room.

"Cards to the players."

"One," said Pork Chop. He discarded a deuce and was dealt a nine. Five, six, seven, eight, nine: he hit his straight!

"Two." Cody held his openers: bullets, and the jack of hearts. He picked up his first card: ace of hearts. His mind became awake. Three aces. Great! He slid the final card into his hand and fanned it. Impossible! Peeking out from behind the jack, like a hesitant showerer in Phys Ed 101, was the fourth ace!

"Dealer stand pat." Big Handy had dealt himself a full boat, kings and tens. "Bet yer openers," he instructed, feeling expansive.

"Check to the power," Cody fished.

"Ten," bet Big Handy, not wanting to scare anybody out.

"Your ten and ten," upped Pork Chop.

Cody considered the hand. Both Pork Chop and Big Handy figured they could beat his opening pair. He'd held three cards to plant three of a kind in their mind. It didn't plant, or they figured they could beat three of a kind. Pork Chop had drawn one card. Probably holding two pair. Or the makin's of a straight or flush. Whatever he was hoping for in the last draw, he must of hit it. Big Handy was another story. Didn't draw a card. He might be holding a straight or a flush, maybe even a full house. But . . . Cody had four of a kind! His strategy should encourage everyone to stay in the game as long as possible.

"Your ten and ten more," Cody said, and laid his money on the pile.

"Here's your twenty, boys, and twenty more," bumped Big Handy.

"Limit's ten," reminded Pork Chop.

"Anybody got any objections to uppin' the ante, last hand and all?" asked Big Handy.

"Okay by me," said Cody.

Pork Chop studied his hand and looked at the pot. "I guess not. That's the last bump anyway."

"What say we skip the bump rule?" suggested Cody.

"Suits me," said Big Handy.

"Well, I'm gonna save my twenny and let you two high rollers fight it out. Fold." Pork Chop threw his cards on the pile.

"Your twenty and twenty more," said Cody.

"And twenty."

"And twenty."

"And twenty."

"And twenty."

Big Handy dug in his wallet, between his tattered Social Security card and a three-year-old prophylactic, and unfolded a hundred-dollar bill. He laid it on the table.

"I ain't got a hunnert," said Cody. "How 'bout this buckle? It's worth a hunnert."

"That buckle ain't worth a dead horse at the dog track! Tell you what, pipsqueak, I'll take the boots for a hunnert."

"Hell, these are three-hunnert-dollar Leddys!"

"All right, all yer cash and one boot."

Cody counted out thirty-seven dollars, pulled off his boot, and put them in the pot. Then he took off the other boot and set it up on the table.

"Raise you one boot," he said.

Big Handy took off his right boot, then stood up and undid his buckle.

"Call and raise you a buckle."

"Your buckle and a shirt."

"Your shirt plus a watch."

"Your watch and a pocketknife."

"Match yer knife and up you a pair of Wranglers."

"Your Wranglers and . . . and, uh . . ." Cody looked around the room.

"How 'bout my thirt?" volunteered Smila.

Cody had temporarily forgotten sweet Smila. He and Big Handy sat across the table from each other. Each wore his hat, underwear, and socks. Big Handy had on his left boot. Pork Chop sat at the table, guarding the pile of money and clothes.

"Depends on whether he can call in like manner," said Cody, lookin' at Big Handy.

"Hee thtill got hith hat!"

All three poker players looked at her like she'd just stepped off a bus from Neptune! Hats wouldn't go unless the game got serious!

"Grenadine, gimme your shirt."

"Handy, honey, all I got's this halter top."

"Fine. I'll bet your halter top and raise my last boot against the shirt and bra. Call!"

"Oh, goody," said Smila, peeling down.

"Why not," said Grenadine.

The four of them were bareback. Pork Chop sat unnoticed and slobbering on the gathering laundry.

"I called. Let's seem 'em."

Cody rolled over the jack, then the ace of hearts, the ace of clubs, the ace of diamonds.

Big Handy was addin' as fast as his distracted mind would let him. *If he paired jacks, his boat is higher than mine; if he didn't, it's just three of a kind....*

The ace of spades rolled over and snuggled in next to his brothers.

Handy froze. His face became ashen! Pork Chop's mouth fell open. The room was silent.

Blotches began to form on Big Handy's naked chest. The redness crawled up his neck until his cheeks were flaming!

"Pork Chop," Cody said quietly, "see if you can slide the pot into that paper bag there." Cody's eyes never left Big Handy's. Pork Chop gently slid the money and clothes into an Albertson's shopping bag. He picked up the boots and gave Smila the armload. He pointed to the door. She eased out to Cody's pickup.

"I'm gonna be goin' now," said Cody without moving.

Big Handy was undergoing a Vesuvian turmoil inside. His lips were twitching, his hands were quivering and his eyes were glazed over like frost on a windshield! Grenadine slipped out and got in Cody's pickup. Pork Chop followed, but watched through the motel window. From his vantage point, he saw Cody slowly rising, never dropping Big Handy's gaze.

Suddenly the table exploded from the floor and bounced off the ceiling! The air was filled with Bicycle playing cards! Cody flew around the room in his underwear like a turpentined cat! King Kong lunged after him! Big Handy picked up the black-and-white TV set and threw it at the careening figure as it climbed the wall above the picture of the matador painted on black velvet! The television exploded against the wall! Big Handy jumped and fell on the bed! Cody jumped on his back and pulled the covers around the prone body, holding the edges together. An eerie ripping sound accompanied the appearance of two giant paws tearing through the sheets!

Cody skittered to the door. He opened it, slipped through and started to close it behind him. Big Handy crashed into the edge of the door, nose first. He shattered his nasal septum.

The wounded bear screamed in pain and frustration! During Handy's temporary blindness, Cody jumped into the pickup with Pork Chop, Smila and Grenadine. They pulled onto the street and passed the flashing red lights of a City of Nampa patrol car.

"I hope Deputy Dawg has a bazooka," Cody said as he shifted into second gear.

9

Friday Night, July 16
Nampa, Idaho

Lick sat in the bar in Nampa on the Friday night after his return. He had not done well in Salinas and was not the best company. Cody had left the bar with Smila.

Lick was in a not-too-enthusiastic conversation with a local divorcee. He was also slightly drunk.

"How old are you?" she asked.

"Thirty-two," said Lick.

"How long you been rodeoing, if that's what you call it."

"Hard since ... since I was twenty-five."

"Why?"

"It's what I do."

"Did you go to college?"

"Yeah."

"Graduate?"

"Yeah, even one year toward a master's."

"And you're still ... still playing cowboy?"

"I said, it's what I do."

"Yeah, but you could probably have a good job."

"I did."

"You married?"

"Nope."

"Were you?"

"Yup."

"Kids?"

"No."

"Well, that's good, anyway."

"Maybe, maybe not."

"I don't understand. Does rodeoing pay a lot of money?"

"I broke even one year out of the last six, but this year I'm doin' okay."

"How much can you make? This year, I mean."

"Thirty, thirty-five thousand, if everything goes good."

"That after taxes and travel expenses, et cetera?"

"Nope." Lick took a sip of his gin and tonic and looked into the green eyes of the woman sitting across from him. She was staring at him like he'd just announced his inclusion in the Guinness Book of Stupidity!

"All I learned in college was how to work for somebody else. Drawin' wages. It's kind of a trap. You graduate and make pretty good money the first few years. You feel kind of a moral obligation to use your education. You get married, buy furniture, buy a car, make house payments, join the Rotary. You become responsible. An upstandin' member of the community. Then later, when you realize what's happened to you and you want to make a change, you can't. You can't afford to take any chances that would jeopardize that regular paycheck. All those people are countin' on you.

"You say to the wife, 'I want to rodeo full-time, before I'm too old to compete.' She says, 'You'll be gone all the time, who'll make the house payments? What about my bowling league, I'm president next year.' You say, 'We'll sell the house, you come with me, give your bowling ball to your sister.' She says, 'What about the dog, our vacation to Yellowstone.' You say, 'We'll take the dog and see a lot more of the country than Old Faithful.'

"But she can't see it. Can't understand it. 'Give up all this security? You must be crazy!' And you can't even discuss it with your folks or the guys at work! They're in the same trap, and the occasional person who thinks your idea is great usually turns out to be crazy, too! It's not something you can talk to people about. Eventually, though, you work it out on your own, and if you're willing to give up everything you've accumulated in life, you just do it and damn the consequences."

"Man," she said, "you are something else. What do you want most? I mean, do you have any specific goals?"

"Yeah. I'd like to make the National Finals."

"The National Finals?"

"Kind of the Superbowl of rodeo. The top fifteen contestants in the year compete at the National Finals in Oklahoma City in December. It's determined by the amount of money you win throughout the year."

"You mean the best rodeo riders in the world only make thirty thousand?"

"No. Some guys make more. Fifty, a hundred thousand. Not many make a hundred thousand, though. Plus they gotta pay expenses."

"Are you going to? Make the finals, I mean?"

"Ma'am, I don't know. I gotta good chance this year, for the first time in my life, and if I ride good, get lucky and don't get hurt, I'm gonna give the big boys a run for their money."

The lights in the dimly lit bar came up. It was one o'clock in the morning.

"Can I take you home?" Lick asked.

"Do you have a car?"

"Nope."

She looked at him for a long moment. He crackled into a slow grin. It was the twinkle in his eye that finally won her over.

"Okay," she said slowly. "I think I'd like to get to know you better."

The digital, phosphorescent clock radio was just posting 2:16 A.M. when Lick closed his eyes and drifted into sleep, folded up against the lady's backside. It was only under these conditions, or when he was sufficiently drunk, that he could go to sleep immediately.

He woke at 7:00 the next morning with the delicious feeling of a soft hand rubbing his neck. What an exquisite feeling to wake up that way. He kept his eyes closed, savoring, and groaned. There is nothing more flattering than the attention of an interesting woman.

"Hey, big boy, what would you like for breakfast?"

"Umm, how 'bout a little more of you!"

This lady looked good in the morning!

Ah, friends, there are time-outs in life. People are allotted more than they use. They should be taken when there are roses to be sniffed. For instance, this lady who looked good in the morning. That is something that never ceases to amaze. There are some women who don't even have bad breath in the morning! It's true! And their shape, the softness of their skin. The hollow spot where their clavicles collide, ankles, fingernails, the undercurve of a breast, an earlobe, a ringlet: all designed to take your breath away. Sigh.

"Will I see you again?" she asked, dropping him off at the contestants parking area where Cody was waiting.

"Do you want to?"

"Yes . . . yes, I do."

"Then you will, but I can't say just when."

"Good-bye, cowboy."

"Bye, darlin'."

Standing there on the grassy roadside in the early morning sun, Lick reflected a moment.

Another good one. I mean a good one! Maybe someday.

He leaped into the pickup. Cody was asleep in the back.

"That you, Lick?"

"Yup. Go back to sleep. I'll drive for awhile."

He switched on the radio. Willie was rippin' through "On the Road Again."

That's right, Willie, Lick thought to himself. *On the road again. Like a goose headin' south, like leaves on the Amazon, like a prisoner who just climbed the wall. Movin' just to feel the wind on yer face.*

He sighed. *Suck it up, cowboy, it's time to go.*

Lick smiled and put the truck in gear.

10

Wednesday, July 21
Kansas City, Missouri

It was in Kansas City that Cody was struck by lightning. The thunderbolt hit him right between the eyes, drove the current down his spine and crackled off the end of his lightning rod! He was dumbstruck; he fell in love!

Not puppy love, or "a walk in the park" love. No gentle tendrils of morning mist, no lingering sunset love. No! This was love right out of the bowels of Mount Saint Helens!

Lilac was twenty-eight, had a smooth forehead and wore a size nine Buster Brown!

After the Wednesday night rodeo, Lick and Cody followed the mob to one of Kansas City's finest urban cowboy dance halls. A little place called Jerry's Sandbox on Main. Cody, who had learned his footwork at community dances as a boy, watched this lovely figure dancing the swing with two or three local boys.

"Save my place," he said to Lick. He made his way to her table, where she sat with two other girls.

"Pardon me, ma'am," he said. "Would you care to dance?"

She looked up at him. She had long brown hair, stood 5'10¾", had limpid pools and lips that fit a Popsicle. The band was on the third line of "Help Me Make It Through the Night." Lilac subtly sized him up and, concluding that he was at least six feet tall, said, "I'd love to."

She stood up and looked at him at eye level. She was long and graceful. More like an impala than a cheetah. More prey than predator.

"How are ya tonight?"

"Fine," she said.

"Man, you are gorgeous!" he said, and he meant it. "You can dance, too!"

"Thank you. You're not so bad yourself." Which he wasn't.

She was a city girl gone urban cowperson. She hadn't grown up learning the mating nuances of the slow dance that is natural to small town girls. However, current began to flow.

She backed up so she could look at his face as they danced.

"What do you do?" she asked.

"Ride broncs and bulls."

"What!" She stopped and looked at him.

"Ride broncs."

"You mean horses?"

"Yup."

"For a living?"

"Well, it's not a real good livin' right now."

"What do you mean? You have a stable or something?"

"No, I rodeo."

"Oh, that's why you're here! Kansas City, I mean. For the Shriners' Rodeo?"

"Yes, ma'am."

"You're kidding. Are you sure you don't sell insurance or work in a bank or something?"

"Nope, I rodeo. Have you been?"

"No. Not ever."

"How would you like to?"

"When?"

"I'm up tomorrow."

"What!" She looked at him long. "You're not kidding, are you?"

"No, of course not. My pardner's back there if you need a reference."

"No, no. I just have to think about it a minute."

They said no more until the dance ended. Cody took her back to her group and walked back to his table in a daze. It wasn't her obvious interest in his uncommon occupation that dazed him. He was always flattered when that happened. It was her. Something about her. Though he couldn't put a finger on the feeling, she had just shot a steel-jacketed, fifty-caliber round through his galvanized aluminum status quo!

How do you describe it? Your chest, maybe your heart, gets light. You can feel your pulse beating in your neck. The sounds around you become muffled. A 747 could land on the dance floor and you wouldn't even turn around! A door opens in the recesses of your brain and the only word that comes to the front is **wonderfantastakemarvelous*!***

Cody sat down completely unaware of his cronies at the table.

"Well, I'll be a certified hellgramite! What a good-lookin' dolly!" LoBall McKinney said, and slapped Cody on the back. "Maybe I'll take 'er fer a spin myself."

"No!" exclaimed Cody. Then, surprised at himself. "Oh, sure, LoBall, whatever."

"Well, if you got 'er all lined up, it don't matter to me."

"No, no. Go ahead. I didn't mean nothin'."

LoBall traveled with two other roughstock riders. Both Cody and Lick liked LoBall, even though he seldom won and wasn't very ambitious. They'd known the blond Kansas bull rider for several years. He was about Lick's height, with blue eyes and a prominent nose. He was of average build, with an inordinate amount of hair in his ears. There were rookies who assumed his name came as a result of some anatomical anomaly. That was not the case. One night, in Garden City, Kansas, he had won $120 in a hand of jacks or back. No one could open; there were six in the game. The worst hand in the game was a nine high. LoBall won it after putting up his bull rope and Buck knife as collateral. He had a little wheel: ace, deuce, trey, four, and five.

LoBall stood up in time to see some big fellow, with feathers in his hat and designer jeans, take Lilac out on the dance floor. For three minutes he put her through the most intricate series of twirls and spins, loops, dips and catches, he had ever seen. She followed effortlessly. Cody noticed, too. His spirits sank slightly.

The band took a break and a jukebox filled in the void. People relaxed.

Cody made his way to her table.

"Can I buy you ladies a drink?"

"Sure, cowboy. Sit down. I'm Lilac, this is Rita and Maribeth. What's your name?"

"Cody."

He was staring at her.

"One white wine, a Michelob light, a gin and tonic, and . . ." she said. He didn't respond. "Cody?"

"What!"

The cocktail waitress appeared at his shoulder. Lilac gave her the order.

"Anything for you?"

"Yes, ma'am. A Velvet ditch. Sorry."

"Are you all right?"

"Yes. Oh, yes. I'm fine. 'Scuze me, I was . . . I was . . . so, you've never been to a rodeo. If yer willin', I'll take you tomorrow. They got good seats for contestants' wives, I mean friends or . . . whatever. You know what I mean."

"What are you doing tomorrow?" she asked.

"Nothin' till tomorrow night." He brightened.

"I mean tomorrow night."

"I'm up in the bull ridin'."

"Are those fellas with you in the rodeo, too?" she asked.

"Those three at the table? Would you like to meet them? All of you?" He turned to Rita and Maribeth.

"Sure, why not."

Cody waved his partners over. They drew up chairs and surrounded the three girls.

"This is Lilac." Cody scooted closer to her, a display of territoriality that would have been noted by any animal behaviorist present. "Rita and Maribeth, this is Lick, LoBall and Franco."

Pretty soon, Cody had his arm around Lilac. Rita and Maribeth were sorted out and spotted between Lick and LoBall, and LoBall and Franco. Another round was ordered as the vociferous vaqueros regaled the maidens with stories of rodeo bravado and derring-do. Cody was sinking into the quicksand of infatuation.

By midnight Lick was drunk, Franco had related his whole

Portuguese lineage, LoBall had eaten eight spearmint Certs and Cody was mired up to his earlobes. We're talkin' cloud nine, straightjacket, last cigarette and blindfold—rapture!

As Cody sat like a space cadet on Pentothol one of the female dancers tumbled into his lap.

"Oh, excuse me!" she said.

Cody helped her lift off.

"Hey, you jerk!"

Cody turned around, still basking in the first plane of anesthesia, just in time to see a right cross four inches from his face!

Friends, forgive the intrusion, but I feel a word is in order here regarding amateur pugilism. Many of us imagine ourselves being forced to fight in defense of a noble cause. We rise to the occasion and vanquish the bully. A small scar, like a saber slash, remains on our cheek as a reminder of that moment of glory.

Or a drunk insults your date. You snort with disdain and walk briskly by, tightening your grip on her elbow. That night you toss and turn reliving what you should have done to defend her honor.

I believe fighting is instinctual. Maybe not as basic an instinct as shopping, but a primitive action just the same. When struck, one strikes back, particularly when the first blow is a surprise.

When you are blindsided at an intersection, you counterpunch.

Cody went backward over his chair and slid like a halibut on a tile floor. He wound up under the next table!

The protagonist, hereinafter known as One-punch Charlie, straightened up. Franco, who was sitting closest to the action, leaped from his chair and jumped on One-punch Charlie's back!

Franco swung both legs around One-punch Charlie's waist and brought his boot heels down on the big man's knees. The men fell forward into the scattering crowd as the band played on—"Hard Hat Days and Honky Tonk Nights." One-punch Charlie might have been a professional football player, because two of his friends fell on Franco like he was a loose ball!

LoBall grabbed one of the big boys by the hair and pulled him off Franco. Atlas turned around and stood up. LoBall let go of his hair. In fact, he couldn't reach the top of his head!

Atlas came up from the basement with an uppercut to the midsection! His fist came knuckle-to-silver with the 1980 Prairie Circuit All Around Champion Trophy buckle that LoBall proudly wore! He broke two bones in his little finger and dislocated the knuckle in his ring finger. The impact carried LoBall two buzzard lengths away!

Lick was on top of the third member of the invading force. Though not as big as One-punch Charlie or Atlas, Billy Goat Gruff surpassed them in ferocious appearance. Billy Goat Gruff was still on top of Franco trying to strangle him! Franco was still on top of One-punch Charlie! They looked like a line of bunny hoppers that had caved in on itself.

Lick had his hands around Billy Goat Gruff's head from behind. He had an index finger up each of Billy Goat's nostrils, pulling them apart like he was setting a gopher trap!

Cody came to with a ringing in his ears. He crawled out from under the table and struggled to his feet. He stumbled and accidentally stepped on Billy Goat's ankle, which was sticking out of the pile like a leg on a soft-shell crab between two pieces of bread.

You could hear the bone snap! Billy Goat Gruff screamed! Atlas spun around and swung on Cody with his broken hand! Cody tripped simultaneously! Atlas connected with Cody's shoulder blade! The long bone in his middle finger cracked at the metaphysis!

Police whistles froze everybody in their tracks! The officers dragged Lick off the pile. Billy Goat Gruff stood up. Tears streamed from his eyes, there was blood on his lip, he couldn't put any weight on his left foot and his nostrils looked like his mother spent the night with a camel!

Franco was flatter'n hammered tinfoil!

One-punch Charlie had two fractured kneecaps and couldn't get up. Cody's eye was swelling and LoBall still couldn't catch his breath. Lick felt suddenly nauseous. He turned to avoid embarrassment and barfed on One-punch Charlie's girlfriend's pantleg, who was kneeling over her wounded gladiator, cooing.

LoBall did the talking.

"No, sir."

"No, sir."

"No, sir."

"Nobody's fault."

"Not much damage, really."

"Yes, sir. Well some."

"We'll pitch in for the chair."

"Yes, sir."

"Tonight? Yes, sir. Out of town. Yes, sir, by dawn."

"Would you mind giving us a few minutes' head start before you release King Kong and Rambo."

"No, sir. Didn't mean to be a smart-aleck. No, sir, I guess they can't travel too good, anyway."

"I just thought—"

"Yes, sir. We're going."

LoBall gathered up Lick and Cody. They balanced Franco between them and split like four caroling winos!

* * *

Ten A.M. Thursday found them all bruised, hung over, on greasy beds in room 306 at the Wanderon Inn, off I-35.

Cody was sitting on the bed in his shorts. More accurately, he was sitting on Franco in his shorts. His mouth tasted like he'd been sucking on a roll of pennies.

"Damn, Lick. Damn, damn, damn! Lick, what do I do? How can I find 'er? All I know is 'Lilac.' 'Course, she probably doesn't want anything to do with me after last night."

Cody was having a sinking spell. His left eye was swollen to a slit and purple. It looked like a canned plum.

"Now wait a minute, Cody," said Lick. "You don't know that. She knows where to find you. Didn't you tell 'er you were up tonight? See, you might be surprised. Besides, it don't matter anyway."

"Lick, she was different! Didn't you see her? She was gorgeous. Delicious, and she liked me!"

"So what? There's millions of gorgeous, delicious women."

"Dammit, Lick, she was different."

Cody felt terrible. He hadn't been that close to something good in so long. His ol' heart was aching.

Longing? Loneliness? Love? Lust? Doesn't really matter which. All require that the object in question be present to be satisfied. And she had disappeared!

11

July 22
Kansas City, Missouri

That night at the big coliseum, Cody kept studying the crowd. *Hell,* he thought, *there's no way I'd see her, even if she did come.*

During the calf roping Cody was limbering up. They ran the first set of bulls into the chutes and slid the gates closed behind them. Cody's bull was in the next set. He put on his chaps and tied on his spurs. Looping his bull rope on a board behind the chutes, he rosined up his rope and glove.

Concentrate, he thought. *I know the bull. Bucks out straight three or four jumps, then spins to the right. Sit tight and be ready when he starts the spin. Don't be off balance to the left when he makes his move. Have that right spur dug in on the third jump. Good honest bull. He's not a buckle-winnin' draw, but if he's at his best and I am, we could have a chance at the money. Ridable, but don't take him for granted.*

Cody didn't watch the first six bull riders. He concentrated. *Slow, steady breathing. Relax. A vacuum.*

Then suddenly the gates slid back and the last six bulls rumbled in like boxcars! Bull 655, Tonto, was fidgeting in chute number five. Cody sprang to life! Lick was beside him. Cody dropped the loop end of the bull rope over the right side of Tonto, behind the elbow. Lick caught it underneath, through the boards with the hook. Cody ran the tail of the rope through the loop and tightened it up, testing for size.

Just right.

Just then, LoBall McKinney stuck his head over the chute gate. "She's here, Cody," he said, and then was gone.

Cody looked up, looked around, but saw nothing.

She's here, he thought. *She's here! Concentrate. She's here!*

Number 655 stood patiently while Lick tightened the rope. Cody hit a few more licks on the tail with his rosined glove.

"You're next," Lick said quietly.

"Now your attention, please, to chute number five, a Wyoming cowboy, Cody Wing, up on bull number six-five-five, Tonto."

Cody straddled the bull, sitting well back over Tonto's flanks, his boots on the boards. The calm descended over him like it always did at this particular moment. It was timeless and silent. He slid his hand, palm up, into the flat braided loop on the rope. Lick pulled again. Cody nodded. Then he took the tail of the rope across his palm, wrapped it around his hand, put a twist in it and flopped the tail forward of the handhold.

With his right hand he screwed his hat down, and then spit out his chew.

Tonto, you braymer sonuvabitch, I want the best you've got, he telepathed to the back of the bull's head. Then he smiled. *Perfect.*

He slid up on the rope, leaned forward, pointed his toes and furiously nodded his head!

Ol' 655 tensed. The gate swung open. For a split second, Tonto and Cody sat like a statue of Simon Bolívar in a park in Bogotá, Colombia. Then they burst into the arena under the gaze of 9,652 paid spectators! The first jump and deep breath squeezed Cody's left hand like a vise! Cody was settin' pretty. Second jump he spurred! Up on the third jump, spurring! Down, third jump, set right spur, stay to the right. Uptight on the hump. Into the spin, just like the book said. Spur with the left! Tonto tried to stick his head under his tail! Tight spin. Two spins, three, kick, kick high! Cody felt the kick coming, leaned back, ready, no sweat. Spur on the left, tight on right, two more spins! Kick coming, kick coming now! Tonto became completely airborne in a high kicking spin, Cody spurring on both sides, chaps flying, toes out, silver flashing! At the top of the lift-off the whistle blew!

Tonto came down, off balance, spinning to the right with both hind legs off center. Cody released his grip as Tonto hit the ground hard with his left hip! Cody's hand came free and he rolled off to his left. Tonto was on his feet. Cody was on his knees. Less than five feet separated their noses. For two seconds Tonto stared at Cody, shaking! Then the bull snorted and shook his head! *You did it, Tonto. Thanks!* One of the clowns darted between Cody and his eight-second business partner. Tonto ambled off after the clown.

Slowly Cody became aware of his surroundings. The crowd was on its feet, cheering wildly.

"Ladies and gentlemen . . . Ladies and gentlemen . . . A new leader in the bull riding, Cody Wing with an eight-five score!"

The house came down!

Cody took off his hat and bowed to the crowd. He was still smiling.

He watched the last bull rider. A 72 score.

"Drive safely, everyone and God bless. We'll see you back here tomorrow night. Good night."

Cody was taking off his chaps, spurs and glove and gathering up his gear. He was also soaking up the gladhanding and congratulations. He had made one hell of a bull ride! It had to be Tonto's best ever, too. "Best I've ever seen you ride," Lick had said. It was, Cody knew it.

"Cody. Someone to see you," said one of the cowboys.

Lilac stood in the arena, next to the chutes. He walked through the little gate toward her.

He wanted to run to her, slow motion, two lovers in a field of daisies like in the margarine ads, but he walked. A crooked grin on his face and a fading shiner.

She wanted to run toward him, too, like in the margarine ads. Instead she walked up to him, put her arms around him and hugged him. Her eyes were glistening with tears.

"Hey, cowboy, wanna get lucky?"

* * *

At her apartment Cody got cleaned up. She set him a glass of wine on the bathroom sink while he was in the shower. He was still on a natural high when he came downstairs and found her in lounging pajamas.

She rubbed his shoulders, held his face, kissed his hands and ran her fingers through his hair.

She was the most beautiful creature Cody had ever seen. She smelled like fresh peaches. She was brown and bathing suit white, smooth as a filly's nose and firm as an orthopedic mattress! When she laughed, it was the sound of wind chimes on a Santa Fe patio.

She made love to him like butterfly wings and new socks, like lime juice and icicles, like a hot tub full of maple syrup.

12

Friday Night, August 6
Great Falls, Montana
The Club Cigar

Three weeks after the Kansas City Summit.

10:15 P.M. Mountain Daylight Time (11:15 P.M. Central Daylight Time):

"Hello. Lilac?"

"Yes?"

"Lilac, this is Cody."

"Cody! Where are you?"

"Great Falls."

"Is that near Kansas City?"

"No, in Montana."

"Oh."

"How you doin'?"

"Fine. I'm doing fine."

"You don't sound too fine."

"I was just a little disappointed. I thought maybe you were back in town."

"That's what I wanted to talk to you about."

"Yes?"

"Lick and me will be comin' back to Burwell and Sidney next weekend, and I'd shore like to see you again."

"Where's Sidney?"

"Iowa. Prob'ly two hours from Kansas City."

"I could drive over and see you."

"That would be great!"

"How long are you staying? I mean, could you come back to Kansas City with me?"

"I haven't got it all figgered out yet, but I surely could. We're both up in Abilene on the seventeenth, so I might could stay a couple three days."

"Cody, that would be wonderful! I can't wait!"

"Me, neither!"

"What's that noise?"

"The jukebox. I'm at the Club Cigar. Neat ol' bar here in Great Falls. They claim Charlie Russell used to hang out here. I don't know, everybody in Montana claims to have known him personally."

"What are you doing?"

"Just the usual. Settin' around shootin' the breeze. I just got here."

"Did you ride tonight?"

"Bareback. Might've done okay, too. We'll see after tomorrow night."

"Well, you do good, little buckaroo. Your biggest fan is back here in K.C. rootin' for you!"

"Oh, yeah?"

"You bet!"

"Lilac . . ."

"Yes?"

"Lilac, I really do like you a lot. I've never met anybody like you."

"I think you're pretty special yourself."

"I don't know if I ever thanked you properly for the fantastic time you showed me in K.C."

"Cody, the pleasure was mine."

The operator cut in. "Thirty seconds, please."

"Listen, I'll call you down the road, but save me that weekend?"

"Okay, Cody. I'll be waiting to hear from you."

" 'Bye, darlin'."

" 'Bye."

Click. Buzz.

Cody hung on the phone a few seconds. His heart felt heavy and light at the same time.

"You done?" asked the queued-up cowboy.

"Yeah. Yup, go ahead." He hung up the receiver.

He ambled into the crowded bar. He could picture Lilac. He could almost feel the warmth of lying next to her long browned body. The way she touched him with her long fingernails, tracing patterns on his chest. The way her hair fell around her face, her confident, trusting eyes. Her laugh, really a deep chuckle, that warmed his insides when he heard it. Cody felt a hollow empty longing.

"Hey, you blue-ribbon codpiece! Set yore raggedy ol' butt down here!"

Cody lifted out of his thoughts. "LoBall, what'cha doin'?"

"Set down and have a beer!"

"How you doin', Lo? Haven't seen you since Kansas City."

"Oh, gettin' by. Not winnin' much, though. Don't know how much longer the money will hold out."

"Me, too. Me, too."

LoBall McKinney took a pull on his draw.

Cody contemplated LoBall. He figgered LoBall to be a couple years older than himself, twenty-nine or thirty. Good fellow, honest, easygoing. LoBall was from Oberlin, Kansas, he remembered. Been rodeoing several years.

"Lo, you ever been married?"

"Yup. Twice. One lasted a month. The other a year."

"What happened?"

"Just couldn't quit rodeoin'. They couldn't put up with it."

"Were you in love?"

"You betcher spine-tinglin' cloaca I wuz! The second time, anyways."

"What was it like? I mean, how did you know?"

LoBall put down his glass and stared at Cody. Cody's face was painted a desperate shade of agony.

"You reckon you got bit, ol' pardner?" LoBall asked seriously.

"I don't know. I'm not sure. I don't know what it's supposed to feel like."

"It prob'ly feels different fer everybody. Sometimes it's an atom bomb, sometimes it's a meadowlark's song. Sometimes it sneaks up on you like a sore throat. How do you feel?"

"Well, sort of good and sort of bad. Is it supposed to feel bad?"

LoBall mused a second, wiping the beads of sweat off his glass.

"Yeah, there's a part of bein' in love that's bad. Sad, really. You'd think it would be all happy, but there's a part of it that's sad. Maybe it's suppose to hurt a little. Nothin' comes without a cost. It would be nice if it always felt good, but when you love somebody, when they hurt, you hurt. When they're happy, you're happy. Or you should be anyway. When you get to missin' someone you care about, it's like you peeled the hide off yer heart and all those bad feelin's you never cared about before can slip right in that same hole that love left. It kind of exposes you. You know what I mean? Like before, you were never lonesome or jealous or protective of nothin', so you never had those feelin's, but when you fall in love, you gotta take the bad with the good. Does that make any sense?"

"Sort of."

"Do I know 'er?"

" 'Member Lilac, from Kansas City?"

"Her! Man, do I remember! A died-in-the-wool snowy cottontail!"

"That's her."

"Have you told her?"

"Hell, I've only seen 'er once! Lo, Lick says I'm crazy!"

"Cody. You can't pay no 'tention to Lick. I've known him longer than you, and that pore ol' rat bag is sour on women. He wouldn't know a good one if she danced in his pork and beans!"

"He always has a lot of women. Every town we go to it seems, he has one stashed."

"Yeah, but they don't last long. They figger the pore bugger out purty fast and send him packin'."

"I don't want to end up like that."

"You won't. Somethin' burned him a long time ago. He's runnin' from love and yer runnin' to it!" LoBall thumped his beer down earnestly. "So, how does Lilac feel 'bout you rodeoin'? That's the death of many a cowboy romance."

"I never asked, but you know, I been doin' the circuit hard for nine years and I'm really not gettin' ahead. I been thinkin' 'bout quittin'. Git a job somewheres or go back to the ranch. Maybe goin' to college."

"Yeah, we all think about that some."

LoBall and Cody discussed love on into the night.

12:45 A.M. Mountain Daylight Time (1:45 A.M. Central Daylight Time):

"Hello, Lilac?"

"Cody?"

"Sorry to wake you."

"Ummmm, that's okay. Something wrong?"

"No. I just wanted to talk to you."

"Okay."

Silence.

"Cody?"

"Yeah?"

"What do you want to talk about?"

"Lilac. I . . . me and LoBall, we talked and had a few beers. I . . . I think I might be a little drunk. But not very drunk! Just a little."

"That's okay."

"Lilac?"

"Yes?"

"How do you feel about things?"

"Things? What things?"

"Important things."

"What do you mean, Cody?"

"Things like . . . uh . . . real feelings?"

"Cody. I think people should always be honest with each other."

"Whattaya mean?"

"They should tell each other the truth."

"I'm really thinkin' about you tonight," he said in a quiet voice.

Silence.

"I'm missin' you somethin' awful," he said in a small quieter voice.

Silence.

"Lilac?"

"Yes, Cody?"

"I think I'm fallin' in love . . ." She could barely hear him. The words faded off through Mountain Bell's spaghetti lines into that black space where true confessions and old memories lie around gathering stardust and wait to be recalled.

"Come see me, cowboy. I'll be here."

" 'Bye, darlin'."

" 'Bye."

Click. Buzz.

13

Monday
Great Falls, Montana

Monday morning found the boys' pickup headed south out of Great Falls on Highway 89. Destination: an old friend's place in Hardin, Montana, to lay up for a couple of days before making the Rapid City rodeo on Thursday. Hardin sat on the edge of the Crow Indian Reservation, fifteen miles north of where General Custer fired his last shot.

They hit Interstate 90 at two in the afternoon and headed east toward Billings and Hardin. The freeway parallels the Yellowstone River as it courses toward Billings. Beautiful and clear, the river relaxes the traveler and invites a closer look.

Lick and Cody had both placed in the money in Great Falls. They were in good spirits. Lick because he'd bought a new pair of sunglasses that morning, and Cody because he had been bit by the love bug!

Several miles up the road Bill and Doris Peeler had pulled their motor home off the highway into a rest area that was near the mighty Yellowstone. Doris set out a folding chair and poured herself an iced coffee. Bill lifted his spinning rod off its hook over the door, pocketed a jar of Patooshki Fireballs and started upstream.

"Watch out for Melanie," instructed Doris as the mongrel terrior trotted after Bill.

Porcupines lead fairly quiet lives. They nibble, climb trees and rummage around, mostly minding their own business. They do not seek trouble, no more than a tire seeks a nail. But that does not keep trouble from finding them.

The porcupine that now joins our cast happened to be exploring amongst the willers that populated the bank upstream from the rest area. It had a little sip from a stranded pool of cool water and lay down to sun itself. It drifted off to sleep dreaming porcupine dreams. Twitching occasionally, winking off a fly and lazily flopping its tail. Porcupines are never bored. To their everlasting good fortune, they can't tell the difference between boredom and contentment.

"Pull over up here," suggested Cody. Lick turned leisurely into the rest area. He drove several car lengths beyond the parked motor home with Doris sitting nearby.

Our boys got out, stretched their legs and breathed in the cool air. They could hear the river flowing by like a distant locomotive.

Cody started walking toward the motor home. "Where ya goin'?" he asked back over his shoulder to Lick.

"Oh, just down by the river," said Lick. Both of them knew sometimes you just needed a little time alone. Cody watched him go. Lick was relaxed and thoughtful. He'd listened patiently to Cody's analysis of his fledgling relationship with Lilac. Cody needed to talk. Lick had done his part, he listened.

The river had carved out a good-sized gravel bar. No doubt it had been underwater in the spring, but now it allowed easy access to the river's edge. Lick reached the bar and walked slowly upstream, unconsciously soaking up the scenery, consciously clearing his mind.

Bill was casting into the swift current upstream from the gravel bar. He was methodically dragging his baited spinner into likely looking spots.

Melanie stayed near him but explored the brushy bank, sniffing holes and tracks of the residents who populated the neighborhood they'd invaded.

Porcupine lay on his side deep in sleep in the thick willers.

Lick continued his amble up the gravel bar thinking snatches of thoughts that kept him awake at nights, but quickly putting them out of his mind.

Bill moved downstream along the bank. He could not see Lick standing fifty feet away.

Melanie moved downstream through the brush, still circling.

Porcupine entered the flatline plane of slumber. Lick spotted something sparkling in the shallow water. He squatted at the river's edge and realized it was a spinner with two neon-colored salmon eggs lying in a quiet spot. A ten-inch rainbow trout was treading water two feet downstream from the bait, watching it.

Mesmerized, Lick watched the unfolding drama. He became absorbed as the trout beat his wings in the water to maintain his position. Lick momentarily forgot where he was, who he was, or why he existed. He became, for a brief period of time, *one* with the fish. He squatted on the bank of the Yellowstone hypnotized.

Melanie smelled Porcupine. She crept up to the sleeping rodent and sniffed his nose.

Porcupine opened one eye, spied the dog and leaped up! Melanie was so shocked she couldn't bark! Porcupine shot out of the willers onto the gravel bar! With the predator behind him, Porcupine made straight for the only protective cover on the bank! Melanie recovered her voice just as the trout struck the lure and Porcupine dove between Lick's legs!

Bill set the hook and Lick fell back, straddling Porcupine like a Hell's Angel mounting a Harley!

Porcupine squiggled free and shot into the water like a loose ball in the backfield! Melanie stood on the bank and yapped ferociously! Bill was reeling in his catch and Lick sat frozen in place like a butterfly pinned to a cork board!

Melanie's furious barking subsided but not before Cody and Doris came striding toward the ruckus. Bill was just coming out of the willers with the nice rainbow still wiggling on the end of the line. Melanie was sniffing around Lick, who sat bowlegged and leaned back on his elbows. Porcupine had beached himself and disappeared downstream.

"By gosh, nice fish!" observed Cody.

"Oh, yeah," agreed Doris. "Bill almost always catches fish. We're seniors, ya know, so we never worry about a license. I usually cook 'em. We like fresh fish. Sometimes I use cornmeal and fry 'em. Bill's mother used to do 'em that way with catfish, but I like to bake 'em.

A little lemon and butter, some garlic salt. We've got propane, ya know. Nice stove. Maybe you'd like to . . ."

By now Cody had realized that Doris was a marathon conversationalist. He looked at Lick who, as yet, hadn't moved.

"You all right, Lick?" asked Cody.

Lick turned his head. Cody saw his face was the color of boiled tongue.

Cody put his hands under Lick's armpits and started to lift him up.

"No-o-o-o-o-o-o-o-o-o!" howled Lick.

Lick's eyes were glistening and saliva dribbled from his mouth. It was then Cody noticed the inside of Lick's legs. From knee to shining knee, up his inseam, and arching across his fly, were uncountable protruding spines!

"Dang! Looks like you sat in a cactus!" said Cody, glancing around for a cactus.

"Porcupine," breathed Lick.

"There must be a hundred stuck in you," said Cody in amazement.

"See if you can pull 'em out," said Lick.

Cody grasped a quill and tugged. Lick groaned. The quill remained firmly embedded.

"Jerk on it," instructed Lick.

Cody did as he was told. The quill came out of the skin but lifted the denim up and stayed fast. When he let go of the quill it repenetrated Lick's leg. He shivered with pain.

"Best get you to a doctor," said Cody.

* * *

At 4:45 P.M. Cody was standing at the emergency room admitting desk in Billings Memorial Hospital.

"May I help you?" asked the nurse. She was in her early fifties and cheerful. Cody's mother's age. Her name tag said Betty Jo.

"Well," started Cody, "it's my pardner."

"What's wrong with him?" she asked.

"He had an accident."

"Is he hurt?" The ludicrousness of the question evaded Cody. Besides, it was not his nature to concoct sarcastic replies.

"Yes, ma'am. He was attacked."

"What was the nature of this attack?" she continued, poising her ballpoint above the admittance form.

"It was down by the river," he explained.

"A wild animal? A bear? Mountain lion?"

"No, ma'am," Cody said. "A porcupine."

"Attacked by a porcupine?" She looked up at him above her 1.5x Walgreen half glasses.

"Well, actually he sat on it."

Cody, straight-faced, explained his version of the assault, including Bill's ten-inch rainbow. By the time he'd finished the story, the nurse had dropped her pen, weaved away from the counter and was doubled over in the corner, pounding on the bookshelf breathless with laughter! She scattered paperwork and pencils all over the floor.

"He's out in the truck," said Cody helplessly.

She had another involuntary siege of giggling.

It took a full minute for her to compose herself. As she wrote "Porcupine Attack" under "reason for admittance," tears were streaming down her face.

"We better have a look," she sighed.

Cody led her out to the pickup and opened the back of the camper shell. Lick was bent over the tack box. Cody had arranged a saddle and blanket on the top of it and Lick was laid over it like a roll of carpet on a pack mule.

His legs were spread apart with his buttocks in the air. His hands were braced over the far side.

The nurse peered in and involuntarily said, "Hike!" After a brief moment she recovered and disappeared into the emergency room. She returned with two orderlies and every employee within two miles! As the growing crowd of nurse's aides, residents and ambulatory patients jostled for a better view, the orderlies worked Lick to the back of the truck.

They formed a sling with their arms and carried him like a dead alligator into the large examination room. Unable to lay him on a bed, they set him in the middle of the floor. Lick lay propped up on his knees and elbows as gunshot victims, fracture recipients and alcoholic hallucinators sat up on their gurneys and stared at the human pincushion.

"All right! Break it up!" commanded an authoritative voice. "Nurse, get this rabble out of here! You! Staff, get back to your duties!"

The crowd grudgingly gave way as Dr. Klugman-Smith faced her patient, or more properly, as her patient about-faced her.

"Did he admit himself?" she asked Betty Jo.

Betty Jo had a fleeting picture of Lick coming down the sidewalk, moving crablike through a crowd. She swallowed the bubble rising inside her. "No, Doctor, this gentleman . . ." She turned to Cody and broke into uncontrollable snorts. Holding her sides and finally leaning on an unconscious weekend housepainter, she heaved and tried to catch her breath.

"Cactus?" asked Dr. Klugman-Smith.

Cody stared into the intense brown eyes of Dr. Klugman-Smith, twenty-nine years old, hair pulled back in a bun and in her first year of residency.

"Porcupine."

"How . . ." she started to ask, but the admitting room nurse burst out with a convulsive peal and plunged blindly through the crowd toward the exit!

Dr. Klugman-Smith walked around to Lick's front end and introduced herself. Lick tried to cock his head but all he could see were her white pants and sensible shoes.

After lengthy discussion and some experimentation they managed to roll up a small mattress for Lick to lie over. They lifted him up on an exam table with him bent over the mattress.

After three futile attempts to pull the quills through his jeans, Dr. Klugman-Smith borrowed a set of side cutters from Hospital Maintenance and began clipping the quills where they protruded through the cloth. Each *click* jiggled the needle-sharp points, causing Lick to emit grunts, then cries and eventually whimpers.

Having completed the pruning, they gently pulled down his pants. They peeled loose like Velcro.

Next came his underwear.

Mercifully, Dr. Klugman-Smith summoned the anesthesiologist on duty and put Lick out of his misery.

Lick was back in high school. The big game for the Vega Longhorns. The crowd watched on in the balmy Texas panhandle Friday night. Lick looked down the line to the left, then to the right, and located the linebacker just over the line. "Hup one, hup two!" He felt the center move. His crotch exploded and Lick flew over the goalpost on his back, large antennae bristling on his body like feelers on a lobster!

"Wake up, Lick," a voice said gently. "You're all right."

Lick opened his eyes and Dr. Klugman-Smith stood beside his bed, clipboard in hand.

"You're all right. We got them all out."

As he stared, she became less fuzzy. He remembered where he was.

"Quills have hundreds of minute barbs. You were under anesthesia for an hour and a half. But we got them all. Eighty-seven, I believe they said. We've given you antibiotics and treated you locally but I'm afraid there's going to be swelling. Especially in your genitals. You took several direct hits in the most sensitive areas."

She went on explaining in gruesome detail the importance of bed rest. Particularly to prevent swelling. Prolonged swelling could result in sterility. Inactivity, keeping cool were the bywords. She added she had prescribed a laxative to reduce straining.

* * *

As she left her patient she passed Cody in the waiting room. She tried to speak to him but was seized by what appeared to be a fit, covered her mouth and hurried from the room.

Cody entered and stood by Lick's bed. Lick was on his back with his legs elevated in a sling. He wore a large diaper-looking loincloth.

"Man, who'da thought it," observed Cody. "Well, at least yer not up again till Thursday."

Friends, there are injuries and there are injuries. During my hormone-charged youth, more than once I was able to affect the "Bull Rider's Limp." In my confused mind I envisioned this limp would illicit sympathy and admiration from the opposite sex.

I assume high school and college football players took advantage of sprains, strains, black eyes and casts for the same purpose.

There are all manner of these "glamorous" injuries that add to the projection of the macho image. Even today at poolside, when someone asks about the scar on my shoulder, I modestly say, "Broke my shoulder . . . [pause for effect] riding bulls."

On the other hand, when one of my real cowboy friends accidentally rode his horse up a guywire, resulting in an equine back flip and human broken ankle, he preferred not to discuss it. Of course, his friends made sure everybody in the immediate vicinity knew the gruesome details.

Falling off the cookhouse steps, dropping a rock on your foot or sticking a screwdriver up your nose do not qualify as glamorous injuries. Nor, I might add, does sitting on a porcupine.

14

Monday Morning, August 9
Kansas City, Missouri

"Guess who called this weekend?" Lilac addressed the question to her nine-to-five confidante and fellow secretary, Maribeth.

"Robert?"

"Nope."

"Tim?"

"Nope."

"Who?"

"Cody."

"The cowboy!" said Maribeth knowingly. "Is he coming back to Kansas City?"

"This weekend."

"No kidding! Wait a minute, you . . . didn't you have something planned? Tickets to Air Supply?"

"They weren't firm. Tim said he'd call if he could get them. But I guess I'll be busy."

"Serves him right."

"Oh, he's all right. He's a good time."

"Cody," mused Maribeth. "I'll never forget that fight at Jerry's. What a night."

"Maribeth, you should have seen him ride that bull. It was beautiful!"

"Beautiful?"

"It's hard to explain, but that's the only word that comes to mind when I remember it. Guess I've always thought of rodeos as horrid, like bullfights, but I'd probably go to a bullfight now."

"Not me. They kill the poor bull." Maribeth scowled.

"Maybe you're right, but it's the same kind of thrill. The challenge."

"Turns you on, huh?"

"How many people do you know that make a living pitting themselves against something that can kill you? Where your only defense is your own instincts. How many? I can't think of another person I know, personally."

"Oooooh, you got it bad! Did he tell you all that?"

"No. He doesn't talk about it that way. He talked about it, but like he was rebuilding a motor or outlining a sales pitch."

"Like being married to a race car driver or a boxer?"

"Or a matador. But let's not be getting marriage into the conversation," cautioned Lilac.

"Not the marrying kind? Just like every other eligible, conceited chauvinist within ten years of our age!"

"I dunno," answered Lilac, ignoring the diatribe. "He's kind of a drifter. He's had lots of jobs, but only long enough to finance his rodeoing. But, you know, Maribeth, I could almost sense something in him that made me think he's looking for a change."

"What do you mean?"

"The way he talked about his family's ranch back in Wyoming."

"Wouldn't that take the cake? Suave, sophisticated city girl marries Wyoming rancher ... Git along little doggie!" Maribeth laughed.

"There's something about him I really like."

"His cute little buns?"

"No. No, it's like ... well, he's real. Right down to his filthy chewing tobacco and the cow manure on his boots. I never thought about cowboys bein' real. Almost makes you believe there is a Roy Rogers."

Maribeth shook her head and smiled affectionately at her friend. She thought, *I hope this knight in shining armor doesn't have feet of Nike. One of us deserves a break.*

15

August 12
Rapid City, South Dakota

I'd rather eat barbed wire than listen to disco." Cody read the bumper sticker on the pickup in front of them. They had picked up Interstate 90 eight miles north of Sturgis, South Dakota.

"Man, what beautiful country!" Cody remarked as the tan hillsides, dotted with clumps of evergreens, surrounded their pickup. Chocolate chips in raw cookie dough.

Lick had good memories of Rapid City. His first big win this year was the Winter Show at the Civic Center, back in February. That thought gave him temporary respite from the current problem gnawing at his nerve ends. One of his special lady friends lived here. Chadron was her name. He saw her two or three times a year and usually stayed with her when he was in Rapid. Last summer she had resigned herself to him and his ways. Part of her feelings for him had died with the realization that her long-term future probably did not include him. But she decided she could handle her own heart and should enjoy as much of him as he let her.

Four days had passed since the porcupine incident. Lick was recovering. He could sit without much pain, though wiggling still hurt. Most of the swelling had gone down, with the particular exception of his dangling participles. They were several shades of bruised blue and yellow. Although they were swollen, he thought it was less than yesterday.

It was also painful, quite so. Movement—walking, for instance—

was awkward. He had been forced to draw out of the bull riding in Rapid City. He remembered Dr. Klugman-Smith's admonition that if he didn't take it very easy, permanent damage could result.

Lick knew Chadron would be disappointed. He'd talked to her last week and they had planned the weekend together. Now he'd have to explain ... *Explain what?* he thought. *That even being near her could render him sterile and forever at half-mast!* "And why?" she would ask, taking it all very personally. Lick could not think the scenario through.

Rapid City sponsors two big rodeos during the year. This summer show was part of the Central States Fair. The boys pulled into the contestant parking off Omaha Street at 6:30 P.M. They gathered their gear. Cody was up tonight.

"Lickity!" Chadron Borglum ran up and gave him a big hug.

"Chadron. How'd you find us so fast?" Lick asked.

"I was watchin' the contestants' entrance and recognized your pickup. How you doin'?" She hugged him and gave him a big kiss. "I've got a great time planned after the rodeo," she said. "Relaxing ... good company."

"Great. I'm ready fer that, Chadron. I need to visit with you about somethin'."

"Fine. We'll have plenty of time. I've got to get back to the booth. I'll catch you after the bulls. Do good, darlin'. Seeya!" She took off.

Following the show Lick found Chadron and they left the rodeo grounds in her car. If she noticed that Lick had drawn out of the bulls, she didn't say anything. That wouldn't have been her style.

"Cody's not coming with us?" Chadron asked. She was a nice-lookin', twenty-nine-year-old brunette who worked for the Rapid City Chamber of Commerce. She'd been ranch raised, a west river girl. She was easygoing and classy.

"No. He's doin' somethin' else."

"Okay." They headed north, out of town. "Let me tell you what's been going on ..." She talked. He remembered one of the many reasons he kept coming back to roost on her bedpost. She relaxed him. Made him feel comfortable. Even their silences were comfortable. She didn't let him get away with half explanations and she encouraged his dreams. She loved him. She had said it. He did not respond in kind. She had only said it once, and not at all in the last several months, but he knew. She let him tell the truth about his feelings, or lack of them, and she never held it against him. He would miss her.

"Now Ron and Rayla are nice folks. You met them last time you were here. He's a rancher and I go out to their place a lot. She's become a pretty good friend, and you'll like them."

They took a right at Piedmont and wound up the road into the hills.

"Tonight," she said, "we're having barbecue and hot tub!"

"Boy, that sounds great!" said Lick. Dr. Klugman-Smith had suggested cool baths. This might be therapeutic if the water wasn't too hot.

"They've got plenty to drink and I brought some scotch... You've got a bathing suit?"

"Yup."

Ron Rant and his wife, Rayla, turned out to be all Chadron said they were. A young ranching couple on the family ranch. He was confident, good with cattle and had done some punkin roller rodeoin' when he was younger. He had the makin's of a dignified, successful livestock man.

The hot tub was in the backyard, on a green lawn surrounded by a rail fence. A big Hereford bull stood sleepily watching the party over the top rail. The half-moon silhouetted the hills and trees surrounding the ranch.

Everybody got mellow and Lick almost fell asleep in the temporary arms of Cutty Sark's peace of mind. Ron and Rayla said their friendly good-nights about 12:45 A.M. Chadron snuggled under Lick's arm. They soaked up the hot tub, the crickets, the clean smell and the moonlight for fifteen minutes. Silently.

Chadron started taking off Lick's bathing suit.

"Darlin', I . . . I can't."

She stopped.

"I mean, right now."

She stared at him.

"I'm on medication."

"Are you all right?"

"Yeah, I just have to take this medicine and the doc said no sexual activities for a while."

"What's wrong? Something serious?"

"No. It's just for a few days."

Chadron Borglum had never been married, had an article published in *Scientific American,* or received more than a C in calculus. But she had always done well with deductive reasoning. A selection of possible multiple-choice answers were lining up on the left-hand side of her brain. Some were less than pleasant to consider.

She looked at him sternly, an unfriendly combination of suspicion and injury flickering in her eyes. In spite of knowing better, she hoped the explanation would vindicate him.

"Well?" she prompted.

"Ya see, Chadron, this is gonna sound funny . . ."

Oh, great! she thought. *I share him with who knows how many other women. I get to see him twice a year. I'm ready to pounce on him like a rutting elk and he's gonna tell me a funny story.*

". . . but, last Sunday, after Great Falls, Cody and I were drivin' up I-90 toward Billings. The truck was runnin' good . . ."

Good, you moron, she said to herself. *Great start. Now we're gonna have a travelogue with color commentary by Mr. Goodwrench.*

". . . and we stopped above the Yellowstone—River, that is—and I was walkin' along the riverbank there . . ."

If this has anything to do with laser beams, white buffalo or Jules Verne, it's over, she thought.

". . . so anyway I sorta bent down, squatted actually, and was lookin' at a fish there in the shallow water . . ."

This certainly sounds plausible, she thought. *Although he hasn't said a thing about talking to the fish.*

". . . and the next thing I knew . . . yer not gonna believe this . . ."

Somehow, she said to herself, *I think you're right.*

". . . I sat on a porcupine."

He *was* right.

Lick went on embellishing his explanation, the trip to the doctor, the long ride to Rapid. He offered Cody as a witness and Doris and Bill, though he couldn't remember their last name. The whole story made him sound like a second grader with a huge imagination trying to explain why he had chocolate on his face.

Chadron sat stone-faced.

She slid out from under his arm and looked at him for several seconds. The flames were working across her chest and nibbling at the backs of her ears.

"Sorry," he said lamely.

"Escuse me a minute." She stepped out of the hot tub and walked into the house.

The light clicked off on the back porch. He heard her coming.

"Lick," she said quietly, "close your eyes and slide your head under the water."

He did, without questioning. He could feel the Jacuzzi jets buffeting his wrinkled body. The sound was muffling his thoughts. He stayed under as long as he could hold his breath. He surfaced and opened his eyes. The water looked dark in the moonlight. He heard car tires crunch on the gravel drive. As Chadron backed out, her headlights shined across the hot tub. He raised his hand just as the lights turned and left him in the dark. His hand looked . . . black?

He stood up in the hot tub. Shivering in the chill, he saw a box propped up on the edge. He held it up to the moonlight. RIT Permanent Dye . . . deep purple. He looked at his arms, his feet, his legs, his belly. In the dark he looked black!

He grabbed a towel and rubbed hard on his forearm. No change!

"Damn!" His predicament sharpened his focus. *Let's see . . . I'm ten or fifteen miles from Rapid. I'm freezing and I'm the color of a wino's shirtfront!*

He found his clothes in the garage, dried off and dressed. On the way out of the ranch he checked a pickup for keys and found none. It took him an hour walking bowlegged to get back to I-90. He stopped several times in the moonlight to catch his breath. It was actually funny if you thought about it. At one point, he sat on a rock and laughed. Ridiculous!

Hitching was unsuccessful. People don't pick up hitchhikers at night, no matter what color they are! By daylight he was strolling through the long shadows of the fairgrounds. He couldn't find Cody's pickup, so he slipped into one of the show barns and fell asleep on the straw.

"Mommy! Mommy! Come look at the funny man!"

"Sshh. Don't wake him. Maybe he's sick."

"Mommy, he's purple!"

"What's goin' on here?"

"I don't know. He doesn't look right."

"He's . . . he's purple!"

"He's okay, isn't he? Alive, I mean."

"Yeah. He's breathin'."

"Maybe we'd better get Security."

"Good idea."

* * *

"Paging Cody Wing. Will Cody Wing please report to the security building."

* * *

"I'm Cody Wing. Somebody paging me?"

"Yessir. Just a moment."

"Cody Wing?" asked the security guard. "We have a man here asking for you."

"Is it Lick?"

"Follow me."

The hallway was crowded. People were taking turns looking through the safety glass on the closed door.

"Excuse me," said the officer as he led Cody through the milling mass into the large office.

Lick sat on the edge of a small steel-and-Naugahyde sofa. He looked like the Minnesota Vikings' dirty laundry!

"Lick?"

"Cody! Boy, I'm glad you showed up. Get me outta here!"

"What happened?"

"I don't want to talk about it!"

"The pickup's outside, c'mon."

The crowd parted in front of the Incredible Hulk! The waves of people gathered in the halls and on the front steps gave way as the convict was hurried to the waiting pickup.

Cody went around. Lick's side was locked. Of course. During the six months it took Cody to slide across and unlock the passenger side, Lick heard the murmurs of the crowd:

"Mommy, he looks like Billy's Popsicle tongue!"

"Shhh, he's probably on drugs!"

"See what happens if you don't eat broccoli!"

"I think it's New Wave, Martha."

"Maybe he's an extraterrestrial?"

Lick slammed the door. "E.T., home."

16

Saturday, August 14
Burwell, Nebraska

By damn, Lick, you oughtta marry *that* ol' girl!" Cody was weak from laughter as Lick recounted the story of Thursday night's adventure. "She's got fire! She'd keep your sorry butt in line!" He continued to laugh and wipe the tears from his eyes. Lick was laughing too, as they drove through the morning sun. Since dawn they had been under the protective gaze of the hundreds of windmills that dot the Sandhills of Nebraska. Now they were driving through miles of cornfield city blocks. They had overnighted at the Remington Arms in Ainsworth, where Lick bought a new razor and shaving kit. His old one had disappeared with Chadron, somewhere in Rapid City. This morning they were ten miles outside Burwell, on Highway 91, when a policeman pulled them over.

"Something wrong, Officer?" asked the Purple Phantom, driving.

The officer looked at Lick's Technicolor face and hands. He leaned over and looked at Cody. "Can you drive this rig?"

"Sure, but what's up?" asked Cody.

"You just follow me into Burwell. You," he said to Lick, "come with me."

"Why?"

"Don't argue, boy. It's nothin' serious. Just for your own protection." He installed Lick in the backseat of the patrol car. Lick asked questions. The officer avoided them. The corn was as high as an elephant's withers along the road.

The Nebraska State Patrol car pulled through the square in Burwell, stopped in front of the Corner Bar and turned off the siren. The contents of the bar poured out into the street.

Lick stared out the back window. Jerry O'Haca opened the door and, with a regal gesture, invited Lick out.

* * *

Lick stood on the sidewalk and turned like a heliotrope. "We've been expecting you," said Jerry. He was wearing a purple armband.

Everybody was wearing something purple. They looked like a group of Texas Aggie alumni gone awry on St. Patrick's Day! "I drove all night to set this up, ol' pardner!" said Jerry.

"Thanks!"

"The least we could do! Okay, boys, bring 'em out!" The crowd parted for the coups de grace: personal, passionate, violaceous cheerleaders! Two bouncing, heavy-hipped, Nebraska darlin's marched to the front of the crowd, each carrying a picket sign. One sign said STICK WITH on the front and LICK on the back. The other said LICK on the front and STICK WITH on the back.

They each wore snakeskin boots, mauve leotards, cutoffs and puce knit bikini tops. Silk lilacs were embroidered in their blond manes. Wyla had a small butterfly tattooed high on the right breast, flying into the breach. Twyla had a small snail tattooed high on the left breast, inching into the chasm. Lavender eye shadow and mulberry lipstick completed the ensemble.

"These are your bodyguards!" declared Jerry. To the polychromatic sisters he said, "Girls, never let him outta yer sight!" To the clamoring multitude he said, "Make way for the king!"

Wyla took Lick's left arm and laid her butterfly in the crook. Twyla took his right arm and laid her snail in its crook. The spectators made way.

An old sofa had been placed across two tables in the bar. Lick and the pulchritudinous purple duo were lifted to the throne.

Flam Leetsdale, rodeo photographer, posed him. The rainbow amazons snuggled closer. Everybody bought him a drink.

"A toast!" ordered Jerry. "To the only purple cowboy in the P.R.C.A.!"

Lick's guardians drank demurely as Lick was toasted. Repeatedly. By noon, his five senses were reduced to one and a half.

"How you doin', pardner?" asked Cody.

"Gettin' severely drunk," Lick answered.

"Remember you gotta bull this afternoon."

"Right!" Someone brought him another Velvet ditch.

The lovely maidens kept Lick pressed between them. Each had a hand on his respective thigh. They were wearing identical perfume, Cinnabar, and had begun to perspire.

"Are you really purple all over?" asked Wyla, draping Lick's left arm around her shoulders.

"Yup."

"Even ... down there?" asked Twyla, placing his right arm around her shoulders.

"Yup."

Lick darted his head to the snail and caught a drop of sweat before it cascaded into the gorge. Pictures of a chameleon from an old *National Geographic*, spearing a mayfly, flashed before his eyes.

"Thank you," she said.

Twyla held a fresh draw to his lips and he sipped the brew. She sucked the foam off his mustache and wiped his chin with her knit bikini top.

"Ooooh." She giggled.

"Let me help," said Twyla, maneuvering into position.

(When asked to recall this particular day to his grandchildren, Lick would always smile. Only the warm sensations, devoid of detail, would come back. But that was enough for an old man.)

They made Lick Unofficial Grand Marshal of the parade. His throne was put on the back of a flatbed truck. He and his tinted attendants variously sat, stood and reclined, depending on the wishes of His Highness.

By the time the parade wound through the arena to begin the grand entry, Lick was bareback, blithering and had peed his pants! Fortunately no one could tell, because at least two six-packs had been poured over his head in tribute! He stood, with the aid of his twin entourage, and greeted the crowd, Caesar-like. He raised his glass in recognition of his subjects in the stands. The flatbed lurched! Lick fell backward, his body in rigor, over the back of the sofa, as if someone had toppled a statue of Cortés, sword upraised, coming into Tenochtitlán!

Lick was flying I.F.R. while Cody was pulling his bull rope. "You sure you wanna do this?" Cody wasn't completely sober himself. Matter of fact, it was the drunkest rodeo either of them had seen since the Indian Rodeo in Mescalero, New Mexico.

"Ladies and gentlemen!" Emerald Dune worked his malleable audience. "You are about to see a first. Nebraska's Big Rodeo presents the world's only purple cowboy . . ." The cheering crowd drowned out Emerald's FM stereo voice. He fine-tuned the volume and went on. "The world's only purple cowboy up on bull ninety-seven D, called Chadron Borglum!"

Lick looked up and caught Emerald's eye.

"Chadron Borglum, in chute number three!"

Lick went back on autopilot. He nodded his head. The spinnin' bull crashed out. Lick stuck to him like road kill skunk on a radial tire! He rode 97D automatically, every nerve and muscle firing! His body a well-oiled machine, oblivious to the emotions of its operator! 97D ducked and spun, dove and stuck! Lick rode him with no mercy! Lick never heard the buzzer. He bailed out to thunderous applause! He lifted his hat, displaying his purple hair. A row of white teeth gleamed under his purple mustache.

He threw his hat in the air! It was his last conscious act.

The night never ended. Lick woke. It was daylight. He didn't know which day. He was in a bed. He didn't know which bed. He lay on his back.

Swatches of vividly colorful memories flipped through his mind like pages in an *Omni* magazine:

Lying facedown on the bakery counter.
Standing on top of a human pyramid on somebody's lawn.
Directing traffic in a policeman's hat.
Swimming?

Seeing double images and adjusting the knobs for better reception.
Roman riding?

His clothes were neatly laid over a nearby chair. His hat gently placed on a dresser. A purple knit, double-barreled slingshot hung from each bedpost.

There was a long scratch running diagonally across his belly. *Surely,* he thought, chuckling at his early morning wit, *this deserves a purple heart!*

17

August 14
Coffeyville, Kansas

Dodge Brown was scared. He was teeth rattlin', knee knockin', hair raisin', bed wettin' scared! Because he was a local boy, he was allowed to enter the Coffeyville, Kansas, rodeo without being an official card-carrying member of the P.R.C.A. He had been on six bulls in his life. He hadn't decided to rodeo until his nineteenth birthday, last May. He worked for a seed corn company and had just gotten engaged to Dee Dee Stufflebean. This Friday night Dodge Brown was scheduled to buck out on none other than Kamikaze!

Dodge needed no description of Kamikaze's bucking prowess or nasty disposition. Even if he hadn't read the *Sports News*, several cowboys had volunteered their opinion to him this afternoon. It was unanimous; they all suggested he draw out.

Normally, it was unthinkable in the derring-do world of rodeo for cowboys to suggest something as tenderfooted as turning out your stock as a result of fear. Stock was often turned out by cowboys who were scheduled to compete when they got a "bad draw" (a bull or bronc they didn't think would score high enough). They would bypass those rodeos completely. They paid a fine in those cases. But Kamikaze was becoming an ominous phenomenon.

The *Pro Rodeo Sports News* had carried six stories between March 15 and July 28 mentioning the notorious bull. Although the *Sports News* carries pertinent information vital to scheduling for the rodeo cowboy, it contains feature stories as well. When a cowboy is seriously injured it is worthy of mention in the *Sports News*. Kamikaze guaranteed several bull riders press coverage they hadn't sought. But bad news travels fast.

***The Nampa Press Tribune*, July 14:**

> Manly Ott, presently ranked fourth in the Pro Rodeo Cowboys Assn. national standings in the bull riding event, was injured last night during the first performance of the Snake River Stampede. He was bucked off before the whistle blew. Officials at Mercy Hospital said he suffered a broken jaw and neck injuries, but is resting comfortably today. The bull that inflicted the damage to Manly Ott is stock contractor Bobby Monday's bull number 1020, called Kamikaze. In the rodeo business, bulls are not usually named and only go by a number, but this bull has gained a reputation and therefore a name. Kamikaze has been on the rodeo circuit for four years and has never been ridden. He has been selected the last three years by the cowboys as a National Finals bull. Kamikaze, according to the cowboys interviewed last night, has a tendency to inflict a heavy toll on those bull riders unlucky enough to draw him. More than five cowboys have been seriously hurt this year attempting to ride him. Snake River Stampede performances continue through Saturday night.

***Associated Press Wire*, July 20. *Los Angeles Herald Examiner*, *Omaha World Herald*, *North Platte Telegraph* and *Kansas City Star*:**

> In the world of professional rodeo, a certain bull is developing a considerable reputation. Kamikaze, who has been bucking for four years, has thrown off every cowboy who has attempted to ride him. He is dangerous, as demonstrated by the fact that he has injured numerous of those bull riders seriously. The latest is Manly Ott, a bull rider ranked nationally in the standings.

***The National Enquirer*, July 30:**

BULL POSSESSED BY DEVIL!

> In rodeo circles, there is a bull called Kamikaze. He strikes fear in every cowboy who attempts to ride this 2,000-pound demon! He has horns over two feet long and an evil eye! He has crippled and maimed many of those cowboys who have been brave (or foolish) enough to climb on his back. He has never been ridden! One cowboy is quoted as saying, "He is the Devil!"

If Dodge Brown read the papers he should have been scared. He did and he was! Dee Dee had tried to talk him out of it.

"Dodge, draw out, honey. You might get hurt and it's not worth the chance."

"But, Dee Dee," protested Dodge, "what if I can ride him? What if? Beginner's luck. I just might be the one who does it. That would be fantastic, with all the gang there watchin'!"

The professional traveling cowboys, who often don't have occasion to discuss much with the local entrants, went out of their way to suggest he draw out. When Dodge told them he figgered on going ahead with it, they just shrugged their shoulders.

Kamikaze wasn't givin' it much thought. He spent the afternoon lazin' around the pens behind the buckin' chutes. He didn't brother-in-law much with the other bulls. He assumed the status of Peckin'-Order Potentate regardless of the company he was in.

If you had a mind to explore the anthropomorphological aspects of Kamikaze, you could compare his thought processes to a piece of heavy construction equipment. A bulldozer, perhaps, or maybe a backhoe with tracks and a three-yard bucket.

Those machines exude power. They have the ability to be surprisingly agile. They are capable of some first-class destruction. This is the basis of their personality.

Just as cables and hydraulics tend to create wear with use, so did memories erode wrinkles in Kamikaze's cerebrum. Each cowboy who mounted him left a unique fingerprint on his brain. Each new trick was printed in his playbook. The counterpunch was programmed.

He didn't know Dodge Brown from Chevy Impala. But unless Dodge tried something no previous rider had done, Kamikaze was prepared.

Kamikaze ambled over to the water trough and took a drink. Several cowboys were leanin' over the fence checkin' out the stock. He studied them for a few seconds. He knew them as interlopers in his territory. He knew them as lightweights who put a rope around his girth. He knew them as frightened rabbits on the arena floor.

But they kept puttin' their hands in the fire.

Like moths, he concluded.

Before the bull riding, rodeo clown and bullfighter Herman Hammer hunted up Dodge for a little chat. "Listen, cowboy, I can't tell you how to ride him 'cause nobody ever has, but when you hit the ground, hit it runnin'! This bull's turned real mean and will try and eat your lunch, so git down and git on the fence! We'll be right there to help you."

Kamikaze was in the second bunch of bulls to be loaded into the chutes. Dodge tried to concentrate. He got some help setting his rope and waited for the announcer to call his name.

"Out of chute number four, a local cowboy from right here in Coffeyville, Dodge Brown, up on three-times National Finals bull, Kamikaze! If this young cowboy rides this bull, he will be the first in the world to do it!"

The crowd let out a cheer and silenced. Dodge nodded his head and the gate swung open.

Kamikaze flew out of the chute, spinnin' like a merry-go-round! Dodge hung on for the first whiplash. The second 180° found him airborne, headed for the fence like a guided missile! He crashed into the gatepost on chute number five, six feet above the ground! Kamikaze wheeled back to his right. He caught Dodge between his horns and threw him ten feet in the air like a rag doll! Dodge, arms flailing, came down over Kamikaze's back! Kamikaze whirled and hooked him as he slid off his rump! Dodge rolled into a ball while Kamikaze continued to gore, pound and drive him into the ground!

The clowns were desperately trying to get the bull off the downed cowboy, but Kamikaze was single-mindedly grinding Dodge into little pieces of arena dirt. Finally Herman Hammer jumped on Kamikaze's back! The bull hooked back toward the new rider! During the momentary distraction, Herman's bullfighting pardner, Smack Knuckles, somehow managed to drag Dodge's inert body out of the eye of the storm. Kamikaze threw Herman off like a slingshot. Herman raced to the arena fence! Kamikaze caught him mid-leap on the inside of his right thigh and lifted him clear over the six-foot steel wire fence! Herman landed in the first row, between two old men from the Elks Club Rehab Center.

* * *

At 11:16 P.M. that night, the emergency room doctor came into the waiting room and told Mr. and Mrs. Brown and Dee Dee that Dodge had died during surgery. The boy had a concussion and severe internal injuries. The doctor was sorry.

18

Sunday, August 22
Denver, Colorado

Lyra stood at the edge of the crowd looking at the stage set up in the middle of the street. The band onstage called itself Night-Train Express and they could give a wino a headache! Night-Train Express was building a bluegrass cosmorama: flat pickin' rainbows, fiddle contrails, waves of doghouse bass and a five-string meteor shower! Lyra's eyes wandered casually to the crowd at the base of the stage. She saw the back of a familiar head.

"Lick, you no-good cactus eatin' dog kisser!" she said to herself in surprise.

"What did you say?"

Lyra turned to her left. A dark-haired woman with freckles and blue eyes was staring at her. She held a little girl by the hand.

"Nothing." Lyra laughed. "I just saw somebody I knew."

"Did you say 'Lick'?" asked the mother.

"That's the lowlife's name."

"Is he by any chance a bull rider, this Lick?"

"Yes. Do you know him?"

"Where is he?"

"Over there right under the bandstand. To the right."

The mother looked in that direction. "Yep. That's the Lick I know."

Lick was leaning against the stage looking up at the band. He had a beer in one hand and a blonde in the other.

"My name is Cherry Hills and this is my daughter, Teddy."

"Lyra Block."

"Have you known him long?" asked Cherry.

"Off and on a couple years. He usually calls when he comes through town."

"You live here in Denver?"

"Yes. How 'bout you?" asked Lyra.

"Here, too. I've only known him six or eight months. Seen him three times. I guess he calls me when he doesn't call you."

"Looks like he called somebody else this time." Lyra stared at him again.

Cherry looked over his way. "Lyra. You know what I'm thinking?"

Lyra looked out of the corner of her eye. They both slid into a "why not" sort of grin.

"It would teach the worthless rapscallion a lesson," said Cherry. Then quickly, "You're not serious about him are you?"

"Serious! I see the scoundrel when he comes to town, when *he* wants to! I'd be crazier than he is if I took 'im seriously! How 'bout you?"

"Well, I admit the first couple times I thought he had potential. He's got a little money, or seems to, the way he spends it, and he treats my kiddo like a princess."

"And the princess's mama?"

"Yes. He does have his way."

"I know. I know," said Lyra.

"We always seem to have a good time," said Cherry.

"The loony fool does make you feel like a woman. So many of these men—I should say, boys—don't know the first thing about it. Good ol' Lick."

"Wait a minute, now," said Cherry. "We both have him pegged for what he is, right? The original wild goose. A shirttail in the wind."

"Motion and no emotion. No commitments. Yeah, we both got him pegged."

"So I think we should go over and meet the blonde. What do you say?"

"Right on, sister!"

"Why don't we send Teddy over to see Uncle Lick first? Then we could walk up together!"

Night-Train Express climaxed! "Earl's Breakdown," the last song of the set, broke into a thousand pieces and sizzled into the afternoon sky like a drop of water in a skillet of hot grease!

Cherry, Teddy and Lyra wended through the people seated on the street between them and the bandstand.

"Look at the boobs on her!" exclaimed Cherry.

"No matter. When she's forty, they'll hang like a four-dollar drape!"

"Mama," said Teddy excitedly, "there's Lick!"

"You wanna run up and say hello?"

"Oh yes! Can I?"

"Sure, go ahead."

Teddy ran through the visiting crowd toward him.

"Lick! Lick!"

Lick looked down. "It's me, Teddy!" cried the little girl. He picked her up in one arm.

"Teddy Bear, you little punkin. How you doin'? How nice to see you! This is Wanda. Wanda, this is Teddy."

"Hello, Teddy," said Wanda.

Suddenly, Lick looked around. "Where's your mama, darlin'?"

"Oh, she's comin'. We were wondering when we'd see you again."

"Oh, yeah?" said Lick.

"Oh, yeah?" said Wanda.

"Lick! How nice to see you," said Cherry, blindsiding him. He jerked his head to the left.

"Lick, you ol' coyote! You've been gone so long!" said Lyra, blindsiding him again. He jerked his head back to the right.

"Lyra. Cherry. What a nice surprise!" His face was the color of eight-and-a-half-by-eleven erasable bond.

"Uh, Wanda, this is Lyra and Cherry. Cherry, Wanda and Lyra. Lyra, Cherry and Wanda."

"Hello." Puerta Vallarta sunset.

"Hello." Ski condo fireplace.

"Hello." Ice fishing on Lake Superior.

Now, this might be a good time for the reader to pause and give some thought to a solution to Lick's dilemma. The plausible alternatives are few, the fatal, many.

1. ***He could try to explain: "Wanda, these are two old friends of mine from high school. We were on the track team together. Lyra was a runner, Cherry a sprinter, and I was in the broad jump. Ha, Ha."***
2. ***He could faint. Then just lie there till they all drifted away. Difficult to do with a Teddy Bear in your arms.***
3. ***He could offer no explanation.***

He chose number 3. He zip-locked his lips.

"So . . . Wanda, where are you from?" asked Lyra sweetly.

"I live here now, but originally from Louisiana."

"Louisiana. How nice. And you, Cherry?" continued Lyra.

"I live here. Teddy and I." She smiled at Teddy, who was taking a sip of Lick's beer. Cherry bit her tongue and smiled.

"How 'bout y'all, Lyra. Lyra? Is that right?" asked Wanda.

"I'm here in town. How long have you known good ol' Lick?" Lyra spoke as if he were a picture on the wall, a deaf-and-dumb watercolor.

"Probably a year, I guess. August of last year," answered Wanda.

"Oh, really?" said Lyra.

"Oh, really?" said Cherry.

"Have you known him long?" asked Wanda.

"Couple years," answered Cherry.

"We certainly have somethin' in common." Wanda was a good ol' girl, and not stupid, despite the opinion of many less well-endowed snipers. "My feet are killin' me and I've had about all the music I can stand. What say we go sit down and have a beer?"

"Wanda," said Cherry, "I think I like you."

"Lead on, McDuff! Lick, bring Teddy and come along," instructed Lyra.

"Uh, Cherry," mumbled Lick, "how 'bout Teddy and I walk around the booths for a while. We'll find you under those umbrellas?"

"Okay, if it's okay with Teddy."

"Oh yes, Mom! Can I, can I?"

"May I."

"May I, Mom?"

"Yes, you may."

"Wow! Far out! C'mon, Lick. I saw some old shoes to try on!" She led him off by the hand.

"That's unfair, you know," Wanda said to Cherry.

"Well, I admit it, but can I help it if he likes kids?" Cherry smiled.

They ordered a Moosehead, a Heineken, a Michelob Light and sat under the Cinzano umbrella on the bar atrium.

"We set you up, Wanda. Just to harass Lick."

"No sweat. I'd have done the same thing. He is the most unreliable lover I've ever had. Any poor girl who thinks she's gonna get him to stay around the house long enough to sprout roots has lost her mind! Besides, what if you were unlucky enough to catch him! Every time he hit the road, you'd worry about him shackin' up or bringin' home something unmentionable!"

Sometimes conversations like this can be awkward. But these three semiworldly, confident women crowdin' thirty, veterans of the Fern Bar Wars, talked like old roommates.

Two beers later, they were like sisters. Nothing like a common affliction to unite strangers.

"Wanda, why don't you and Lyra come to my place and we'll fix a little dinner. I've got hamburger in the freezer. We can stop and pick up some salad makin's. Wait a minute," hesitated Cherry, "that's not fair. Wanda, you're with Lick. Maybe you have other plans?"

"None that I wouldn't change. This is too good to pass up! A rare opportunity! You know, I admit I'm not too hep on sharing, but since we all obviously know him well, what the hell!"

Teddy came up to the table.

"Hello, kiddo. What'cha got?"

"A balloon, Mom. And Lick bought me these shoes, and this hood ornament. He said it's off a '51 Plymouth. See, it's the *Mayflower*."

"Where's Lick?"

"Oh. He said to give you this." She handed Cherry a note that said "Due to a death in the family, I had to take off right away. Sorry, Lick."

Wanda smiled. "Nothin' to it. Ya know, I make some pretty mean coonass chili, if you still got that hamburger."

"You bet! Let's go."

* * *

In the fading afternoon shadows a coward slunk off through the parked cars, crawled under a Falcon Futura and pondered all these things in his heart.

19

Saturday, August 28
Payson, Arizona

Welcome, ladies and gentlemen to the third performance of the oldest continuous rodeo in the world! Fast action, great stock, the best rodeo cowboys and cowgirls here in one of the most spectacularly scenic rodeo arenas in our great land!"

The monotonously beautiful high desert mountains and pine trees surrounded the small rodeo arena, and the temperature at one P.M. was standing at a comfortable eighty-three degrees.

Lick was up in the bulls this afternoon and Cody had entered the saddle bronc riding.

Cody had been as successful riding barebacks these last few weeks as Ned had been lucky in love. Neither had scored high enough to buy a bottle of Absorbine Jr.! Cody decided to switch events to the saddle bronc riding to break his slump.

Neatsfoot Hawkins, past world champion bronc rider and presently leading in the P.R.C.A. standings, offered to help Cody.

"Velvet Snide is a good draw, Cody," Neatsfoot was coaching. "He's predictable, but not that easy to ride. He always takes a big jump out of the chute, bucks to the left three or four jumps, then turns back out to the right. Give him plenty of rein or he'll pull you over his head on the first jump."

"How's the turn?"

"Usually smooth, but you gotta watch 'im. I've seen him reverse directions a couple times an' if he does that, you're on your own."

"Good'nuf. I'll be ready."

Cody set his competition association saddle out on the ground. He sat down in it, stretching the stirrup leathers and adjusting to the feel.

Saddle bronc riders enjoy a certain prestige in rodeo circles. Ridin' a saddle bronc is like playing the guitar: it's the easiest thing to do poorly and hardest thing to do well. Neatsfoot was one of the best. He came from Texas, though lots of the good ones grow up in Montana or the Dakotas. . . . He was a personable fellow and had pizzazz. Announcers liked him, rodeo advertisers invested in him, women adored him, men admired him and the crowd loved him! He always put on a show. His personality showed in his work. None of this was supposed to affect the judges' evaluation of his ride, so they said it didn't, but when all was done and said, Neatsfoot was good for rodeo. He stood out like a penguin in a patch of sandhill cranes!

* * *

Velvet Snide was nineteen years old. Born on the Pine Ridge Indian Reservation near Red Shirt, South Dakota, he ran free until he was four years old. They gathered the band that year, branded him and cut him. During the next two years they broke him to ride. But Velvet Snide, whose name at the time was Yellow Star Thistle, had one flaw that predisposed him to verbal abuse by the tribal leaders: the sonuvamare loved to buck! Not maliciously, just gloriously, enthusiastically, with the same joy a peregrine falcon feels when he stalls at fifteen hundred feet, folds his wings and free-falls from the sky!

After two broken arms and futile incantations, it was decided by the tribe that he should be taken to the bucking horse sale in Miles City, Montana.

Yellow Star Thistle distinguished himself and was bought by T. Tommy Calhoot, entrepreneur and stock contractor from South Dakota.

In the last thirteen years, Yellow Star Thistle was selected by the rodeo cowboys to go to the National Finals four times and was Bucking Horse of the Year twice. T. Tommy still owned him. At

Yellow Star Thistle's peak, Tommy changed his name to Velvet (as in Black Velvet) Snide, in response to a little advertising campaign sponsored by a national distiller of white lightnin'.

Velvet Snide was in chute number two (there was no number one). Neatsfoot helped Cody get saddled and adjust his hack rein. He threaded a little hank of mane through the braided rein to mark his grip.

T. Tommy rode up to the side of the chute where Cody was waiting his turn. "You got a good one there, son. Watch his first big jump outta the box."

"Yeah, thanks." Cody knew T. Tommy was rooting for the horse. The better ol' Snide bucked, the more the stock contractor's inventory was worth.

"And now in chute number two, Cody Wing, Ten Sleep, Wyoming, on a past Bucking Horse of the Year, Velvet Snide!"

Cody took the rein in his left hand and stuck his toes out over the points of the shoulders. He leaned back and nodded his head. The gate swung open. Velvet Snide rocked back on his hind legs and slammed his butt against the back of the chute! He uncoiled and leaped out! Cody and Snide were airborne!

Lean back an' touch 'im when he hits the ground, Cody thought.

Wham!

Pull. Cody brought his spurs from the points of the shoulders plum back to the cantle.

Reach and pull. Three successive jumps and Cody was in perfect rhythm. When Velvet Snide had his tail in the air, his hind feet out behind him and his front feet planted, Cody was ramrod straight, toes out, spurs at the points, and his free arm out behind him held high. When Snide's front feet left the ground for the next ascent, Cody raked his rowels along Velvet's side as far back as he could reach. But something went wrong when Snide made his right turn. Maybe he didn't signal? Maybe T. Tommy had offered Velvet Snide a raise in hay? Who knows? Regardless, Cody was in his backswing when the ol' palomino made a 90° swivel and stuck his nose to the ground. Cody failed to make the swivel and lazy-Susan'd to port side. Velvet Snide took the rein, jerked Cody out over the swells and punched him headfirst into the dirt.

Lick ran over to his crumpled partner. "Jeez, Cody, you all right?" Cody's hat was down over his ears. If his upper plate hadn't stayed in place, he would have bitten off the end of his nose! He stretched his neck and pounded his smashed hat back into a reasonable facsmile of its original shape.

"Yeah. I bit my tongue."

They stepped back over to the fence and watched Neatsfoot make a classic ride complete with flying dismount.

Lick was rosining up his bull rope when LoBall McKinney came up to him. "Howdy, Lick." Lick nodded.

"Listen, Lick. You are really hot this summer. You are flat tearin' 'em up. *Sports News* got you ranked eighteenth now. I ain't doing worth a dang. I wonder if you would watch me ride and see if you could give me a pointer or two? I'm up tomorrow, if yer gonna be around."

"Yeah, I'll be here, LoBall. I don't know what I can tell ya, but I'll watch."

Lick already figured he knew part of LoBall's problem. He just didn't want to win bad enough. He wasn't stayin' with the rough ones when the goin' got tough.

These last few weeks Lick had become possessed. He was quieter, didn't party as hard, and got more nervous before each ride. Cody even told him he was losing his sense of humor! But he was winning, winning consistently.

L92 rumbled into the chutes. Lick's bull. Not a real big bull, kind of a brangus-looking critter, with no horns and a little hump. But he would give a man a good spin.

Lick was concentrating while Cody helped him pull his rope. He still had his mind on it when he and L92 made their grand entry into the arena. Lick rode him automatically. When the whistle blew, he reached down with his right hand to free his grip. L92 kicked and flipped Lick over and off! Lick somersaulted out over the bull's right shoulder, but his left hand didn't come free; he was hung up! L92 continued to buck, jerking Lick around like a tetherball tied to the bumper of a low rider!

The two rodeo clowns were right square in the middle of the dance floor! Bucko Bailey was across the withers from Lick, jerking on the tail of the rope, trying to free Lick's hand!

Wang Snaffle, the other bullfighter, was in front of L92, slapping him on the muzzle to keep him from hooking Raggedy Ann and Raggedy Andy! Bucko gave one mighty yank and they both fell away! L92 wheeled, swinging his head like a scythe, and caught the stumbling duo! Lick took the hardest blow. Wang raced back into the gap and drew L92 off toward the gate. Bucko put his arm around Lick's waist and drug him to the fence.

"Git the doc! Siddown, Lick. Git the doc, he's bleedin'!"

The paramedics slapped Lick on the stretcher and carried him to the ambulance. Cody jumped in the back with them and they sped off.

"What is it, Doc?"

"Might be broken ribs, maybe a punctured lung. See those bubbles of blood in his nose? Punctured lung." The paramedic put his stethoscope to Lick's chest.

"Yeah, could be a punctured lung."

20

September 5
Hereford, Texas

Lick got out of the hospital and, for lack of a better place, went home. The doctor in Payson had said he was lucky. *Just what I was thinkin'*, thought Lick.

The punctured lung turned out to be a bloody nose, but his bones didn't fare as well. His take-home pay at the Payson Rodeo had been two broken ribs and two weeks off.

Despite his outward nonchalance, he fretted about missing the five rodeos from which he'd been forced to withdraw. He would have felt that way regardless of his success. But this year, with less than three months to go until the National Finals, he was ranked in the top twenty money winners. To make the finals he had to finish in the top fifteen. Every ride was important.

Home wasn't one of the several places he'd lived in as a boy but where Mom and Dad lived. They had a small but nice house three miles from Hereford, Texas. It had one good outbuilding, eighteen acres of dry-land pasture and a fair set of corrals. They rented.

Lick enjoyed visiting with them both. During the first couple days after Papa had gone to work riding pens in the feedlot, Lick and Mom talked. He looked at photos of his brother's children, old pictures of his parents' youth, of Grandpa Elojio, snapshots of his own youth. His mother had saved Lick's baseball cards. There was a time when he was twelve years old he could name virtually every lineup in the major leagues. Now he couldn't name all the teams. Lick had still never been to a major league game.

"Lloyd's in Amarillo now," his mother informed him.

Lloyd had been his best friend in high school and college. Lloyd had carried their pack of Winstons under the dash of his Ford pickup.

"I thought he was in Chicago."

"Well he's back. He's doing well, I hear. He works in some fancy office building, your papa says. *Pero quien sabe?*" she added, reverting to her father's native tongue. "You should maybe go see him. You can borrow the Galaxy. Your papa saw him go into the office at the feed yard a couple of months ago. So he said hello and Lloyd asked how you were doing. He gave your papa his business card, maybe it has the phone number."

That evening Lick called his old friend and made plans to meet him for lunch the following day.

Lick borrowed the Galaxy and drove to Amarillo. The offices of Hammell, Hammell, Loon and Garvey were on the fifth and top floor of the Luckinbaugh Building downtown. They were commodity brokers.

Lloyd was sincerely delighted to see Lick. To Lick's modest surprise, Lloyd introduced him to everyone in the office and included a flattering discourse of Lick's rodeo career. He was even up-to-date on Lick's present standing and genuinely proud of his friend.

Lloyd had not changed. He had always been a nice person. They went to lunch at a Mexican restaurant. Both ordered a beer; Lloyd loosened his tie.

"Gotta wear the damn thing. Part of the game. Anyway, how are the ribs?"

"Oh, they're healing," said Lick, again surprised that Lloyd knew. "A hazard of the profession."

"You don't know how I envy you," said Lloyd. "Not the ribs, but the rodeo."

Lloyd had been a calf roper. They'd both been on the college rodeo team.

"Whattya mean? Looks to me like you're doin' real well for yourself. Chicago and all. Now you get to come home and have the best of both worlds. How old are your boys now?"

"Six and eight. Both good athletes," Lloyd said proudly.

"Roping already, I bet," said Lick.

"No. T ball and tennis. We bought a house in town. They don't have much interest in horses or rodeo. I wish you were closer. Maybe you could inspire them."

"No more than you, Lloyd."

"Yeah, but I'm so busy. Sometimes I just stare out the window and wonder where you are. Wish I could be with ya goin' down the road."

"It's nice," admitted Lick, "but it's not too lucrative. Takes all your winnin's just to buy the gas."

"I guess. But a new town every night, seein' new country, breathin' real air. Psychin' up to ride. Havin' a beer afterwards. Yup, you sure got it made, my friend. I'm happy for you."

"You ever hear from Alma Lee?" asked Lick.

"Yeah, as a matter of fact I saw her couple weeks ago. She lives here in Amarillo. She said she was workin' in a travel agency."

"You mean she quit teachin' school?"

"Must have. She's married again. Third time, I think."

Alma Lee had been Lick's first love. Their romance spanned his senior year in high school and first year of college.

"So," said Lloyd, "when are ya crackin' back out?"

"I'm gonna try and make Pendleton next week."

They sat silently a minute.

"What are you doin' next week?" Lick asked Lloyd. "Shoot, ya might as well come with me. My pardner's in Iowa right now. I'm gonna meet him in Denver next Monday, then we're headin' west."

Lloyd began to marshal the reasons he couldn't go.

Lick persisted. "You'd like Cody. Good boy from Wyoming. Pretty solid. Kinda like you, I guess. He laughs at my bad jokes and has bailed me out more times than I can count."

"Gosh, Lick, I'd love to, even for a few days, but I can't."

"Aw, that's okay," said Lick. "Just thought it would be fun."

"No, Bea and I have plans. Big shot financial consultant from Wichita is going to be at the office for three days puttin' on a seminar and I'm his host. Oughtta be pretty good for business. Plus the oldest has tennis. Anyway, it would be fun, but I can't."

"No, I guess not," said Lick, feeling a little wistful for his ol' friend and their lost opportunity. "So," he continued, "how do I find Alma Lee?"

Forty-six minutes later Lick walked through the door of Professional Travel. He was in a large open room with three desks, each piloted by a woman talking on the phone. He walked straight to Alma Lee's and sat opposite her in the client chair. She glanced up at him, did a double take, covered the mouthpiece and whispered, "Lick?"

He hadn't seen her for thirteen years. He'd envisioned her as having grown fat or gray or covered with warts. He was wrong! She stood, still shouldering the phone, and stepped to a file cabinet. She looked magnificent! August 12. He remembered her birthday. She'd be thirty-three now.

She sat back down and looked at him as she continued talking on the phone. She had her dark hair pulled back tightly, exposing her large ears. She used to wear her hair in such a way as to hide them. Now they stuck out like wings on a hang glider! She exuded confidence.

She rang off, reached across the desk, grabbed his hand and without a word pulled him into the adjoining storage room. She closed the door, threw her arms around him and kissed him! An onlooker would have thought she was tryin' to lick barbecue sauce off his face! He reciprocated! Within seconds they were rolling on the floor, exploring remembered delights!

They had parted years ago as teenage virgins. Not uncommon then. The world had changed in the intervening decade.

Spent, Lick looked down at her. "Sorry about the button."

Alma Lee was crying but smiling. That's exactly how Lick felt.

They shared an innocence. A secret intimacy with each other that jaded maturity steals from the young. *I can't believe we were so naive* sums up this retrospective wonderment.

"Gosh, Lick, I'm a married woman!" she said, amazed at her own behavior.

"I know."

They stood. He buttoned the front of her blouse. He grasped her skirt belt above her hips and straightened her gig line. She slid her shoes back on and handed him his hat.

"How do I look?" she asked.

Lick thought: *Like a polished masthead on a clipper ship! Like Jayne Mansfield on the hood of a '58 Cadillac! Like Joan of Arc in a bikini! Like a tall iced tea to a thirsty man!*

"Best I ever saw," he said, and he meant it.

They walked through the office to the parking lot. He started the Galaxy. She stood by the driver's side.

"Can I see you again?" he asked, looking up into her eyes.

"Nope," she said, then shook her head, folded her arms across her chest, turned and walked back to her office, never looking back.

He made it to the first stoplight before his eyes began to burn.

* * *

Lloyd stood in the kitchen as Bea was chopping lettuce for their dinner salad. The boys were in the den in front of the television. Lloyd was sipping a whiskey and water and telling Bea about Lick's visit.

"He wanted me to come with him for a week. Well, I've got Fred coming for the seminar and Jason's got a tennis match so I told him no. But I thought about it."

Bea kept chopping lettuce. "What a life he must lead. I feel sorry for him."

"Yeah, I guess yer right. Is your Junior League still planning the fund-raiser? Next week, isn't it?"

21

September 7
On the Plains of Northeastern Colorado

Rock Rypkima, pure Hollywood, walked with Bobby Monday out to the big metal barn behind the rodeo contractor's office. Trailing them were a cameraman and a sound person. The sound person's suitcase bore the stencil PROPERTY OF ROCK TELEVISION PRODUCTIONS.

Rock had to pace himself not to walk ahead of Bobby.

"What we do on 'Those Amazing Animals,' " he was explaining, "is try to entertain the public's curiosity. Kamikaze is certainly famous, but not necessarily a household word." Rock ran his fingers through his silver hair.

Bobby wasn't prone to saying much, so he didn't. Rock felt obligated to fill the silence. "This is certainly a desolate place. Is Brush the nearest town?"

"Yup."

They walked around the barn to a set of corrals. Horses were in several pens. Big heavy horses, unshod, and others, not so big, stood around variously dozing and balancing on three legs. Other pens contained bulls, lying on their briskets or standing. As the crew walked down the alley, the bulls cast them indifferent glances and went back to contemplating the nice day.

"Here he is," said Bobby, stopping.

"Which one?"

"The spotted one."

"Well," said Rock, nervously fingering the gold chain around his neck. "Somehow I'd pictured him bigger." He looked around. "Get your camera set up here, Clint. Maybe get up on this fence behind us so we can get Bobby, here, with Kamikaze in the background."

Rock warmed to the task. He was the producer and though he didn't know anything about rodeo, he knew about filming.

"Bobby, I'll just ask you some questions and we can edit what we don't need."

Kamikaze watched the cameraman move up on the fence hefting the heavy videocamera. A woman scurried behind him. Bobby stood across the fence with another human. The bull knew Bobby. He fed him and made him get in the truck every now and then. Kamikaze recognized his voice. Bobby never got on his back. Kamikaze never associated him with the bull rope or the ride.

Kamikaze kept a suspicious eye on the cameraman. He could sense no fear emanating from the man, but his machine seemed to intrude into Kamikaze's space. It was an uncomfortable feeling. Like someone was sizing him up, but in a different way from the bull riders.

A big glass eye was staring at him. He stared back but the big eye never blinked. It was not intimidated. Kamikaze took a step back. His instinct put him on guard. *Danger,* he thought. *Big eye. Bad intentions.*

"Listen, mister," said Bobby, "I'm havin' second thoughts about doin' this."

"Why?" asked Rock, rapidly calculating the cost of the filming crew's airline tickets from Los Angeles to Denver, the rental car and incidentals.

"This bull is just a poor dumb animal. He happens to be good at what he does. He just doesn't like people. I've seen some of those rags print trash and TV shows like '60 Minutes' crucify innocent people just to get a reaction. Rodeo is my life. It's Kamikaze's life. You might glamorize him or make him look like a monster, neither of which is true."

"No, no, this is a family show," assured Rock. "I think this will make a good segment and show rodeo in a good light. No sensationalism, but some pizzazz."

"Okay," agreed Bobby.

"Beautiful, baby, beautiful!"

One week later. 7:45 P.M. on television sets across the U.S.A.:

Anita, what have you got for us now?"

"Barry, we have a story that is chilling. On the plains of eastern Colorado resides a killer! A killer that is allowed, even encouraged, to maim and cripple humans and never be punished!"

A close-up of Kamikaze's cold eye filled the screen. The camera backed up to reveal the head. The eye was flat black. The camera panned from Kamikaze's horns, over his hump to his rump, then back to present a full body shot.

Anita continued. "Kamikaze is a rodeo bull. What all you urban cowboys will recognize as the model for your disco mechanical bulls. Once every ten days to two weeks, at a rodeo somewhere in the American West, a cowboy bets he can ride this beast. Sometime's he bets his life." She paused dramatically and the camera focused on her serious face. "In August this year, a nineteen-year-old young man named Dodge Brown was killed trying to ride Kamikaze. Kamikaze has never been ridden."

"Bobby Monday is Kamikaze's owner. We asked him how he could, in good conscience, continue to include this dangerous animal in his rodeo performances."

The television screen switched to Bobby leaning against the fence, Kamikaze standing placidly behind him.

"... bull riding can be dangerous ..."

"... certain risks are taken by anyone climbing down on the back of a bull ..."

"I do it for the money ..."

"... sorry for the young man and his family."

"... it's a business ..."

It took a lot of editing to get that thirty seconds, and the cuts between comments were choppy. Bobby, who was never very genial anyway, came across hard.

The film cut to a short interview with the Browns and Dee Dee Stufflebean, who was presently dating a brick salesman in Coffeyville. Next was an action shot of Kamikaze at last year's National

Finals Rodeo, over which a list of Kamikaze's casualties was read.

The report concluded with a repeat of Bobby's last comments. "It's a business ... do it for the money ..." The camera stayed on the bull's owner while he spit a brown stream of Red Man at his feet. There was a final close-up of Kamikaze's eye.

"Wow! Anita, that's scary!" said Barry.

"Yes," she said grimly. Then she turned to the audience. "It makes you wonder what they do to him to make him so mean."

"Golly, you're right! Makes you wonder. But stay tuned right after this commercial message to see a dog that actually talks on the telephone! Those amazing animals! What will they do next?"

22

September 19
On the Road Between Othello and Puyallup, Washington

"Cody, I've lost it."

Cody let his runnin' pardner ramble on.

"I had a real shot at the Finals. Now I can't git back on track. I couldn't ride a broken-mouth ewe!"

The headlights sliced a half-moon piece of landscape out of the rainy night like a cookie cutter. The cab defroster warmed Cody's stocking feet, propped up on the dash.

"And today," Lick continued, "I had a money bull and what did I do . . . got my two-bit, no-tryin', sorry ash can bucked off!"

"How's the ribs?" asked Cody.

"Feelin' better all the time. They hurt o'course, but a lot better than three weeks ago. No, I can't blame it on the ribs. I've just lost my luck."

"It wuddn't ever luck to begin with."

"Well, whatever it wuz, I ain't got it back."

"Lick, I think you're tryin' too hard."

"Whaddya mean?"

"Ever since late summer, when it began to look like you had a chance, you been real serious. You been a little hard to live with, too. I'm not complainin', I can stand it, but I think now it's interferin' with your ridin'."

"Well, I am serious! I wanna win!"

"I know, but somehow you gotta relax and let the ol' Lick come back."

"The ol' Lick," Lick said sarcastically, "never made the Finals."

"Well, that's just what I think, anyway."

"What do you suggest I do?"

"Number one: ride the best you know how, but when it's over, forget it. You been layin' up in the motel or the back of this pickup, evenin's. Early! You just lay around and think about it till your nerves git shot! I admire you cuttin' back on the booze, but that don't mean you have to give up partyin' with yer friends."

"Jeez, Cody, while I was laid up down at Mother's, I got to figgerin' how much I was drinkin'. I think maybe I got the makins of an alcoholic."

Neither said anything for several minutes.

"Find a spot and let's sleep a little," said Cody.

Lick pulled off Interstate 90 at the next rest stop. The boys parked and laid out their bedrolls in the camper. They cracked the cab window an inch and stretched out.

Cody dug a nearly full fifth of Black Velvet out of his war bag. He took a pull and passed it to Lick, who hesitated, then followed suit.

"Somethin's eatin' you, Lick. Maybe it's the Finals jitters, maybe more, I dunno."

"Cody," Lick said quietly, looking at the camper top, "I'm thirty-two, nearly thirty-three. I've put seven years of my life into bull ridin'. I gave up everything I had to do this. Job, career, family, home. I got nothin' to show fer it except broken bones."

Cody let the echo of the words slip out through the cracks around the camper's open roof vent before he replied. "Remember that time in Jackson when you tackled the bank robber? Jus' clotheslined that big skinny kid? Man, he didn't know what hit him! You settin' there on his chest pointin' his own gun up his nose! He was sure scared! Then the sheriff come runnin' up and arrested *you*!"

"Yeah, the buggers didn't have any sense of humor." Lick smiled.

"How was you to know it was a play for tourists!" chuckled Cody. "An' how 'bout in Phoenix when you took off yer boots and stepped into the lobster aquarium!"

"Yeah, Karen Kay was there that night. Matter of fact, I believe that's when I met her for the first time. Boy, now she was a darlin'! A real keeper. Ya know, Cody, she used to rub my back till I fell asleep. I've reduced everything I know about women to that one single thing!"

"What? Rubbin' yer back?"

"Not just rubbin' yer back, rubbin' it till you fall asleep. When someone makes you feel so comfortable that you forget all the reasons you should be on guard or stayin' awake so you don't miss nothin'! When you feel so relaxed you don't care if you miss it and you know she's kinda watchin' out fer you! You just fade off with her squeezin' the ache and the tired out of you. The perfect woman. You show me a woman that doesn't do that and I'll show you one you got to watch out for!"

"You reckon you'll get married again?" asked Cody.

"I imagine. Hell, I hope so, but now I jus' take it a day at a time. How's Lilac?"

"Good. She's good, Lick."

"She's all right, Cody. I doubt a feller could do any better. You gettin' serious, ain't you, pardner?"

"Could be. It's a little soon to tell."

The conversation ceased. Each mind wandered off into the land of Muzak. God had put them on hold.

" 'Night, Lick."

" 'Night."

"Lick."

"Ummm?"

"You're gonna do all right."

23

September 24
Northern New Mexico

Lick was sober. The first-quarter moon was shinin' its chaste eye down on his stocky frame. They'd made an easy pull down from Washington State. They were both up tomorrow night in Albuquerque. The New Mexico State Fair and Rodeo, a mighty rich one. For a seventy-five-dollar entry fee, the winner might make three to four thousand dollars. At ten o'clock they were about twenty miles south of Farmington, New Mexico, on Highway 44. They were both sleepy, so they pulled over and Cody got in the sack. Lick took a little walk.

Along the vast northern New Mexico roadside he stooped and picked up an old bottle. It was rectangular and flat. He unscrewed the cap and held it to the faint moonlight. Vicks Formula 44. He sat down on a rock and listened to the sounds of the night. Humans had been here for centuries in this high desert land, hundreds of years before Columbus or Alan Alda. Absentmindedly he rubbed the dirt off the encrusted bottle. A whiff of dust puffed out of the top. Mist that smelled vaguely of Vicks VapoRub began gathering from the dust. The mist coalesced into a face. Lick watched, fascinated.

The face was scrinching and grimacing like a baby waking up. It appeared to be floating. The eyes blinked open. It yawned and smacked its lips. Somehow it steadied itself above the bottle. It was the face of a cowboy who'd seen better days. The face spoke to no one in particular. The voice was gruff and had all the enthusiasm of an airport ceiling announcer.

"Rub ol' Pinto, my fine friend,
What's mine is yours, until the end."

The face looked up with tired eyes and studied Lick a few seconds. It glanced around and seemed relieved that Lick was alone. The ragged voice became more pleasant.

"Man, oh man, I'm glad it's you.
I could really use a chew."

Lick handed the gauzy figure his can of Copenhagen. The oldtimer rapped a little "shave and a haircut, two bits" on the lid with his knuckles, and put himself a big pinch in his lower lip.

"I smoke clouds to clear my head,
I drink rain before I bed.
Thunder helps me say my vowels,
But Copenhagen moves my bowels."

Without speaking he excused himself. He reappeared momentarily.

"Uh? How are ya this evenin'?" asked Lick. It was all he could think to say.

"Pretty good, I could be worse.
It's hard to talk in rhyming verse."

"You always gotta talk in rhymes?" asked Lick.

"When I don't, my tongue gits tied.
It hurts my throat and pains my side."

"Are you some kinda genie?" asked Lick.

The old figure gave Lick a withering stare with one half-closed eye. His black hat was dusty and sweat stained. There was a ring binder memo pad sticking out of his brush jacket pocket. His face was wrinkled and whiskered. The Copenhagen crumbs clung to his teeth when he stretched his thin lips back. The missing teeth, or rather the few remaining incisors, made him look like a jack-o'-lantern.

"Genie? Genie! Bite yer tongue!
A genie couldn't cork my bung!
Guardin' misfits' what I do!
I'm a hangel, true and blue!"

"What's yer name, brother angel?" Lick was gettin' interested.

"Hoon, brother, it's Calhoon.

Common as a plastic spoon.
'Merican as pecan pie
But Pinto's what I'm goin' by."

"Pinto Calhoon, guardian angel," mused Lick. "Do you do day work by the hour, by the job, 'er what?"

"By the job, but not too long.
I've helped Willie write a song:
'Hangel Flyin' Near the Ground.'
Helped Ali regain his crown,
Helped Knievel cross the Snake,
But everybody makes mistakes."

Lick and Pinto visited awhile in the starlight. It turned out Pinto was born in 1866 in Bonham, Texas. His real name was Barker Francis Calhoon, but not everybody was privy to that information. He had ridden in the Oklahoma land rush of '89, but staked out the site of what was to become Noble, Oklahoma, and ended up with nothin'. He moved around the country a lot, but wound up on a little two-bit ranch north of London, Texas, in 1897. Pinto raised Spanish goats, ran his quail traps and gathered wild cattle.

Somewhere along in the twenties he died of complications resulting from an armadillo bite. Not that anyone ever knew exactly what had killed him, but if they had, they wouldn't have believed it anyway.

Now he was in the "hangel racket," as he called it. He wanted to have "Wings West" printed on his business cards, but Gabriel, the only five-star angel in the regiment, had nixed it, on account of that name being taken by a small commuter airline in California.

The last job he had was for an eight-year-old boy named Jeffrey who had found him in a discarded can of Right Guard (he had been left in a Super Eight Motel by a nervous lover who had gotten his wish with Pinto's help). While under Pinto's watchful eye, Jeffrey came down with tonsillitis and made an F on his spelling report card. However, he did teach his dog how to "siccum" and won $2.35 at recess playin' three-card monte. Pinto was better at some things than others. The tonsillitis was how come he came to wind up in a cough syrup bottle. But he was growing weary of Jeffrey. Hell, he wasn't even old enough to buy beer! Pinto was glad to see Lick.

"I've kinda tol' ya what I do.
Anything I could do fer you?"

Lick pondered a moment. "Well, ya know, Pinto, I'm on a circuit, ridin' bulls. I was doin' good, had a chance to make the Finals. Then I got hurt at Payson. Since then I ain't done good enough to pay my entries. My pardner, Cody, says I'm tryin' too hard. I sure wanted to go to O.K.C., but I gotta git winnin' again."

"Well maybe it ain't meant to be.
At Payson's where you needed me."

"How the hell—'scuze me, how was I supposed to know! Ain't there somethin' you can do now?"

"It just so happens there might be
But what, jus' yet, ain't come to me.
But you could surely help me out
My liver's suffered from a drought.
'Cause milk was all that Jeffrey drank
My belly's gettin' mighty lank.
Let's tend to business, first things first;
A little drink to whet my thirst.
Another thing, if you don't mind,
Accommodations you might find.
Some other place to keep my mug
An' git me out this stinkin' jug!"

Lick opened his Copenhagen can and Pinto Calhoon took up new residence.

"Ride 'em hard an' make 'em buck
Rub ol' Pinto fer good luck!"

Cowboys do believe in luck and superstition. Lick had acquired his good luck charm and he was ready for Albuquerque.

But what about you, steady reader? Do you believe in luck and superstition? Do you always bet your favorite number? Do you knock on wood and throw salt over your shoulder! If so, you are predisposed to believing in the likes of Pinto Calhoon.

Because the real question is, oh, ye trusting, are you willing to follow me further into the depths of this tome knowing that Lick's good luck charm is a . . . what shall we call him . . . a ghost? So

far in this story, I've only asked you to believe that bulls can think. Not a big stretch of the imagination. But now I'm asking you to give legitimacy to a run-down crackpot of an angel. I'm trying to seduce you into believing in his existence like you believe in Moses, Superman or President Buchanan.

When you say your prayers at night do you stop and consider that possibly no one is listening? No! You charge on, blessing this and blessing that, asking forgiveness, seeking comfort so that you may go and sin again.

So following my logic, if you do believe in a higher being, an extended batting slump, hot dice, momentum, Shem, Ham and Jafeth, a kiss for good luck and avoiding black cats, you could give Pinto and me the benefit of the doubt.

It will sure make tellin' this story easier.

24

Saturday, September 25
Albuquerque, New Mexico

Cody and Lick slipped into the rodeo office at the fairgrounds. "Elveeta, you big dumplin'!" said Lick.

"Lick, honey! Good to see ya! How's the ribs?" Elveeta was rodeo secretary for Bobby Monday's Stock Contracting Company. She was in her late forties and had been Bobby's secretary as long as Lick had been a card-carryin' pro rodeo cowboy.

"Comin' along okay. Still can't raise my arm all the way, but other than that, no complaints. I haven't done much good since Payson, though. That's where I got hurt."

"You've got a chance here," she said. "Do you know what you drew?"

"Nope, never called. We been up to Othello and Puyallup."

"You've got P77!"

"No kiddin'?" said Lick. "Ol' Sunset Strip. All right!"

"You stick a ride on him and you ought to be in the money," she said. "Here's your number." She handed him the nine-by-eleven placard to pin on his back.

"What about me, Elveeta?" asked Cody.

"Let's see here, Williams, Wilson, Wing . . . You've got—" A look passed over her face like she had just seen her ex-husband in a crowd.

"You've got ten-twenty."

"Ten-twenty," Cody repeated. Lick looked at his pardner.

"C'mon, Cody," said Lick, leading him to the door.

They glad-handed acquaintances and friends all the way back to the pickup.

"What'ya think?" Lick asked Cody.

"I admit it's a little spooky."

"Yeah. The trash bag's a bad draw." Lick didn't want to encourage Cody one way or the other. Pride is a strange thing. If you're a professional rodeo hand, you live or die on the draw. The chance of Cody ridin' Kamikaze was real slim, and his chance of gettin' hurt was in the definite realm of possibility. Lick didn't want to see Cody get hurt, but he didn't intend on offending him or making his decision for him. If the situation had been reversed, there would have been no question: Lick would try Kamikaze, but he didn't know whether Cody would.

"I reckon I'll try him," decided Cody. Cody and Lick had both tried 1020 before, but not this year. Not since he'd gotten so mean.

They spent the afternoon visiting and waiting for the evening show to begin. Cody got plenty of advice on how to ride Kamikaze. Most of the professional bull riders were careful to circumvent any warnings. Those were unnecessary. They just gave him tips on the bull's bucking pattern and how they'd handle him.

Manly Ott, presently ranked third nationally, in spite of his injury and layoff at the hands of Kamikaze in Nampa in July, went over the bull's bucking technique with Cody.

"He's the wiliest bull I ever saw," said Manly. "He actually thinks. He deliberatedly works you into position, catches you off guard, and dumps you, hooks you or twists you. I've never seen any other bull quite like him. He sideswiped me on the chute in Nampa, not so's the judges could see, but just enough. Got me a skosh off balance, then proceeded to hook me and buck me off. If . . . er, when you make the whistle, get off and run like hell! Fells and Dingo are clownin', so you couldn't ask for none better."

An hour before the rodeo began, Cody was on his way over to the corrals to look at Kamikaze. He spotted Emerald Dune enchanting a group of rodeo queen contestants.

"Cody! How you doin'?" Emerald waved him over. Emerald was dressed in a white satin shirt with kumquats on the yoke. It was unbuttoned to the xiphoid. His designer jeans were tucked inside his python-and-grizzly-bear boots. His Western hat was furry; it looked the way your tongue feels on Sunday morning.

"Girls, this is Cody Wing, bull rider extraordinaire."

The girls giggled appropriately in their color-coordinated boots, Western suits, gloves, makeup and hats. They were sweating more than a bachelor at a wedding.

"Howdy, ladies." Cody doffed his sombrero.

"You up tonight?" asked Emerald.

"Yup."

"Well good! We'll be watchin', won't we, girls?" They smiled and nodded. Cody strolled off when Emerald started into his description of the best banana flambé he ever tasted on Basin Street in New Orleans.

Lick returned to the camper and pulled his can of Copenhagen out of his hip pocket. He rapped the "shave and a haircut, two bits" out on the lid. That was his signal to Pinto Calhoon, G.A., so he didn't have to appear every time Lick helped himself to a chew.

He opened the lid and the dusty mist gathered above it. Pinto appeared in the camper.

"Afternoon, an' howdy do!
Somethin' I kin do fer you?"

"Well, for starters, is there some way you could take a shower? My chew's been tastin' like VapoRub."

"I reckon so. It's been a while.
A little scrub can't hurt my style.
I'll rinse off from front to hind,
But first, let's hear what's on yer mind."

"My pardner, Cody, has drawed a mean mutha. A bad news, triple X, meat eatin', cowboy hatin' spotted braymer! The big-horned head buster killed a kid here a while back and he's hurt plenty others. Cody's gonna ride 'im, but he is sure gonna need some guardin'."

"Guardin' two's against the rules!
It's bad enough just guardin' fools."

"Pinto, he needs it bad. I'm not kiddin' 'bout this bull. Couldn't you jus' help him fer a measly eight seconds? See that he don't git hurt. You know what they say about rules."

"This job don't come without its strings.

Gabriel might clip my wings.
He's mighty strict and has his ways
But he don't work on Saturdays.
What he don't know can't be a crime,
I'll put it down as overtime."

"I'm sure beholden to ya, Pinto. One other thing. I'm up tonight. Got a money bull. If I kin jus' stick it to 'im, I'd be back in the money. I'd appreciate any protection you could give me. By the way, is there anything I could do fer you?"

Pinto closed his eyes in thought. He raised a dirty fingernail and spoke.

"I've helped some folks adjust their fate.
You could bring me up-to-date."

"Fire away," said Lick.

Pinto got out his ring binder memo pad and fished a two-inch pencil out of his jeans. Little scraps of paper fell out of his memo pad like confetti as he thumbed through it. There was a movie ticket stub for the premiere showing of *Rocky III* in Cape Girardeau, Missouri, the address of a Gypsy palm reader in Pittsburgh, and a red business card that said MARIA, LATIN SPECIALITIES, ELKO, NEVADA. His questions concerned people he'd had occasion to offer his services to over the years.

Pinto had gotten mixed up with an ambitious yacht captain from Atlanta during the America's Cup. He had promised the captain he would try to get his face carved on Mount Rushmore. Lick told him that as far as he knew it was the same fearsome foursome etched in the mountain.

"Oh, damnation, sakes alive!
I thought I'd talked 'em into five.
It's my style they try to cramp.
I'll put Ted Turner on a stamp!"

He licked his pencil and made a scratchy, spidery note in his memo pad.

Mario Puzo, author and Hollywood producer, had wanted a leading man for his movie *The Godfather*. He'd asked Pinto to use his influence and obtain Marlon Brando for the leading role. Pinto had gotten confused and brought him Marlin Perkins instead. He had even worked out a side deal with Mutual of Omaha to insure the National Park facilities surrounding Mount Saint Helens. Lick told him Brando had gotten the job, not Perkins.

"Lick, ol' boy, that makes me sad.
Marlin wasn't all that bad.
Could milk a bear, from underneath!
And he'd agreed to fix his teeth.
I trust a man who's good with stock.
He promised me a Piece of Rock!"

Pinto went down the list of those he'd taken under his wing, so to speak, for awhile: Gary Hart, Donald Trump, Anita Bryant, John DeLorean, John Erlichman, Zsa Zsa Gabor's eighth husband, George McGovern, the Seattle Mariners and Kuwait!

Lick answered each question as best he could, and told him what had come to pass. It was a ragged litany and pretty poor references if one was looking to employ a guardian angel. But it didn't faze Lick a bit. He felt fortunate to have Pinto on his team. After all, according to the odds, Pinto was due for a winner.

25

September 25
Albuquerque, New Mexico

Lick and Cody watched the rodeo from behind the chutes. The other roughstock events at the New Mexico State Fair and Rodeo, bronc and bareback riding, each had two goes. A contestant entered and rode two horses on different days. Due to the large number of entries, the bull riding was a one-header. As the time drew near, the bull riders gathered in the contestants' area behind the chutes. There was a fifth-string banjo tension in the air. Fells Wingtip, rodeo clown and bullfighter, was talkin' to Lick. Others were rosining their gloves and ropes. Cody was doing stretching exercises.

The first load of bulls rumbled into the chutes. The sliding tailgates behind each bull rolled shut with a clunk. The bulls rattled and banged against the boards.

"Seventy-seven's out first, down here in four," Bobby Monday shouted to the scrambling bull riders. He was on horseback in the arena. "Whoever's got 'im, get crackin'!"

Cody's bull wasn't in the first bunch. He knew it wouldn't be. Bobby saved his best for last.

Cody and Manly Ott dropped Lick's bull rope over his bull and looped it. Lick climbed over into the chute and gently placed a boot on the bull's broad back. Then, still supporting himself on the chute, he knelt on 77. Ol' 77 wasn't known as a chute fighter; still, it was good table manners to let him know you were there. Lick adjusted his rope forward until he was satisfied.

Lick was concentrating. He dropped his legs down and scooted up a little.

"Pull! Pull!" he told Cody, who was bent over pulling the tail of his rope. "Good!"

Lick took his wrap and pounded his gloved and rosined fist closed. Sunset Strip was a half Charolais, half Braymer polled bull. He weighed in at 1,840 pounds. That's two hundred and four barn cats, seventeen grass-fat lambs, eleven Saint Bernards, six mule deer, three Berkshire boars, one and a half moose, one Budweiser Clydesdale or half a hippo! The book on the big white bull was that he was a spinner. To the left.

"You ready, Lick, we haven't got all night," chided Bobby Monday from the arena side of the chute. Lick ignored him. *Remember,* he thought, *whose side Bobby is on.* He slid up on the rope. Ol' 77 had his nose to the ground.

Lick took his right hand off the chute and rubbed the Copenhagen can in his shirt pocket. *Ride 'em hard and make 'em buck. Rub ol' Pinto fer good luck.*

He put his free hand back on the railboard, his only escape route.

"Git his head up," said Lick.

Cody slapped the back of the bull's head three times. He raised his head. Lick dropped into the vacuum of concentration. He spit out his chew.

"Cowboy up," said Manly into the whirlpool surrounding Lick's senses.

"Do it, Lick," encouraged Cody.

Lick nodded his head.

The chute boss, afoot in the arena, who had been watching Lick intently, slipped the latch and pulled the gate wide open instantly. Bull 77 roared into the arena! He took two short jumps and flung himself into a whirling dervish! He spun back to the left. Lick sat tight. *Squeeze,* he thought. He squeezed his legs. *Lift*; he lifted up on the rope. The split second before the huge body jerked him into another 180° whiplash, the massive head feinted in the direction of the intended orbit. Lick kept his eyes glued to the back of the bull's head. Reaction time was measured in nanoseconds. The hulking ropes of muscle beneath the rolling skin flexed and stretched beneath Lick's seat. He bit in with his left spur at the precise moment and spurred with his right. His right chap leg flapped furiously! Watching the great white head for that same moment to reappear, he bit in and spurred again!

Everything became slow motion. He was on a gently turning merry-go-round. He became aware that it was taking longer and longer between his opportunity to spur. He waited patiently. The bull was rocking gently. At one moment, he was high in the sky, climbing, climbing, then the gentle roller coaster ride back to Earth. Time to spur again. The great muscles bunched and released in waves beneath him. Lick felt a tremendous sense of satisfaction course through his body. *Hey! This is what I do,* he thought. *This is what I'm here for. Nobody can take this away. I am there.*

The buzzer rudely interrupted his magic moment! He descended into reality. Ol' 77 was jerking and pounding him! He was still spinning hard to the left. Lick needed to go off into his hand, to the left, to prevent hanging up. The eye of the hurricane, however, was also on his left, so he reached down with his right hand and loosed the wrap. He opened his palm and bailed off the right side.

Fells and Dingo were right there to take 77 off the rider. Nonetheless, Lick hit the ground running and sprinted to the fence. It wasn't until he was safe that he realized the crowd was on its feet, cheering. The cowboys, his peers, on the fence, were all grinning ear to ear like a photographer had ordered them all to say "Wheeze!"

His mind began to pick up Emerald's creamy smooth, spreadable voice: ". . . *like it!* That's rodeo at its finest! Let's see what the judges say."

Each of the two judges were allowed to give a maximum of 25 points to the bull and 25 points to the rider, for a total of 100 points. They told the runner their scores, he tallied them up on a small blackboard and held it up for Emerald to see.

"Ladies and gentlemen, your new leader in the bull riding here at the New Mexico State Fair and Rodeo, an eighty . . . three!"

The crowd's hoopin' and hollerin' refilled Lick's confidence tank. It went from two quarts low to overfull! Just that quick he was back on the trail to the National Finals and Pinto was goin' with him!

Cody was behind the chutes, stretching. He was definitely scared. His movements were mechanical, his skin was blanched. Lick put a hand on Cody's shoulder, stopping his leaden exercise. He spoke quietly into Cody's ashen face.

"Cody, I know this is gonna sound like I been smokin' pigweed, but I want you to do somethin' fer me."

"What?" Cody was rigid as a bathroom tile.

"I got a good luck charm."

"What?" His eyes were all pupil.

"I'll tellya 'bout it later. His name is Pinto. He's in my Copenhagen can."

"What?" Cody was still unable to blink.

"Just rub ol' Pinto fer good luck." Lick proffered the can. "Jus' do it."

Cody rubbed.

Lick slapped Cody gently on the cheek. "C'mon, pardner. You kin ride this bag o'bones. He's jus' like any other bull. You've rode a million of 'em. You're jus' the cowboy who can ride him. Now git yer rope, here he comes."

Cody's spring was one turn too tight. *Just relax,* he told himself. *Sure,* he answered. He had drawn ol' 1020 two years ago but he honestly could not remember the ride. He'd gotten bucked off, of course.

Cody watched Kamikaze come into the chute. The big spotted braymer fought it all the way. He banged his horns on the planks and the iron pipe. He kicked the tailgate repeatedly.

If yer tryin' to make me nervous it won't work, Cody telepathed to the back of Kamikaze's head.

Loud teeth, noted the bull.

Matter of fact, continued Cody's brain waves, *this may be our big night, Hog Belly. I am so psyched I b'lieve I could ride a beach ball in a hurricane. I'm stuck to you like glue. When I'm done they'll retire you to a dairy! Little kids will ride around on your back for a nickel apiece! You'll be known as Bozo the Stumbler!*

They'll put mascara on your face and paint your hooves red. Dress you in frilly stuff and puff up your tail with hair spray.

You'll remember tonight, Burger Brain. Yer all downhill from here!

Lick interrupted. "Okay, pardner, it's time."

Cody eased over into the chute. As soon as he touched the bull's back, Kamikaze started throwing his head. Cody dropped down on his back.

"Pull! Again!" he instructed Lick. "Again, okay."

Cody's hand was set. He slid up on the bull rope. Kamikaze smashed Cody's leg against the gate. Cody nodded his head. The gate slammed open.

Kamikaze didn't move a muscle! The crowd was silent, anticipating.

Hog Belly? came the low-frequency waves from the bull.

They rolled into Cody's autonomic receptors and printed out, *Watch this . . .*

Suddenly Kamikaze bellowed! A fearsome, bone-chilling, neck-tingling, malevolent warning! The long inhuman wail echoed eerily through the lighted arena!

Kamikaze dropped to his knees! The ground man started to close the gate. With less than three feet left to secure the latch, Kamikaze rose like a missile fired from a nuclear sub and crashed out of the chute, knocking the gate man on his back! He bucked two spectacularly high jumps and stopped stock-still!

Bozo, hey? Kamikaze thought. He was stopped no more than half a second, but it was enough. He knew what he was going to do next. The hapless Cody didn't have the slightest idea. Kamikaze reared up like Trigger. *Bulls don't do this,* thought Cody as he slid perceptibly back off the rope.

Syonara, hawk bait! A quick gyration to the right and Cody hit the ground with both hands! He was up and on the fence before Kamikaze completed his circle.

Cody clung to the highest rail panting like a hot dog. He watched over his shoulder as the massive bucking machine trotted toward him. The muscles rolled and bunched beneath the skin. The almost Appaloosa spots that covered his hide would have made him appear clownish except that your stare was drawn to his face.

The spots had arranged themselves into dark furrowed brow lines like a blindfold over both eyes. His muzzle was black. He looked like a gargoyle wearing a Lone Ranger mask.

He stopped and looked up at Cody. Cody was quivering slightly. Their eyes met, Cody's fearful, Kamikaze's deep and inscrutable. *Burger Brain? Humph.*

The big bull swung his heavy head toward the out gate and trotted off. Cody sagged.

* * *

Lick patted his pocket and let out his breath. "Thanks, Pinto." There was a faint effluvium of VapoRub in the air.

26

September 26
Albuquerque, New Mexico

The bull riding championship of the New Mexico State Fair and Rodeo paid $4,503. The win put Lick in eighteenth place in the world standings. It brought his total to $24,376. The men in nineteenth and twentieth place had $23,455 and $21,512, respectively. The man leading the bull riding had collected $73,295 to date. But the key number was fifteenth place. To compete in the National Finals Rodeo, held December 4 through 13, you had to be one of the top fifteen money winners in your event. There are approximately 8,500 card-carrying members of the Professional Rodeo Cowboys Association. Three to four hundred of these men and women made enough money to rodeo full-time.

The man standing in fifteenth place had earned $27,225.

At the conclusion of the Grand National Rodeo held in San Francisco's Cow Palace October 29 through November 7, the annual professional rodeo season ended. Competitors' earnings would be tallied and the top fifteen would be invited to the Finals.

Lick and Cody regularly studied the *Rodeo Sports News* to plan their itinerary. Each rodeo had a deadline to enter. On average the rodeo secretary required ten days' notice. The major rodeos needed to be entered thirty days in advance. The P.R.C.A. had a computerized system in Colorado Springs that helped these traveling athletes keep up and get entered. It required only a telephone call.

While Lick was laid up in Hereford with his cracked ribs, he had planned his schedule up through the Cow Palace in San Francisco.

He drew a big calendar that covered the last six weeks of the season, from September 26 through November 7. He wrote down every rodeo scheduled on each day that had a winning payoff of a thousand dollars or more.

He planned to go to Memphis, Pine Bluff, Oklahoma City, Omaha, Bonafay, Waco, Texarkana, Little Rock, Minot, Portland, Dallas, Billings, Bismarck and San Francisco. He and Cody hashed it over and figured which ones Cody could enter and still be able to drive to the events Lick would be flying to.

He calculated the required entry fees: twelve to fourteen hundred dollars, and commercial flight expenses another fourteen hundred. Plus his share of the gas and incidental costs. He'd have to win along the way. He had less than two thousand dollars in the bank.

Some cowboys earned over fifty thousand a year competing at a hundred rodeos. Many rode in a lot more and didn't make that much. Lick usually averaged a hundred and ten. If he was going to make the Finals, he was really going to have to press in October. The other bull riders ranked fifteen through twenty knew the same thing. It was going to be tight.

Cody drove Lick to the airport in Albuquerque this fine Sunday morning. Lick climbed aboard the big silver bird to Memphis, the start of a meandering odyssey that would cover thirteen hundred miles, give or take flat tires and lost luggage, in less than six weeks.

27

Friday, October 1
On the road from Oklahoma City to Omaha

"What's botherin' you, Cody?" asked Lick. "You ain't said five words all mornin'."

"I feel kinda rotten 'bout last night," he answered.

"What! I wish you'da said somethin'! I'da gladly swapped you. That dolly I's with couldn'a been over twenty-one. Like talkin' to a recorded message!"

"I didn't mean Harvetta. She was real nice. Matter of fact, I didn't even sleep with her!"

"Well, no wonder you feel dumpy."

"No, I woulda, but she didn't want to. But I would have. All the time I was talkin' and huggin' her, I kept thinkin' 'bout Lilac."

"You jus' didn't git drunk enough. That's simple," said Lick.

"No, dammit! That's not it. It's not that simple. I've got the lonelies all the time. I keep wishin' I was with her, or she was with me." Cody sighed. "Lick, what would you think if I was to git married?"

Lick looked over to the passenger side. Cody was sitting up on the edge of the seat, hands clasped and looking like Father O'Flanigan at a paternity suit.

"Married?" asked Lick.

"Yeah, married."

"Hummm, I don't know. I guess it has to happen to everybody at least once."

"I'm thinkin' 'bout askin' her."

"When?"

"I'll see her Sunday night, spend two or three days at her place before I meet you in Texarkana."

"No, I mean when would you git married?"

Cody loosened up a little and smiled. "I thought maybe during the Finals. Have a big blast. The folks could come down."

"You gonna quit the circuit?" Lick asked, keeping his eyes straight ahead.

"Yep. If I get everything set. Maybe I'll go back to the ranch. Dad's gonna be fifty-eight next month. He could use the help. Long as we had a place to live, I'd be okay."

"You reckon Lilac could handle livin' out like that?"

"Yup, but I never asked her yet. Both her folks are dead. She's got a brother in Saint Louis and an ex-husband in Omaha. There's nothin' keepin' her in Kansas City."

"In that case, I say ask 'er! We'll have a celebration like you never saw. We'll party till our knees are sore!"

"You really think I should?" Cody asked, brightening.

"Ya damn right! If that's what you want, go after it!"

28

Monday, October 4
Waco, Texas

Lick had flown into Waco from Bonafay, Florida, and was watching the last of the bull riding. He felt a hand on his shoulder. He turned his head. Cody was standing there. His clothes were rumpled, his eyes bleary and bloodshot.

"What the hell!" said Lick. "I wuddn't supposed to see you till tomorra!"

"She turned me down, Lick. I ast 'er and she turned me down."

"Cody, I'm sorry!"

"I ast 'er Sunday mornin'. Saturday night had been so wonderful. We talked and everythin', so the next mornin' I ast 'er. She said no. I drove straight through."

"Let's git a room somewhere," said Lick. "You look like you been drug through a knothole. Get some rest. It'll look better in the mornin'."

Lick grabbed his gear and they took the pickup to town. They found Franco and Pork Chop at one of the overcrowded motels and moved in. Cody went right to sleep.

Lick took Franco and Pork Chop to Acosta's BBQ and Cantina. They sat around licking their fingers and discussing Cody's plight.

"I was there when he met her that night in Kansas City. Had the big fight with the football team," remembered Franco. "A girl that good-looking is sure to have all kinds of men chasing after her. Maybe she doesn't think he's good enough for her?"

"That's crazy!" said Lick. "Cody's one of the best men ever strapped on a pair of spurs! You guys know that!"

"That's fer sure," said Pork Chop. "He'd give you the shirt off his back. He never gets mad."

"Boys, I know him better than anybody," said Lick. "He is a genuine, silver-plated, good ol' boy. Good hand with stock. Got good folks. He's talented and he loves her!"

"Maybe something is the matter with her," volunteered Franco.

"Dang sure must be!" said Lick indignantly. "If she can't see he's a good man, she needs her head examined! If he was like me, or even you, Franco, I could see her passin' 'im by, but not Cody! I know fer a fact he'd be true to her and treat 'er right!"

This tawdry triumvirate sat and extolled Cody's virtues and questioned Lilac's wisdom until 11:30 P.M.

"We oughtta call her," suggested Pork Chop.

"Better yet," said Lick, "we oughtta go see her, and there's no time like the present! Any y'all feel like goin' fer a drive?"

Pork Chop agreed to stay with Cody until they got back. Franco and Lick had both drawn bucking stock for the following night in Waco. They took Cody's pickup and started north on I-35 at 12:01 A.M. digital time.

It was 110 miles to the Dallas–Fort Worth airport. They pulled into American Airlines's unloading zone at 2:35 A.M. The earliest flight was number 298, departing at 7:00 A.M. Lick bought two tickets at $124 each. They buzzed and jangled their way back and forth through the hijacker's keyhole until they were depleted of any pig iron, hubcaps, Copenhagen lids, belt buckles or live ammunition. They lay down in the waiting area. It was furnished in neon gloomy.

"Lick, how do we know how to find her?"

Lick slid his hat back off his eyes and looked at Franco, "What?"

"How do we find her?"

"I guess I don't know. I never thought of that." He looked puzzled.

"Maybe Cody's left her address in his truck," suggested Franco.

"We better take a look!"

In the jockey box was a map of Kansas City. It was fresh. Up at the top was written "L.H. 1918 N. 76th Dr. Apt. 26."

"L.H. That's probably her," said Franco. "Did you find anything else?"

Lick was scouring the jockey box for scraps of paper in the dim interior light. He crawled over into the camper and searched, to no avail.

"Well," Lick said, "if that's all we got, then it's enough."

Tuesday, October 5
Kansas City

"Wait here," they said to the cabdriver.

Lick and Franco tromped up the stairs to Apartment 26. It was 9:36 A.M. Nobody was home. A neighbor walked down the stairs. She knew where Lilac worked. God often takes care of the innocent well-intentioned. Lick had her explain it to the cabbie. The meter already read $22.50.

Lilac and Maribeth looked up in surprise as the two disheveled figures pushed open the glass door into their office. The invaders were dressed like cowboys; both needed a shave. They looked like they'd wadded their shirts up and carried them in their pockets for a week! They were vaguely familiar to Lilac. They stomped over to her desk.

"Lilac?" asked Lick.

"Yes?"

"We need to talk to you."

"What? Why?"

"It's about Cody."

"Oooh, now I remember. You're Lick and I know you too."

"Franco, ma'am. I met you during the Shriners' Rodeo," said Franco.

She looked back at Lick. "What about Cody?"

"He's plum lost his mind over you."

"We talked. I hope he didn't do anything foolish."

"Foolish! He fell in love. That night at the bar he fell in love! From the very first. I thought he was loony, no offense, like somebody spiked his punch!"

"Did he . . . did he tell you what he did?" she asked.

"Yup. Said you turned him down."

"I told him I just didn't think our life-styles were compatible. I knew it would hurt him, but it's the truth."

"Lilac," said Lick, "I don't know what I can do to make you change your mind, but I'm here to tell ya, if you let him git away, you'll be kissin' off just about the most decent, honest, sincere, hardworkin'—"

"Brave, kind, considerate . . ." interjected Franco.

". . . Lovin', true-blue, intelligent, talented . . ." continued Lick.

". . . Bronc stompin', bull ridin' . . ." added Franco.

". . . good-hearted man I have ever known!" said Lick. "And I've known a few!"

"Is he outside?" asked Lilac.

"He's asleep in Waco, Texas."

"How'd you get here?"

"That's not important. What's important is that his ol' heart is achin'. He thought you felt the same way about him."

"I really care about him. He's everything you said. He makes me happy. I love his singing, and he is so considerate."

"He's willin' to quit rodeoin' for you! He's ready to carry you back to Wyoming to his ranch. He'd do it, too!"

"I know. He told me."

"And you still turned him down!"

"I've only seen him four times! I'm not sure how I feel. What if I don't like Wyoming? It would be worse to go and then be unhappy."

"Who says?" asked Lick. "Go. If it don't work out, it don't work out. You can always leave."

"That would hurt Cody."

"Worse than he feels now?" asked Lick.

"Yes. And what if he's not ready to settle down? What if he stays on the ranch for six months and get restless and wants to rodeo again?"

"So what. Go with him."

"I can't live like that."

"Like what?"

"On the road. No security. I want a man who's home with me. A home, a family. Besides, I like to work."

"You can work."

"I can get a job in Ten Sleep, Wyoming?"

"I said you can work!" said Lick. "Lilac, I wanna tell you from the heart, there's not many men I'd be standin' here for. Matter of fact, I can't think of a single other one! No offense, Franco. I'm not real gung-ho on anybody gettin' married. Most fellers that get turned down, I figger it's just their good luck, only they don't know it. But some men are the marryin' kind. What I'd call good family men. They're true to their wives, they like workin' in one place. They're good with kids, they belong to the volunteer fire department, the Kiwanis Club and the church. They're dependable husbands and pillars of the community. Everything I'm not. But I can recognize one when I see him. I've lived with Cody for nearly two years and he's real. You couldn't go wrong."

"That's very touching, Lick," Lilac said. "It's also quite a tribute that you would come up here from Waco to speak for him. You must think very highly of him."

"We're friends. You can't be more than friends."

"I told him I enjoyed seeing him, but I honestly didn't think there was much future in our relationship."

"Well, Lilac, if you can't see a future in that kind of man, maybe you don't deserve one that good!" Lick turned to go, then looked back at her. They held each other's eye for several seconds. She didn't blink.

"C'mon, Franco. We're wastin' Cody's time." They walked out.

29

Tuesday, October 5

Franco and Lick took Delta and Henry Ford from Kansas City to Waco. They were back at the motel by 6:00 P.M. Pork Chop came out to the pickup.

"He's been in there all day. Won't eat nothin'. I had some good tequila, 'bout half a fifth. He drank it all," Pork Chop reported.

Lick went into the room.

"Cody, how ya feelin'?" he asked.

Silence.

Cody didn't say a word. He wouldn't even look at Lick. Lick came back outside.

"He won't talk to me," he said.

"He hasn't said a word all day," said Pork Chop.

"Keep an eye on him, will ya, fellers? I gotta think a minute," said Lick. He climbed into the camper.

"Shave and a haircut, two bits," he telegraphed on his Copenhagen can. Pinto formed into his seedy image. Lick wrinkled his nose.

"Jeez, Pinto! Why don't you take that bath like I asked you? You smell like a three-day-old Absorbine bandage!"

"You woke me to tell me that!
Kiss my foot, you little gnat.
I'll git by, I don't need you.
I've got better things to do!"

"Aw, hell," said Lick. "Cool down. I'm just edgy. I got another problem."

"Might've guessed, you worthless whelp.

You only knock when you need help."

"It's Cody again."

"Your ears bad? I've told you, son,
My license's only good for one."

"I know, I know! But hear me out! Maybe you can give me some advice." Lick told Pinto of Cody's love affair, his expectations, his tragedy and his present condition.

"You got any suggestions?" he concluded.

"Seems to me, if I hear right,
Cody needs a bride tonight.
From my view, it matters not
Who it is or even what."

Pinto drifted back into his can.

"What?" Lick sat and absorbed the wisdom of the spirit who had advised the designer of the sleeveless parka. After due consideration, he came into the room and presented his plan to Franco and Pork Chop.

"Cody's getting married tonight," he announced.

They produced a bottle of distillate from the mescal plant (a variety of the maguey) on the way out to the rodeo grounds. Each took turns nursing the morose Cody Wing while the others competed. Word spread among the cowboys.

At the conclusion of the rodeo the stands emptied and fifty or so cowboys and cowgirls gathered at Cody's pickup.

Lick stood in the back of an adjoining pickup bed and explained Cody's turn for the worse.

"We need a bride and a preacher," he said.

The crowd raised their beer cans in agreement.

"Part of y'all scatter and find a suitable bride for this, the finest of our lot. Emerald," he said, and pointed to Emerald Dune, rodeo's answer to Jimmy Swaggert (radio evangelist and cousin to Jerry Lee Lewis and Mickey Gilley), "have you ever performed a wedding ceremony?"

"Nope, but I'd sure be willin' to try," declared the announcer.

"Good. I'll be best man. Gather up some bridesmaids and a bouquet of flowers. Turn on the lights in the arena and we'll make a wedding chapel in front of the chutes."

Half an hour later the wedding committee was interviewing prospective brides. Chaco Tortuga had offered his roping horse, Branch. A dogging steer had been considered. Wyoming Montana escorted a fourteen-inch Brazos River carp to the reviewing panel. Someone brought in a possum that had laid in the fast lane for three days. Twenty-three-year-old Nostra Fillip had offered her forty-five-year-old body as Cody's Cleopatra. She was placed on the list between the carp and the possum.

Good ol' LoBall had finally returned from his citywide search with what all agreed to be the best selection. He had found her at Piggly Wiggly, looking back at him in the fresh meat department. Her skin was smooth to the touch. She had a long tapering neck and shapely legs. And her breast: pulchritudinous and white as porcelain!

"What's her name, LoBall?"

"Butterball!"

Since Cody could not stand of his own accord, a rope was looped under his arms and draped over the chute braces under the announcer's stand. Butterball was similarly strung by the tail, eye level to the oblivious groom.

A small bouquet of shin oak twigs were placed in her enlarged giblet holder like roses in a vase.

Butterball rotated gently on her supporting string. One of Cody's toes reached the ground and he hung and swung slowly, inscribing a meandering infinity sign in the arena dirt.

Lick and LoBall stood solemnly next to the swiveling Cody, occasionally pressing the fifth of Cuervo Especial to his slack lips.

Nostra Fillip, Branch the roping horse, and a hog-tied Spanish goat were the bridesmaids. They stood at Butterball's side.

Flujencienta Rojas was recording the wedding ceremony for Polaroid posterity.

Emerald took his place in front of the bride and groom.

"Ladies and gentlemen," he began, casting a puzzled glance at the bridesmaids, "we are gathered here, an' it ain't often that so fine a group is ever gathered as this. . . . Gimme a little swig, there, Lick. Thanks. It ain't often that we poor peripatetic souls, who make our meager livin' gettin' pounded and pummeled by all manner of mean, ugly and often stupid brutes, are given the opportunity to pay tribute, and I do mean tribute! It is an honor that we are here to witness, to attend the uniting of our friend, one of us, the nearly great Cody Wing, and his darlin' bride, née Miss Butterball.

"Usually when one of our kind gets hitched, he slinks off like a hip-shot coyote and winds up in an ol' bore hole plowin' ground or settin' posts. Neither of which—I say, neither of which—is a suitable or worthy end for the great American cowboy!

"Do I hear an amen!"

"Amen!"

"Gimme another shot of Crow. Thanks.

"Now we are here to join this man"—Emerald was looking at the back of Cody's head at the moment—"and this turkey in the time-honored, civilized institution of marriage.

"Who offers this bride to be wed?"

"I do," said a thick voice near Lick. Lick smelled VapoRub in the air.

"Before I unite this beautiful couple, is there anyone among you who has any objection?"

"I think it is preposterously silly."

All eyes turned to the rotten apple. It was Ned! Big Handy Loon was standing behind Ned. Big Handy placed a bear claw on each side of Ned's hat brim. He pulled it down with so much force, the brim tore off Ned's hat and encircled his neck like a wreath! The crown completely covered his eyes and bent his ears out like a rabbit standing on his head.

"Any other objections?" asked Emerald.

"None," said Ned.

"Do you, Butterball Histomoniasis, take Cody as your lawfully wedded spice?"

"She does," said Nostra Fillip, always the bridesmaid.

"Do you, Cody Wing . . . turn him around this way, Lick . . . do you, Cody Wing, take Butterball as your lawfully wedded turkey?"

A thin glimmer of light shown in Cody's eyes, like a night flight over Yaak, Montana, at 35,000 feet. His lips began moving. The sound was out of sync with the picture. "Lilac? Is it you-o-o-o?"

"The ring please." Lick peeled Cody's Timex off his limp wrist.

"You may place the ring on her, her . . . uh . . . ?"

Lick helped Cody manipulate the expandable watchband over Butterball's upraised thigh.

"I now pronounce you man and turkey. You may kiss the bride."

Lick turned Cody toward Butterball. He pressed Cody's head to Butterball's cool, inviting skin. Cody licked her.

Nostra began to cry.

They carried Cody and his bride to the camper, placed them side by side on a pillow and left them to consummate their union in privacy.

The reception continued until dawn, when Lick climbed into the pickup and pointed it toward Texarkana.

30

October 6–23
On the Road

Cody did a lot of hurting the next three weeks. Lick pushed him hard and kept his mind occupied. They made the Texarkana rodeo October 6, then Little Rock, Minot, Portland, Dallas, Billings, and rode October 22 in Bismarck, North Dakota. Cody missed Minot and Portland. Lick had flown to them.

Lick regained his confidence and was back on track. Cody drank more than usual for him, philosophized and carried his heart around gently. He wrote twelve songs in the two and a half weeks! Songs with titles like: "You've Put My Heart on Hold," "You Kissed My Lips Then Kissed Me Off" and "Another's Feeling You and That's Why I'm So Blue."

Lick even got into the songwriting mood. All he could create was the first line and Cody thought he had heard it somewhere before. It went: "I'm so miserable without you, it's like you never left."

The two friends spent many hours and miles discussing Cody's love life. Lick didn't hesitate to give advice. Fortunately, Cody knew when to listen to him and when not to.

31

Sunday Afternoon, October 24
Kansas City, Kansas

Lilac's dog barked like a seat belt buzzer in a '73 Lincoln. She slid off the couch, turned down the game and answered the door.

"Cody!"

"Hi, Lilac." He stood in the doorway, hat in hand.

"I . . . I wasn't expecting you."

"I wanted to talk to you."

"Of course. Come in!"

The lazy afternoon sun made her front room warm.

"Something to drink, or eat, maybe?" she offered.

"No thanks. I don't plan to stay long, but I . . ." He'd practiced all the way from Bismarck how he was going to address her. "I think I might have been too soon, uh, too hasty, in asking you to consider marrying me." He blushed. "It's just that I never felt like this about anybody. I figgered you had felt the same way, but I had no right to assume that . . ." He hesitated. She looked at him, bright-eyed, not speaking. He hurried on. "And I wondered if maybe we could forget I asked and we could see each other again?"

Lilac smiled sadly. "Cody, I like you very much. You are a special man. But we don't know each other very well. I don't think I'm prepared to move to Wyoming and live on a ranch . . . with your parents. I'm not sure I would ever be prepared to do it. It's not fair to you to lead you to believe otherwise.

"I'm satisfied with my life, at least right now. Ten years from now I might regret not going with you. But in those same ten years I might regret living in Wyoming. I have to be honest with you. I'm a city girl. You're a country boy."

"Okay, okay," he said. "Could we forget that I asked and just let me see you again, every now and then?"

"One day at a time?"

"Yup. One day at a time."

"No promises? No expectations?"

"This agreement can be canceled on five minutes' notice by either party," said Cody.

"I'd like to think about it," Lilac said.

"Certainly." Cody stood up and turned toward the door, hiding a little tear of disappointment.

"Cody," she said to his back.

"Yes?"

"I've thought about it."

"Yes?"

"Gimme a hug, cowboy!"

Excuse me, friends, but I should like to point out that we are in a critical stage of this relationship.

In the Guidebook of Love: Step one is discovery and declaration. Step two is relax and let it happen. Lilac is having trouble with step two. She is guarding her heart with the regulations set forth in the Presidium of the Practical. These regulations are filed in the brain between "Heartache Memories" and "Status Quo."

They are meant to protect. Lilac knows she should not be tempted by some elusive fairy-tale hints of love ever after. She knows it . . . but she hesitates. She steps back and takes a deep breath.

Cody, on the other hand, never saw the sign that read CAUTION: LOVE AHEAD, USE LOWER GEAR. His emotions boiled out of his heart and rolled like magma over every warning thrown in their path. His love was uncontrollable until she simply held up her hand and stopped his landslide halfway down the slope. Cody's chest is fluttering, his mind is teetering, he is balancing on the edge of his heart. He gains control of himself, steps back and breathes deeply.

Love is so fragile at this moment that the weight of an old boy-

friend's finger on a touch-tone phone can make it dissipate like morning fog.

Even a single reference to a future filled with new adventure can drive the timid heart to retreat to the comfort of familiar pillows.

At this moment the door to love is ajar.

They both sighed. Cody touched Lilac's long fingers. They stepped through the door together.

Monday Morning, October 25
Kansas City, Missouri

"Cody came by yesterday," said Lilac.

"Oh, really?" said Maribeth.

"Yes. We've agreed to see each other, without any strings attached."

"Do you think you can do that?"

"I think so. He seems willing. I told him I just wasn't ready for a deep relationship."

"Is he?"

"Yes, very much so."

"He's about the only man I know who is!"

"He invited me to come to Wyoming with him for Thanksgiving."

"You're not going, of course! You told me how you'd probably hate Wyoming."

"Well, I . . ."

"If I were you, I'd sure avoid the temptation," said Maribeth with a sly smile. "It would be terrible if you liked it."

Lilac looked at her and grinned.

32

Saturday, November 6
Grand National Rodeo at the Cow Palace
San Francisco, California

It all came down to the last bull ride. Shang Lutz, according to Lick's calculations, was three or four hundred dollars ahead of him in the national standings. Shang was in fifteenth place, Lick in sixteenth. The bull riders in seventeenth, eighteenth, nineteenth and twentieth had been eliminated during the first two goes at the Cow Palace. Both Shang and Lick had been sent preliminary invitations to the Finals in OKC. The man who finished sixteenth would be notified after this rodeo that his only official capacity at the Finals would be hawking Snow-Kones in the cheap seats!

* * *

He and Shang would find out which bull they had drawn tomorrow morning. Tonight Lick had no intention of doing anything that would violate his training rules.

At the end of the rodeo tomorrow night Lick would slide from the statistics or be standing where he'd never stood before.

His good intentions included a glass of warm milk and a good night's sleep.

He had good intentions but weak resolve. He rose from his insomniac's bed at 1:30 A.M. and prowled the hotel hallway until he found a party in progress.

* * *

6:36 A.M. Sunrise slid in around the corners of the hotel curtain and woke him. Cody was snoring in the other bed. Lick lay under his covers, shifting uncomfortably, unable to go back to sleep. At 8:30 he got up, fuzzy-mouthed, eyes burning. He rattled around the room like a man in a motorized wheelchair.

After several busy signals, he reached the rodeo office to ask about his draw for that evening rodeo: 007LB10, not good news. He was a mediocre bull. If Shang drew a better bull in the short go, Lick's chances of going to the National Finals would be about as good as being appointed ambassador to Great Britain. Lick left the room without waking Cody. He went out to the sidewalk and wandered up the street.

"Shave and a haircut, two bits." He put in a call to his guardian angel.

"Ah, my friend. Bee-yoo-tee-full day!
Looks like it's all goin' our way!"

"Pinto," asked Lick, "what's that smell?"

"Polo, son, Polo cologne.
Only the best fer yer chaperone."

"Shore is potent stuff. Guess it's better than VapoRub, though."

"A pleasant change, to say the least.
Polo tames the savage beast.
Prickly pear and cactus claw
Tell me, son, who'd you draw?"

"007LB10," said Lick glumly. Pinto whipped out his ring binder memo pad and flicked through the lined pages. A yellowed black-and-white photograph of the Birdman of Alcatraz fluttered to the sidewalk.

"Oh, Oh, Seven, L, B, Ten.
Not too good my bumbling friend."

"I know," Lick sighed. "This is it. Tonight. For all the marbles. I have to finish higher than Shang Lutz in the short go and the average. Otherwise, we don't go to OKC."

"What do you intend to do?
You drew the bull, it's up to you."

"Ride him, I guess."

"You're dang right! You ride 'im hard!
Ride that bull an' I'll stand guard.
Spur 'im like a hurricane
Was in your shorts and in yer brain!
Lock up tight! Make 'im buck!
Only you can change yer luck!"

"What if Shang draws a better bull?"

"You bet yer wad he's tryin' to!
Just do the best that you kin do!"

"Right. Yer right, Pinto, ol' man. I'm the only chance I got." Lick smiled a little.

"By the way, I like yer new perfume. Even if it smells like a debutante's laundry."

"You measly, weasly parasite . . ."

Lick just snapped the lid on tight.

* * *

The Cow Palace crowd was big and rowdy at the Sunday night performance. This was a big money show and important to plenty of cowboys who knew it was their last chance to make the Finals.

Lick had spent the afternoon in his room sleeping and forcing himself to rest. He hadn't eaten all day. Now he stood in relative calm behind the bucking chutes waiting for the bulls. His was in the first load. Shang had drawn W6, ShugaVelvet, an eliminator, hard to ride. If Shang could ride him, he'd probably beat out Lick. Lick's bull did not have a reputation for winning rodeos, but he should be easier to ride. Lick was talking to Shang while each buckled on his chaps and readied his gear.

"I'd almost trade you, Lick," said Shang.

"I was thinkin' the same thing," Lick replied. "I been on W6 twice. Bucked off both times. He fights the chute."

"Yeah, I know. It's not my first time on him. I had him in Fort Worth."

"You ever been on LB10?" asked Lick.

"Rode him once. Drew him again, but turned him out. Best I

recall, I marked a fifty-eight. Couldn't get him to do much. It would help if the clowns turned him back, otherwise he'll go straight."

The first load of bulls rumbled into the chutes.

"Guess I better get to work," said Lick.

"Lick . . ." started Shang. Lick looked at him. They held each other's gaze. The space between them was filled with mutual respect.

"Yes?" asked Lick. Shang stuck out his hand and Lick shook it.

"Ride 'im, cowboy."

"Thanks."

33

Sunday Night, November 7
After the San Francisco Rodeo

Lick and Shang each did the best they could. They played out their small drama at the far side of the bigger stage. They had record crowds at the Cow Palace. A seventeen-year-old girl on a big rangy horse won first in the barrel racing. A spectator was mugged in the parking lot. Manly Ott, bull rider, continued his slump.

Lick rode his bull. He scored an anticlimatic 63 points. He and Cody stood on the deck behind the bucking chutes and watched Shang Lutz ride. ShugaVelvet lived up to his reputation. He bucked hard, spun crooked and tried to kill Shang after he bucked him off. But buck him off he did, four seconds into the eight-second ride.

Cody was ecstatic! He was so happy for his friend he could barely contain himself! He pounded and hugged Lick, stepping on his toe and mashing his hat! Lick just stood there with a supercilious look on his face, a little embarrassed.

Lick's qualified ride placed him in the average, which upped his total winnings for the year to $33,763. That was $632 ahead of Shang, who fell to sixteenth place overall.

They saw Shang Lutz a few minutes later behind the chutes.

"Good ride, Lick," said Shang. "Congratulations!" His goodwill was genuine. Shang was twenty-three years old and destined to attend several National Finals in years to come.

"Thanks, Shang. You almost rode 'im, didn't ya?"

"Yeah, almost. Next time. Tear 'em a new one in Okie City. You deserve it." Shang shook hands and headed off.

"Let's git on with the party! We're gonna celebrate tonight!" said Cody.

"You go ahead. I'll be there in just a minute."

"Okay, pard."

Lick walked into the arena. It was over. Cowboys, spectators and maintenance people were moving in all directions, like they had someplace to go. He felt small in the big coliseum.

Lick spoke to himself in a small, quiet voice. "You made it. You may not have deserved the good luck, but you made it.

"Lord, I owe ya. You've always been there. I know I'm not always there for you. But every time I need to talk to you, you listen. Sometimes I know you're tryin' to call me and the line is busy. My life's good. I'm a simple man on a lucky roll. I know I'll have to pay you back sometime. Maybe I'll be ready when the time comes. Anyway, for now, I thank ya for standin' by me. Amen."

Lick stood there another minute or two until the nagging emptiness sent him trotting after Cody and the security of friends. Victory and achievement were meaningless when you couldn't share them.

Lick climbed into the pickup with Cody.

"Pardner, I wanna be the first to toast ya!" Cody uncapped a fifth of Jim Beam and made it bubble. "I'm so proud of ya, I could bust!"

"Thanks, Cody." Lick took a swig. "Where to?"

"The party, where else!"

34

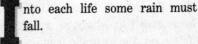

November 18
Houston, Texas

Into each life some rain must fall.

Sympathetic reader, have you ever been the helpless victim of some grand design? Does the term "eminent domain" make you shudder? Did the new truck bypass leave your little Main Street business high and dry? Did they find an endangered species in your pasture and condemn your farm? Did they raise your taxes? Close your bank? Cancel your favorite TV show?

And who did these deeds that so affected you personally? The answer is, dear friends, the infamous "THEY." They who are the wheelers and dealers, the seedy and greedy, the lickers and stickers, the kissers and pissers!

The honor bending, condescending, all important, influential, anonymous* They. *When* They, *these influential people, do something, they usually make waves. Innocent bystanders get washed away with the tide. That is not to say that influential people are mean-spirited or uncaring. They are simply unconscious of the far-reaching consequences of their little amusements.

In Houston, on this November night, a thunderhead was building that would nearly drown our bull ridin' hero.

Read on. . . .

Clive McDill was a good man, with eight grandchildren, 136 oil wells on three ranches and a standing order for two new Cadillacs every October.

He loved his grandchildren, his oil wells and his Cadillacs. He was a charter member of the Texas Cattle and Oil Club. This year he had assumed the chairmanship after fellow member Billy Ray File had been appointed ambassador to Lagos.

The Texas C & O, as it was called, was as exclusive as the Association of Left-handed Astronauts Who Have Walked on the Moon.

Clive brought the meeting of the Texas C & O to order. Twelve men sat around the conference table on the thirty-fifth floor atop the Texas Red Petroleum Building. The reflection of Houston's night lights sparkled on the large window at the end of the room. An elegant stained-glass light fixture hung over the shiny oak table, giving the impression that one was in a pool hall and not a corporate boardroom.

Bourbon and scotch were in crystal decanters on the side table. Cigar smoke made its presence known in spite of the humming air-quality filters.

"Boys," said Clive, "y'all know how much fun we have bettin' the ponies at Ruidoso, an' how we been lookin' fer another little event we could calcutta."

The members nodded noncommittally. Each year before the quarter horse futurity at Ruidoso Downs race track in New Mexico, they held their own private betting pool. The starting horses in the race were auctioned off to the highest bidder. The members would begin with the favorite horse and bid amongst themselves, continuing until all of the entries were bought. Then all the money would be pooled. After the race, those who had bid the highest for the horses that won, placed and showed would divide the pool. These were rich men and the pool was deep.

Clive continued. "The committee, Bosco, Jim Bob Tom Ed and me have come up with a possibility that might be right down our alley. Jim Bob Tom Ed, would you kindly explain our proposal to the boys."

Jim Bob Tom Ed Luckett, cattle rancher from Crane, Texas, rose. Jim Bob Tom Ed ran twenty-eight-and-a-half cows per oil well on his place south of Midland and made a pretty good living. "Thankya, Clive," he drawled. "We figgered we could pick an event at the National Finals Rodeo next month, say the bull ridin', and calcutta the fifteen finalists. Each one of us could buy a finalist, maybe two, and the winner would be determined by the amount of money won by the rider during the ten days at the National Finals. Each rider starts out even. Pay three places in the calcutta: win, place and show."

"What they've won to date, the rest of the year, don't have any bearing on the calcutta?" asked Dicky Lee Limenuts, president of Dicky Lee's National Gas and Brangus.

"Nope. 'Course, the bull rider with the best record goin' into the Finals might bring a little more in the auction," answered Jim Bob Tom Ed. The good ol' boys around the table chuckled.

Smiley Horrocks pushed his 6'4" lanky frame back from the table. "The cowboys don't know nuthin' 'bout this and we don't tell 'em, right!"

"Right. Anybody caught tryin' to interfere will forfeit his membership in the Texas Cattle and Oil Club.

"Everybody understand the rules? Good."

Ah, sure . . . we all understand, don't we, fellow readers? We understand the good ol' boys are just havin' a little fun. How could it possibly affect the little people? Wait and see.

Clive handed each of the members a list of the top fifteen bull riders showing their standings going into the National Finals and the amount of money won by them to date. He let everybody study the list for a few minutes.

Halfway down the table Hoss Bendigo sat beside his cousin, Jaybo Marfa. Hoss was trying to explain the proceedings to him. Abandoning the details, he concentrated on coercing his not-too-bright cousin to buy the second bull rider to be auctioned off. Hoss, himself, planned on being the highest bidder for the number-one-ranked bull rider.

A flicker of understanding crossed Jaybo's eyes and he took the bait. Jim Bob Tom Ed stood up and terminated the table talk.

"You ready, Sam?" asked Jim Bob Tom Ed.

"Yup, if y'all are." Sam Houston Pinzgauer, auctioneer, Longhorn raiser and offshore drilling magnate, stood up.

"Okay, boys. We're gonna go down the list, one through fifteen. All bids are final and we'll need a check by December first. Clive is keepin' the books."

"First up for bids is Smokey Brothers. Won eighty-one thousand, two hundred and thirty-nine dollars this year. What am I bid? Will you bid twenty-five thousand? Twenty-five, bid twenty-five, twenty-five. Thank ya, Hoss, now fifty . . ."

Smokey Brothers brought $210,000.

One hour and fifty minutes later, Clive handed a typed copy of the calcutta results to each member. The bids ran from $210,000 for Smokey all the way down to $18,000 for Lick in the fifteenth place.

The total pot, which would be split 50-30-20, was $1,859,000.

On the way to their car following adjournment of the Texas C & O, Hoss was givin' Jaybo the "Good Dog" treatment. "Ya done jus' right, cuz, we got the number-one and number-two cowboys in the pot. One of us is bound to be in the money. Ma's sure gonna be tickled!

" 'Course, if it gits right down to it we might have to hedge our bets a little. A little burr under the blanket, so to speak." Hoss chuckled.

"Ya really think Ma will be tickled?" asked Jaybo, who always worried what Ma would think.

"You betch'er hat!" answered Hoss.

"That'll be great, if Ma's tickled," concluded Jaybo, smiling. "Jus' great."

35

Wednesday, November 24
Worland, Wyoming

The boys had ridden in three more rodeos before the Thanksgiving lull: Brawley, California; Sioux Falls, South Dakota; and the American Royal in Kansas City. Then Lick took off to spend the holiday with a belly dancer in Hailey, Idaho.

Cody stood in the small airport waiting room in Worland, Wyoming. It was 11:15 A.M. The airplane was half an hour late.

"Frontier flight 915 from Denver now arriving."

The reliable Convair 580 touched down. Smoke puffed off the tires on impact. It taxied up and shut down the props. Lilac was third and last to debark.

Cody saw her and his heart skipped a beat. Her long brown hair was pulled back behind her ears and blowing in the wind. She was a tall woman, but she walked erect, shoulders back, with long strides. She had on a long coat and dark pants. She was wearing fashionable Western boots.

"Hi, Cody." She smiled.

"Hello, darlin'." He gave her a hug.

He shuffled a minute. "You got bags?"

"Two. I didn't know what to bring, so I brought more than I'll need, I'm sure."

"That's okay. We've got plenty of room."

He tossed her bags in the back of his blue pickup and they drove east toward the Bighorn Mountains.

"I'm a little nervous, Cody."

"I know, but it'll be all right."

Meeting potential in-laws. What could be worse? Possibly taking the final exam in bio-chemistry? Contracting malaria? Stacking twenty tons of moldy hay? Scheduling a hemorrhoidectomy? Spending the winter in a sheep camp? Given a choice, most normal people would rather be stabbed to death with a table fork than meet potential in-laws!

It is no wonder Lilac has butterflies. In her worst nightmares she envisions them living in a cave cooking big hunks of antelope liver over a cow chip fire. The father-in-law belching and grunting, the mother-in-law shuffling around shooing bats off the skewer while the children skitter and screech like Rhesus monkeys!

She realizes that the mother-in-law will only be pleased if the new daughter-in-law is like her. The father-in-law may have a different opinion depending on his relationship with the mother-in-law. Assorted aunts, uncles and grandmas can all sway the evaluation. Younger siblings can bolster or erode a family's approval. Did she pick up the baby? Did she help with the dishes? Did she listen to Uncle Albert's jokes? Did she like sister's corn bread?

Potential wives are usually evaluated as potential mothers. First impressions aren't formed on the fact that the candidate may have a Ph.D. in nuclear physics or own her own shoe store. No. First impressions hinge on the initial response to questions that often begin:

"My son tells me that you are a supreme court justice, the first person to cross the Pacific in a hang glider and have been nominated for the Nobel Prize in literature. That's nice . . ." says the mother-in-law, who hesitates, then, ready to resign herself to disappointment, reluctantly continues, "But can you chew buffalo hides and make your own jerky?"

Lilac knew all these things and pondered them in her heart.

"Cody, we're still on one day at a time, right?"

"Yes, ma'am. I'm not tryin' to put any pressure on you. I hope you have a good time. I've told the folks that you're just a friend, so they shouldn't harass you too much.

"Knowin' them," he continued, "they'll just fit you right in and you'll feel comfortable."

"Good." She reached over and kissed his cheek. "It's nice to see you, cowboy. Where will we be sleeping? What arrangements, I mean."

"You might be in Kaycee's room, my little sis. I'll be on the couch. Sorry."

"That's okay. I understand." She slid over and sat next to him.

The weather was clear and fifty-two degrees. They turned off onto the ranch road. Cody took them up another side road up a draw. He stopped at the base of a little meadow. The sun was shining through the windshield. He took out a mattress from the camper and covered it with his bedroll. He laid them out in the meadow. He and Lilac lay on their backs, side by side, looking up at the sky.

The sky was blue. Migrant clouds stood at parade rest, like cottonwood silk on a municipal swimming pool at dawn; no ripples.

"Lilac, this is what I love. This is where I belong. My roots are in these mountains and hard ground. I've banged around the country these last few years and seen all of it I care to see. I'm tired of it. I'm tired of the long nights, the bad whiskey and the endless road. My body hurts, neon gives me a headache.

"If I'd been one of the best, maybe it would be different. But my bones ache, I live from one rodeo to the next, always bettin' this one will make me enough to enter one more.

"I'm ready to come home. I'm ready to try and amount to somethin'.

"Lilac, I love you. I love you more than anything I've ever seen, known, tasted or rode. Since I met you, I know what it means to love.

"I wanna marry you. I want to have kids. I want to teach 'em to ride colts, track lion, punch cows, rope steers, play guitar and love this wild Wyoming country. I wanna sleep with their mama every night.

"I know we've got a deal. I'm not gonna back out on it. I promise not to talk about it again, but I want you to know how I feel. You are the best thing that's ever happened in my life."

Cody's open-faced honesty and quiet confession pierced Lilac's self-defense. He touched her heart. She squeezed his hand and lay there in the feather bed of his love.

He rolled onto his side and unbuttoned her coat. "We're not in a hurry," he said.

★★★

"Mama, this is Lilac . . ."

"Come in, sugar, outta the chill. Call me Chick. Roscoe and the boys are up on Willer Crick. They'll be in by supper.

"Have you kids eaten yet? Probably not, huh? Cody would never think of stoppin' off for a bite. Worse than his dad! Can go for three days without thinkin' of eatin'.

"You've been comin' this way a long time, haven't you, darlin'? You know that though, of course.

"Sit down, honey, I'll heat up some Hamburger Helper and stringbeans. You like peach cobbler? Cody's favorite. I always make up two or three when he comes home.

"Cody, put her suitcase in Therm's room. You two boys can sleep on the sofa.

"Now, Lilac, tell me about yerself. You sure are a pretty thing."

Lilac spent five days bein' tossed and tumbled amidst the busy, happy Wings. They assimilated her like a snowflake on Powder River Pass! She was asked to help. She made the turkey dressing and pumpkin pie. She learned to play dominoes and rode to the head of Cedar Creek. She saw her first elk, mule deer, antelope, porcupine, jackrabbit, eagle, buzzard and pheasant. She ate her first venison and Rocky Mountain oyster. She talked for hours with Cody's little sister, Kaycee, who was hungry for sophisticated conversation.

Lilac was taken to a real country dance, met someone who had never heard of Neil Diamond and did something on horseback she didn't know you could do!

36

Friday Night, December 10
Oklahoma City, Oklahoma

Lick had a room reserved at the Sheraton during the Finals. Cody was staying with him. Cody saw to it that Lick was sober, rested, and celibate. Pinto saw to it that he was safe. They kept his socializing to a minimum and his partying proper. Lick could have applied for membership in the Campfire Girls!

Friday night they were all back in the room by 10:30 P.M. watching a "M*A*S*H*" rerun. Lick had ridden his bull earlier that night and won second in the go round. It paid $2,439.

Lick was sore. He had climbed on seven bulls in seven days. Not just your everyday run-of-the-mill eighteen-hundred-pound thrashing braymer, but each one of the top hundred bucking bulls in the rodeo game. They had been selected to represent the best stock the rodeo contractors had to offer. After all, it was their showcase, too!

Every person competing, be he roper, rider, dogger or roughstock rider, was wound up and ticking like a two-dollar watch! A high sense of drama hung over every conversation, keeping the cowboys on the edge of hysteria. Friends, supporters, fans and family suffered the tension vicariously.

The physical pain and nervous exhaustion was cumulative. It was the true test of Ban and Certs! Each competitor had to bring himself to a mental and physical peak nine days in a row. Hallways and rooms began to smell of liniment and DMSO. Rolaid wrappers piled up in the butt cans.

At the coliseum a training room had been designated. In the hour or two before the rodeo it filled with contestants. Roughstock riders, mostly. There was so much black and blue, bandages and tape, and creaks and groans a visitor would think he was in a battle zone!

Allow me, friends, if you will, to expand on pain, on playing hurt. Rodeo is not a team sport. If the quarterback injures his elbow and is on the bench for three weeks, the game still goes on, the team still takes the field and the quarterback still gets paid.

If the bareback rider injures his elbow no team physician writes him an excuse. His game is canceled. His horse is turned out and his money goes back in the pot.

National Finals: ten performances, nine days in a row, ten chances to win. Chances to win, did I say? Fifteen first-class cowboys ride. Each performance pays only the top four places. Even if you rode your bull every performance, you could still score out of the money.

And even if you don't score you still get beat up. Playing with pain? You have no choice. The coach can't pull you out; you're the coach!

I could turn around and tell you that they don't do it for the money. You'd laugh, unless you'd climbed mountains, danced in a chorus line or circumnavigated the Earth in a one-man sailboat.

Grit, drive, desire and determination fuel the fire that burns inside the gladiator until it is so intense that pain is overcome. Each night, for each performance, he must stoke that mental fire.

High risk? Mental fire? Playin' hurt? Low pay? What kind of game is that!

It's rodeo. The cowboy's answer to organized sports.

Lick had drawn seven bulls up through this Friday night. He'd made the whistle on six head. Three other bull riders had ridden six bulls: the first- and second-place bull riders in the world standings coming into the National Finals, Smokey Brothers and Lennox Wildebang, and the fifth-place finisher, Wyoming Montana.

Although all four men had ridden six bulls so far, Smokey was ahead in the average for the National Finals Championship. Their scores for each ride were totaled to determine their standings in the average.

At the conclusion of each performance, the cowboys drew for tomorrow's bull. Officially forty-five rides remained, forty-five bulls to be drawn for, including the Bucking Bull of the Year, number 1020, Kamikaze. Some poor, unlucky, hind-tit sucker was going to draw that cowboy killer and put his body on the line! It gave each potential victim a queasy feeling. But this queasiness didn't last long among these brave vaqueros. The odds against drawing Kamikaze were fifteen to one.

CL75, Bugger Velvet, had bucked off Lick in the third round and reinjured his ribs. He'd been wrapping them faithfully before each ride, but each successive night the pain grew worse. Cody had been taking care of Lick like he was an only child.

Cody put down the telephone. He'd turned down a party invitation for him and Lick.

"A little drink would relax ya, pard," Cody said, pouring Lick a shot of Johnny Walker Red over ice.

"Thanks." Lick grunted.

"Still hurtin', huh? Does it hurt to breathe?"

"Yup, but I'm all right."

"Ya damn shore are! You're doin' fastastic!" Neither alluded to Lick's present status in the top four: bad luck.

"Any suggestions 'bout tonight?" asked Lick.

"Hell, you're ridin' better than you ever have! Those ribs must be forcing you to stay over yer rope!"

"When's Lilac comin'?" asked Lick.

"I'll pick 'er up tomorrow at noon."

"You gotta place to stay? You can stay here, ya know, if Lilac can handle it."

"We'll see. Nothin' fer you to worry about." Cody paused. "I never did thank you for goin' up to Kansas City after I'd . . . I'd made a fool of myself."

"No sweat. Didn't do much good anyways."

"Maybe it did. She's comin' here and she went to Wyoming with me for Thanksgiving."

"How was that?"

"Thanksgiving? Good, I guess. She got the full dose. She knows what it would be like if she ever decided to marry me."

"You still tryin' to talk 'er into it?"

"No. We don't discuss it. I promised her I'd not mention it unless she wants to talk about it."

"You've been pretty straight-arrow. Maybe it's to help me, but if you wanna snort in some ol' dolly's flanks, don't let me stop ya!"

"No! You're not stopping me. I just don't feel the urge. Actually, it's helpin' take my mind off it, stayin' here and keepin' you outta trouble."

"You reckon she's bein' as true and pure as you?" asked Lick.

The question hit Cody like a fist in the chest! He hid it well. "I don't know. She's made it clear we've got no hold on each other."

Lick laughed. "Well, you're a better man than me! Matter of fact, I could use a little lovin' right now! This place is crawlin' with sumptuous darlin's, one of 'em with my name tattooed on the inside of her upper lip! I've been here a week and been brushed up like an ol' bull in the willers!"

"You're winnin', pardner! Maybe what yer doin' is the right thing."

"I don't know, dammit. I ain't been drunk once, loved at all and I've slept more than a man in a coma! I'm supposed to be enjoyin' this! This is my last fling!"

"Last fling?" asked Cody. "You gonna quit after this?"

"I been thinkin' on it," Lick admitted, mad at himself for the slip of the tongue. "I'm gettin' too old to keep hurtin' this bad. But I don't know what I'd do. Bull ridin's the only thing I'm half good at. I figger I'm good for another year or two, unless I get hurt again." He sighed. "What about you? You still goin' back and run the ranch?"

Cody shook his head slowly and said, "It all depends on Lilac."

37

Saturday Morning Early, December 11
Oklahoma City, Oklahoma

Hoss Bendigo pulled into a handicapped parking space and turned off his lights. The Eldorado glowed silver under the vapor lamps in the parking lot. No one else was visiting the Cowboy Hall of Fame in Oklahoma City at 4:30 in the morning.

"Are you sure these guys are reliable, Hoss?"

"Shootfahr, cuz, 'course I am! The lawyer gimme Slyzack's name and he personally picked 'em fer us."

"But Slyzack's locked up in La Tuna!"

"These peckerwoods are from Dallas, the Big D! They're hand-picked! And only a thou a day. Not much to protect our investment."

"I wished Ma wuz rightcheer. She'd know if we wuz messing up."

"Shootfahr, trust me, Jaybo," encouraged Hoss.

Hoss and his cousin, Jaybo Marfa, had inherited their oil ranch in Wharton, Texas. Hoss was smart, but shady; Jaybo had trouble keeping score in the game of life.

Jaybo's real name was Jim Bowie Marfa. His mother, now deceased, had been president of the Daughters of Texas in 1951 and a shrewd businesswoman. In addition to her son, whom she called JayBoy, she had raised her nephew, Hoss, as her own, after his mother ran off to Shreveport with a wildcatter. A group of lawyers, friends of Jaybo's mom, now ran the company.

"So what's these two Dallas woodpeckers gonna do?" asked Jaybo.

"Git out yer list, Cuz. I'll 'splain it to ya. I bought Smokey in the calcutta. You bought Lennox. Number one and two. We paid over two hundred thousand apiece, right?"

"Now . . . try to understand this, Jaybo . . . each bull rider's been on seven bulls. They've got three to go. Our boys have ridden six bulls each. There's only two other riders who've ridden six bulls each. Follow so far? So, just to help *our* boys out, we set a few traps along the way for them other two cowboys. Nuthin' serious, just kinda a wrench here an' there to make sure they don't ride as many bulls. See?"

Jaybo thought it over. "I'm not sure I understand, Hoss."

Hoss sighed. "These boys from Dallas toss a few tacks in the road. Apply a little gentle pressure, you know. Then we win. You wanna win, don'cha?"

" 'Course I do, Hoss. You know that."

"Well, then, trust me. Have a cheroot."

As Jaybo lit up, the plan disappeared into his cranial vault like a firefly into a black hole.

"That must be the cats there," observed Hoi Solomon Rosofsky.

He sat at the wheel of a rented four-door AMC Concord. The heater wasn't working and Hoi Sol was cold. He steered toward the parked car. "Man, look at that Cadillac! Nice set of wheels. Might git one like that myself someday, but in panther black."

Hoi Sol was not talking to himself. His traveling companion, Thorhild by name, sat hunched in the passenger seat. Thorhild bent his head slightly to keep from touching the headliner and his knees pressed against the dash. He had thick, very light blond hair, ice-blue eyes, a cross tattooed on his thumb and a nose like a gravy boat.

"Nice of Slyzack to throw a little work our way," continued Hoi Sol. "I'll tell ya, bro, it's been thin. Things are changin'. I mean, when was the last time we rousted some liddle mom-and-pop business. Hell, everybody's carryin' firearms! The corner drugstore now belongs to an international conglomeration that doesn't give a flyin' filch whether they get held up or not!

"And when was the last time you broke somebody's arm? Everybody's got a lawyer! I don't know what it's all comin' to, ya know? We're losin' our traditional values. Extortion, a little payola, some strongarm. Now they steal more with computers than you can make hijackin' an armored car!" He sighed sadly.

"Maybe it's drugs or TV preachers. Somethin' has taken folks' minds off unscrupulous behavior or petty revenge." He glanced at Thorhild, who was staring straight ahead. "I mean, nobody robs a church anymore."

Hoi Sol pulled in perpendicular to Hoss's Eldorado. He could see two heads illumined in the front seat. The Cadillac's doors opened. Hoss walked around to Hoi Sol's window.

"Y'all Slyzack's boys?" he asked.

"That's us, brother."

Hoss climbed in the backseat. Jaybo came in after him.

"I'm Hoss and this is Jaybo . . . uh, Jim."

Hoi Sol adjusted the rearview mirror to better see the gents in the backseat. Hoi Sol immediately noticed the Texans' attire. It was Hoi Solomon Rosofsky's curse. He was preoccupied with clothing. He came by this preoccupation naturally. He was descended from a long line of tailors. His grandfather was a Russian Jew who had immigrated to Houston. Hoi Sol's father had learned the trade, moved in the fifties to San Francisco, where he worked for a large dry goods store. His father had made a buying trip to Hong Kong, where he met and married the working daughter of a Chinese haberdasher. They returned to California and soon moved to Los Angeles, where they started their own business making fine men's clothing. Hoi Sol was born thirty-nine years ago in L.A. and grew up on East Eighth Street in the middle of the garment district. As a baby Hoi Sol slept on the cutting table while his mother and father were cutting fine suits. His diapers were tailored from scraps of white silk left over from shirts his mother made.

For the meeting tonight, Hoi Sol had chosen one of his seventeen hand-tailored suits made by Rosofsky's Fine Clothing for Men, Los Angeles. It was midnight blue with subtle metallic green highlights. To compliment the ecru hand-made silk shirt—with stays, of course—he wore an Italian silk tie just a shade lighter than midnight blue with echoes of metallic green. Unseen were the coordinated silk socks and silk boxer shorts, a luxury he'd acquired the taste for while in diapers. A dark homburg and sleek Italian shoes with only four shoestring eyelits rounded out his top and bottom.

He had inherited his mother's dark slanted eyes and his father's thin face. Though he kept trying, he had a horrible time growing a mustache. His chin was slightly recessed and his neck was scrawny. Tonight he wore a long silk-lined cashmere scarf, exactly matching the midnight blue, which he wrapped once around his neck. He had fancied himself a little like Al Pacino in *The Godfather* when he'd checked himself in the dressing mirror earlier.

In fact, he looked more like a weasel in a peacoat sleeve.

Hoi Sol stared at the reflection of the two Texans. Ever since coming to Dallas from Los Angeles via Las Vegas seven years ago, he'd tried to understand the Texans' mode of dress. He'd given up. Hoss was wearing a bolo tie with a turquoise stone the size of a largemouth bass. Hoi Sol was sorely tempted to turn around, reach over the seat and jerk Hoss up by the mink lapels of his hair-side-out Hereford-skin vest and offer some much needed sartorial guidance: "Can't you see that you look like sticky Christmas bows on a naked fat boy? Your hatband weighs more than a carpenter's belt! That elk horn sterling silver belt buckle in the shape of Lake Texoma belongs on a trot line in the Bay of Fundy! Have ye not heard of good taste, understated ostentation, scrofulous affectation! . . . 'Seek elegance rather than luxury, and refinement rather than fashion; to be worthy, not respectable, and wealthy, not rich' . . . In the words of the immortal William H. Channing, '*That* should be your symphony!' "

Hoi Sol considered it, but instead he said, "I'm Hoi Sol and the little guy here is Thorhild."

"Please to meetcha," said Hoss.

"So, what's the job?" asked Hoi Sol, acting brains of this dynamic duo.

Hoss leaned forward. "My cousin and I have a wager with some other gentlemen and we'd like to hedge our bet. There's two cowboys entered in the bull ridin' here at the National Finals that we don't want to win any more money. They've got three more bulls to ride and I'd just as soon they didn't ride 'em. Get the picture?"

"I think so," said Hoi Sol. "You want 'em iced? That'll take more than a grand."

"No, no!" Hoss said quickly. "Just don't let 'em score."

"How do we find 'em?"

"They've got three rides left," explained Hoss. "Two today, Saturday, at one-thirty and eight P.M. Then the last one Sunday afternoon at one-thirty. You boys find 'em this morning and do whatever you have to do. If you keep these two bull riders from their appointed rounds there will be a ten-thousand-dollar bonus. You savvy?" He paused to let it sink it.

"This is real important to me and Jaybo here." He handed an envelope over the seat. "Here's twenny-five hunnert in advance."

"Who are these cowboys?" asked Hoi Sol.

"Give 'em your list, Jaybo. They're number five and number fifteen."

Hoi Sol switched on the dome light.

"Wyoming Montana and Lick . . . ?" he read. "I can't read this. Looks like you spilled something on it!" He looked back at Jim Bowie Marfa.

"That's, uh, barbecue sauce, I think," said Jaybo.

38

Saturday Noon, December 11
Oklahoma City, Oklahoma

Cody had just left for the airport to pick up Lilac. Lick lay back on the hotel bed. He planned on walking over to the coliseum about one-thirty.

The door knocked. He answered.

"Room Service," said the lady.

"I didn't order anythin', ma'am."

"Is this twelve-twenty-five?"

"Yup!" Lick looked her over. She didn't look like a waitress. She didn't look like a maid. She certainly didn't look like a Hutterite missionary!

Lick's visitor smiled. "I was told to come up here and entertain you," she said. Now he knew what she looked like! "Compliments of Cody," she added.

"Well, bless his randy ol' heart! Come on in!"

Willa Dean slid into the room like magma down a slope. She was 5'5" wearin' high heels. But she was a big girl! She shook her long wavy blond mane, then looked at him steadily.

Her fur coat slipped off like a shedding snake's skin.

She was wearing a sleeveless, strapless blouse of some kind. From shoulder to shoulder, acres of porcelain skin filled the landscape and Lick's approving eye eventually disappeared into the décolletage. The silky blouse did little to hide the articulated infrastructure that reached up in support like two catcher's mitts awaiting a pop foul.

A wide elastic belt separated this magnificant top from the equally spectacular bottom. It—the bottom, that is—appeared broad and smoothly encased in a short dark form-fitting skirt that ended just above the knees. This entire display of colossal comeliness balanced on shapely legs as stout as marble columns.

When she walked away it was the driver's-eye view of a wheelhorse pullin' against the tugs.

I know, y'all are trying to envision from my description just how big Willa really was. Surely you appreciate that I would never be so indiscreet as to tell you what she weighed. I have mentioned she was big. Was she fat? Well, I would never describe Willa that way, because I want you to picture her as truly beautiful. Big, and truly beautiful.

If Funk and Wagnall's needed an illustration to accompany the term "seething pulchritude," she would be it.

Lick was impressed.

"Wow," he said appreciatively. "You are amazing."

"Thanks, cowboy. You have somethin' to drink in here?"

"A little scotch do ya?"

"You're talkin' my language. . . . Join me?"

"Oh, I don't know. I gotta ride this afternoon and tonight. I better not," he explained.

"Honey, yer wound up tight as a hippo's girdle. You need to relax. That's what Cody had in mind. A little drink, a hot bath, a little harmless recreation."

"Well . . . yeah, sure. Yer right. Might be just the ticket."

He poured the drinks in the hotel glasses and gave her one. "Sorry, no ice," he apologized. They sipped.

"Let me help you get comfortable," Willa offered. She pulled his shirt off over his head. He put his arms around her waist and squeezed. "Careful," she said. "I'm precious."

A few steamy moments later Lick was in the bathtub. He was breathing heavily and felt light as a bag of jellyfish bones.

"Let me go get our drinks," Willa said.

He lay back in the tub and watched her magnificence depart.

She returned with their glasses. "Drink this and let me give you a scrub."

He downed the scotch in two gulps. Willa picked up his leg and started by soaping his foot, a toe at a time. Then she continued up the leg.

By the time she finished his second leg, he was in never-never land. The particulate count in his hemoatmosphere was registering "Don't go out today!" He was babbling incoherently and smiling when the phenobarbital she had stirred into his drink overloaded his circuits and blew the fuse in his brain! He remained at half-mast.

She put on her blouse and jacket. Then she dialed a hotel number. It was answered on the first ring.

"Hoi Sol? . . . Yeah . . . he's ready . . . Right . . . Bring the money," said Willa.

* * *

Cody kept scanning the contestants' area for Lick. The Saturday afternoon performance was already into the saddle bronc riding.

"Dang, Lilac. Where's he at! Maybe I should check the room again."

"You've already called three times," said Lilac. "Maybe he's visiting with someone. He doesn't have to ride for another hour, you said."

"Yeah, but it's not like him. I'm goin' down and look again."

"Whatever you think, Cody. I'll wait here."

Cody made his way down behind the bucking chutes. Manly Ott had reinjured his neck and been forced to turn his last four bulls out.

Manly was standing with the clowns, rigid in his neck brace. Cody approached.

"Manly."

"Hi, Cody."

"Have any of you seen Lick?"

"Since when? I saw 'im ride last night."

"I mean this afternoon. The last hour or two."

"Nope. Sure haven't."

"No?"

"Nope."

Cody walked all the way back to the hotel room. Lick's gear bag and bull rope were on the floor where he'd put them last night. His hat lay on the television.

His hat? thought Cody. *He must be in the hotel somewhere. Maybe shacked up, the crazy cockeyed lunatic! This is no time to be ruttin' and rubbin' his horns on the tree!*

He had the hotel operator page the restaurant, bar and lobby. No luck, no Lick. By the time he returned to the coliseum, the bull riding had begun. He sat down beside Lilac, agitated.

"Somethin's wrong. I know it. He'd never miss this. Not for all the tequila in Guadalajara!"

Smokey Brothers came out on a big Santa Gertrudis spinning bull. He made a beautiful ride and marked an 83, which would eventually split first in the eighth go-round.

Lennox Wildebang bucked off, and during Wyoming Montana's ride a strange thing happened: his bull rope broke! Just as the gate pulled open, the rope came loose in his hand! The bull threw him into the gatepost and knocked him unconscious. The ambulance had to cart him off.

Bull ropes don't break! Closer inspection by the judges revealed Montana's rope had been cut nearly in two where it was knotted to adjust for length. It was not cut enough to break when it was pulled up to seat the rider, but when the bull took a breath and flexed, it popped like a piece of cotton thread! The judges conferred and decided to say nothing about the insidious tampering unless an official protest was registered.

39

4:00 P.M., December 11
Oklahoma City, Oklahoma

By four o'clock Cody and Lilac were up in room 1225.

"We've got to do something!" Cody was furiously pacing.

"Sit down, Cody," said Lilac. "Let's figure this out." Cody sat on the bed. "All right," she continued, "now it has to be some emergency. How about a death in the family? Maybe he got suddenly ill or an accident?"

Cody jumped back up. "Right. He might have fallen and got amnesia. Or food poisoning. If it was his folks, he'd have left a note. Call the hospitals, see if they know anything. Call the police. He might'uv got in trouble. I'm goin' downstairs and see if the hotel help has seen 'im. I'll be back in an hour."

* * *

Lick opened his eyes. All he could see was white. There was a cloth over his face. He felt a pain in his shoulders. Trying to move his hands to pull the cloth off his face, he realized his arms were secured behind his back at the wrists and elbows. His ankles were also taped. When he moved, the bed he lay on moved!

Clearing his mind, he tried to recall: *Where am I? Oklahoma City. Daylight? Cody left to pick up Lilac at the airport. Room Service. Room Service! Willa Dean! Gorgeous. We made . . . no . . .*

we . . . I . . . took a bath. I musta dozed off. Willa Dean! He smiled. *She must be afraid I'm gonna try to escape!*

"Willa Dean," he called. "Come here, you Greek goddess!"

He heard footsteps. Footsteps on a rug? Someone placed a hand on his blanketed butt and pushed. His bed swayed back and forth! He was in a hammock!

"She couldn't make it," a thick male voice said beneath him.

Lick got goose bumps. The hair stood up on his neck.

"Who is it?" asked Lick, trying to hide his rising panic. *Probably just the boys makin' a joke,* he thought, embarrassed.

"Cody, are you there?" he asked seriously.

"Nobody here but us chickens," said the voice.

"Where am I?"

"With friends."

"Who are you?"

"Friends."

"Well, boys, you pulled a good one on me, but I've got a bull to ride about one-thirty." Lick laughed nervously.

"It's a quarter to five, little buckaroo. I think you missed your appointment."

"What!" Lick tried to sit up and the hammock moved jerkily beneath him.

"I'd be careful if I were you. You're six feet off the ground."

"What the hell are you doin'?"

"We're going to stay with you until tomorrow afternoon."

"But I'll miss my bulls."

"That's the idea, cowpoke."

"But why me?"

"Orders."

"Orders?"

"You need anything, you just call," the voice said pleasantly.

"I have a splittin' headache," Lick heard himself say.

"Good. It'll keep your mind busy." The footsteps left. Lick lay still, thinking. *Me? Why me? Why anybody? What for? Who?* His head was pounding. He quit thinking.

* * *

Cody rejoined Lilac in the hotel room. She recounted her fruitless telephone search.

"Nobody downstairs knows anything," he said.

"Let's add up what we know again," she suggested.

"Okay. He was here in bed at eleven this morning when I left to get you. He left his hat. Very unusual. That might mean he's still in the hotel if he left of his own free will. He took his boots, pants . . ." Cody looked around the room. Lick's pocketknife, change, wallet and Copenhagen can lay on the dresser. "He'd never leave without his Copenhagen! Much less his hat!"

"He might have forgotten them," Lilac offered.

"No way! He was carryin' his guardian angel around in his Copenhagen can! That was his good luck charm!"

"What do you mean?"

Cody tried to explain Pinto Calhoon, G.A., to Lilac.

"What! You don't believe that stuff, too?"

"I don't guess so. I've never seen him, but Lick believed. Enough so's I know he wouldn't go without his guardian angel!"

"I knew you said he was coyote, but I didn't know he was crazy!"

"He didn't leave of his own free will," Cody said, finally facing the truth.

"You mean somebody kidnapped him?" asked Lilac incredulously. "Why would anybody kidnap him? Does he have money?"

"Some, but not enough to hold for a ransom. Maybe it was one of the women."

"What women?" asked Lilac.

"He has had lots of lady friends and they don't always part on the best of terms."

"They'd kidnap him? Personally, I can't see that. Is there somebody else that would want to keep him from riding today? Even as a joke?"

"Keep him from riding today . . ." Cody repeated. Thinking out loud, he said, "If they were gonna keep him from riding today, they'd have to keep him from riding the rest of the Finals tonight and tomorrow, too."

"Why would anyone do that?"

"He's done real well in the Finals so far. He's won a first, a second, and a fourth in the go-rounds and is standing third in the money won. But more important, he's ridden six out of seven, now eight, bulls. Only three other bull riders have a good shot at the top money. The man that rides the most bulls and scores decent usually wins close to ten thousand dollars. Smokey rode today, so he's ridden seven out of eight, Lennox bucked off, so he's still six, and Wyoming Montana, the cowboy whose rope broke and was taken to the hospital, had ridden six." Cody began to pace up and down the room.

"Theoretically, somebody who'd ridden five bulls so far could ride his last three and finish with eight, but the odds are against it. These are tough bulls and the boys are gettin' worn down, beat up and tired." He paused a moment.

"Wonder why Wyoming's rope broke?" he said slowly. "I've never seen that before. He was in the runnin' for the average like Lick. He was behind the other three in total points, but he still had a good shot at it."

Lilac stared at him. "Cody . . . maybe somebody didn't want Wyoming to win. The same somebody who doesn't want Lick to win. Who'd benefit if they dropped out?"

"Smokey, Lennox and anybody else who had a shot at the average. But no cowboy would do that. They just wouldn't." Cody started pacing again. "Smokey's new, but he already has the overall buckle won and Lennox is straight as a Texas ranger. No, I can't believe any of the finalists would resort to . . . to foul play."

"Maybe Wyoming's rope was tampered with," said Lilac. "Both he and Lick were eliminated in what you might call unusual ways. Sounds like more than coincidence to me."

Cody just looked at her without speaking.

* * *

Cody and Lilac attended the Saturday night rodeo. They left a message on the desk that they were expecting an important call. Cody was tense and his concern infected Lilac.

Lick never showed. They watched the bull riding in pain. Wyoming was still in the hospital. Smokey and Lennox both bucked off.

* * *

10:30 P.M. Saturday night. The phone rang in the small motel room. Hoi Sol answered.

"Yes?

"Thanks.

"He's in the next room. He'd come to the phone, but he's, you might say . . . tied up!" Hoi Sol allowed himself to chuckle.

"Right, I'm going by during visiting hours tomorrow to make sure he's still out of the picture.

"Sure. We'll come see ya tomorrow night, midnight. Same place.

"You bet. All part of the service.

" 'Bye."

Thorhild lifted Lick out of the hammock and hopped him to the john for a whiz. They left him taped up and blindfolded. Lick was cramped, but his circulation was still good. They put him back in the hammock and tucked him in. He didn't sleep well.

* * *

Cody and Lilac went back to the hotel room.

"Cody, there's nothing we can do."

"He might call," Cody said hopefully.

She put a hand on his shoulder. He slumped.

"Go to sleep, cowboy. You need some rest. We'll start early and find him tomorrow."

"He's like a brother to me. I don't know what I'd do if something happened to him. He's always been there to help me. Now he needs me, I just know it, and I can't do a damn thing!" Cody felt as useless as a painting in a blind man's house.

"Close your eyes." Lilac turned him over and rubbed his neck until he finally relaxed and slept.

40

1:15 P.M., December 12
Oklahoma City, Oklahoma

"Four . . . three . . . two . . . one . . . cameras rolling!" The man with the earphones pointed at Will Yunk. Will had been World Champion Bull Rider and All Around Cowboy in his day. He used to wear Levis that buttoned up the fly. Later he wore Wranglers that faded after two washings. Now he wore name-brand designer jeans, his own name! He had an entire line of clothing with his name on it: boots, hats, vests, leather coats, fancy shirts and even Yunk Junk. Yunk Junk was costume jewelry for hats. It had become very popular with the straw hat/leisure suit group as well as Oklahoma truck drivers. Their hats jingled and shook like a Moroccan bride with a limp!

It was amazing to most of Yunk's friends that his clothing line showed artistic refinement. They had known him when he wore the same gaudy shirt ten days in a row and never wore socks. Putting an expensive, tasteful, well-fitted Western shirt on Will was equivalent to sprinkling croutons on a cow pie! But Mrs. Yunk, Will's wife, had a good eye for style. She dressed him and ran the business.

Will spoke into the microphone and addressed his taped television audience. "Welcome back to Rodeo TV Network," he drawled. Will turned to his co-anchor, Thermal Bind. "Thermal, the big story here at the Finals is shaping up in the bull riding. Going into this tenth and final go-round, Smokey Brothers has ridden seven of his nine bulls and has the highest dollars. Lennox Wildebang, having ridden six bulls, is second in total dollars, followed by two other cowboys who still have a chance."

"That's right, Yunk," said Thermal, taking the electronic baton. "But neither of them has ridden in the eighth or ninth go. If either of them or Lennox have a chance to win top money, they must ride their bull today and Smokey has to buck off. As you know, Wyoming was injured yesterday in a freak accident and is still in the hospital with a concussion. That leaves only Lennox and Lick with the possibility of catching Smokey. Lennox has drawn a good bull, but, according to our day sheet, Lick has made the worst possible draw of the finals. He's up on Bobby Monday's bull of the year, number ten-twenty, Kamikaze! The reason I say this is the worst draw is that this bull has never been ridden! I wonder if Lick even knows that he drew Kamikaze?

"But Yunk, all Smokey has to do is ride his bull today and he will likely take home the top money," wrapped up Thermal. "We wish all the bull riders the best. And now ... we'll be right back with the calf roping after this word from Hesston. . . ."

41

In the annals of sports history the losers disappear from memory as fast as lightning leaves the sky. Who lost the War of 1812? Who did Jesse Owens outrun in the 1936 Olympics? Quick, friends, name one Superbowl opponent of the '75, '76, '79 or '81 Pittsburgh Steelers. Matter of fact, who lost last year's Superbowl?

There are exceptions to the forgotten-loser rule, mainly those who are notable because their losing was so unexpected: the 1967 Baltimore Colts, Sonny Liston, and Tornado.

They are remembered in part because they were the dragons slain by Joe Namath, Cassius Clay and Freckles Brown.

Tornado was a bull that had bucked out over two hundred times and had never been ridden. Let me allow that to sink in. It would be the equivalent of a pitcher facing two hundred of the best hitters in the league, one after the other, and striking them out . . . every one.

Or the equivalent of Martina Navratilova winning two hundred games in a row. Not two hundred sets in a row, not two hundred matches in a row, two hundred games in a row.

I can't even spell my name right two hundred times in a row!

When Freckles Brown rode Tornado at the National Finals Rodeo in Oklahoma City in 1967, it was Charles Lindbergh, Admiral Perry and Saint George all rolled into one! It was the indelible rodeo moment.

Kamikaze is a figment of my imagination. Tornado is real. So if fiction imitates life we can imagine that if some lucky bull rider were to make a qualified ride on ol' 1020, that cowboy would have a place in fictional history. But Kamikaze would be remembered as well.

None of this was going through his bovine brain as Kamikaze stood in one of the stock pens that were a part of the OKC coliseum. Mount Everest doesn't leaf back through its scrapbook and reminisce about Sir Edmund and the Sherpas. Plymouth Rock doesn't dwell on its place in the brief human history of Massachusetts. It will be there long after the Kennedys have become Republicans.

Kamikaze, however, had a sense that this rodeo was different. It was his third trip to the National Finals here in Oklahoma City. He was familiar with the pens, the chutes, the arena, the crowd and the smell of the dirt.

During an unprecedented ceremonial exhibition he had been run into the darkened arena and spotlighted in front of the crowd. He was not pleased and stomped around swinging his head, holding it high, ears alert to stimuli. He could not understand the dramatic poem dedicated to him and his worthy adversaries. It was meaningless droning. This prerodeo entertainment was the idea of Wooley Boogin, known as the P. T. Barnum of rodeo producers. It was dramatic and pleased the crowd enormously.

To Kamikaze, all this hoopla was an irritation.

On this Sunday afternoon he was aware that he had not done anything yet. Other bulls came and went. He waited patiently. He would be ready if they called on him. No onerous premonitions disturbed him. He had become comfortable in his pen these last few days. He was not nervous.

He could see cowboy after cowboy walk or ride by, sometimes stopping and staring or pointing him out to others. They'd sit on the fence and watch him.

Like birds, he thought. *BOO! They'd flutter away.*

42

Sunday Morning, December 12
Oklahoma City, Oklahoma

Cody had been awake since 5:30 A.M., looking at the ceiling. He and Lilac ordered Room Service breakfast at 8:30. They ate in bed. They went over and over the possible reasons for Lick's disappearance. Exhausted, Lilac asked Cody about Pinto Calhoon. Cody explained again.

"You mean Lick thinks he lives in his Copenhagen can?" asked Lilac.

"Yup."

Lilac slid off the bed, her long nightgown flowing, and picked up the can. She opened it, sniffed the contents and made a face.

"He always taps the top before he opens it," said Cody.

"What do you mean?"

He took the can and did "shave and a haircut, two-bits" on the lid. He opened it.

The strong wave of men's cologne hit her delicate nasal passages.

"Polo!" she exclaimed.

"What?" said Cody.

"Polo's correct! How nice to be whiffed at!
Her olfactory sense is not to be sniffed at!"

Pinto's head and shoulders floated together like a jigsaw puzzle in a smoky room. They formed into his image and rippled.

"Pinto?" asked Cody.

"Pinto Calhoon, please hold the applause.
Guardian angel, but not without flaws."

"Why aren't you guardin' Lick? He's disappeared!" said Cody, obviously disturbed.

"Disappeared? Wiped out in his prime?
How did it happen? I've lost track of time."

"Yesterday morning. He's missed two go-rounds. He's got one bull left and a chance at the money this afternoon!" explained Cody. "I can't find him anywhere!"

"Spare me the anguish, the sentiment, too.
First things first, who the devil are you?"

"Cody. An' this here's Lilac."

Pinto raised a gnarled claw and tipped his hat.

"You're pretty as an Easter ham.
I'm surely pleased to meet'cha, ma'am!"

"Thank you," she whispered, staring.

"Pinto," implored Cody, "do you have any idea how we could find Lick? Any place for us to start? You were in the room, in yer can, when he left. He left his hat, his Copenhagen, his money, even you! We think maybe somebody kidnapped him to keep him from ridin' his last three bulls."

"Other angels, not unlike me,
Are guarding humans constantly.
Perchance another might recall,
So I'll put in a conference call."

Pinto whirlpooled clockwise back into the Copenhagen can like dirty bathwater down a drain. His voice came up from the well:

"If I'm expected to help him, kid,
Gimme a break and close the lid!"

Cody did.

"Conference call? Other guardian angels? I must be dreaming!" said Lilac.

"Do you believe in gravity?" asked Cody. "Evolution? Life on other planets, God, Santa Claus, electricity, ESP? That momentum equals mass times velocity?"

"What?"

"If you do, then it's not hard to believe in guardian angels."

Fifteen minutes ticked by. Cody tapped out Pinto's code. He reappeared, brushing Copenhagen crumbs off his shoulder.

"Did you find anything out?" asked Cody anxiously.

"A Russian ballerina great
Assigned to guard a Viking's fate
Said she might have seen ol' Lick
An' he's taped up and feelin' sick.
He's hangin' in a swingin' bed
With pillowcases on his head."

"Pinto! Did she say where Lick was?" cried Lilac.

"He's with the Viking, she knew that.
But not just sure where they are at.
Some motel that's not too neat.
McDonald's is across the street."

"Anything else?" asked Cody. Pinto shook his head. Cody capped the can and stuck it in his pocket.

"Git crackin', darlin'. We're gonna find our pard if we have to go to every McDonald's in town."

"How do we know he's even in Oklahoma City?" asked Lilac, pulling on her jeans.

"We don't. Grab the phone book."

* * *

There were twenty-eight McDonald's in Oklahoma City.

They drove to the first five. Each was teeming with teenagers like an adolescent anthill. None had "not too neat" motels across from them. It was 1:15.

"Cody, this is not gonna work," said Lilac. "Let's get a cab. The driver should know the town better."

They found a cab downtown. They explained what they were looking for. The cabbie knew of two places that fit the description. Off they went!

The first McDonald's was across the street from a used-car lot. The second one the cabbie took them to was off Fifty-fifth Street, a few blocks north of the zoo.

"That's gotta be it," said Lilac excitedly.

The sign said CHARLIE & DI'S MOTOR COURT. It was 1940s vintage white stucco with scrubby landscaping and a red dirt lawn. There were eight motel room doors numbered 5 through 26. Cody asked the cabdriver to wait and gave him a twenty-dollar bill. Rooms 7 and 18 had the curtains closed. Lilac explained her plan to Cody. He held her purse and coat.

She walked up to room 7 and knocked. An elderly woman answered.

"Towels?" asked Lilac.

"Powells?" said the woman, cupping her ears.

"Towels," Lilac enunciated.

"No Powells around here. They moved."

"No, towels!"

"Bowels?"

"Not bowels, towels!"

"Bowels moved, too. Friday afternoon. Wait a minute." The old lady turned and spoke to someone in the room behind her. "Elsie, there's a traveling laxative salesman here. You need anything?" She turned back to Lilac. "Guess not, honey, thanks anyway." She closed the door on Lilac.

Lilac walked down the row to number 18 and knocked. The veneer was peeling off the wooden door front. It opened and was filled top to bottom, side to side, with Viking!

He was a head taller than Lilac, which made him close to 6'8". As his mama would have said, "A big-boned boy." He was neither musclebound nor sloppy fat. He was clean-shaven with light blond hair that reached to his shoulders. His brow beetled over his light blue eyes. His nose cast its own shadow. He neither leaned nor bent in the doorway. He balanced on the doorjamb, a good portion of his size fourteen triple-E Redwing lace-up boots hanging outside. He wore generic blue jeans and a nondescript flannel shirt the size of a hay tarp. He was tieless.

Thorhild's forehead furrowed as he looked at Lilac.

"Towels?" Her voice sounded like Minnie Mouse.

His head rolled from side to side, like a half-ton wrecking ball.

"Thanks," she squeaked, and walked back toward the office. The door closed behind her.

She ran to the cab! "Cody! He's big as a house!"

"Who?"

"This giant man. He could be the Viking Pinto was talkin' about. What am I saying?" she asked herself in surprise.

"Viking? It's the right place, then! Pinto, you scarpacious ol' sidewinder, you were right!"

They went around behind the long building and peered in the back room window. They could see the hammock and the wrapped carcass through a part in the curtain.

"It's him!" said Cody.

"Is he dead?" asked Lilac anxiously.

"No," said Cody, squinting at the mummy.

"What are we going to do? Call the police?"

"I don't know. Probably should."

They walked around the end of the building. The Viking was walking across the red dirt toward the McDonald's on the other side of the street. A four-door AMC Concord was now parked in front of room 18.

"Come on," whispered Cody.

They ran to the room. The door was ajar. Cody pushed it back quietly and stepped in. He heard that universal sound that supports the flawed concept of biological male superiority. That audible splashing that demonstrates why the human male can remain vigilant even during peaceful moments. That ultimate display of evolutionary distinction between the *Homo sapiens* male protector and his female counterpart: the standing pee.

Cody opened the sharp blade of his Old Timer pocketknife and handed it to Lilac. He pointed to the bedroom and then his wrists. As Niagara Falls continued to resound in the background, Cody pointed to himself and toward his crotch. Lilac nodded to indicate she understood his hand gestures. Of course, had he done the same thing in a crowded restaurant she might have never spoken to him again.

Cody stealthily walked over to the bathroom door. Hoi Sol was unself-consciously tinkling his heart out. A cardigan sweater was draped neatly over the back of a tattered sofa.

That explains the AMC Concord, which wasn't parked there when we arrived, deduced Cody.

Before going into the bathroom, Hoi Sol had changed from the sweater into a forest green silk smoking jacket with maroon lapels and sash. It had been in the latest package from his mother. Knowing he might spend the day lounging about the motel room, he had dressed with the beautiful smoking jacket in mind. An ivory white silk shirt, gray wool slacks and silk tie in the same forest green with a maroon paisley pattern. He accessorized with matching Armani belt and slip-on loafers in cordovan.

Cody studied this well-dressed free-lance felon. He could see Hoi Sol's reflection in the mirror. Hoi Sol had his eyes closed and seemed to be meditating.

Cody put one foot into the bathroom, raised his arm and tapped Hoi Sol on the left shoulder. Hoi Sol turned his head sharply to the left. Cody reached over Hoi Sol's right shoulder and grabbed him by the designer tie! In one swift motion he jerked on the tie and stepped back out the door, pulling the hapless Hoi Sol in his direction.

With his left hand, Cody closed the bathroom door, slamming it on the tie! Cody hung on to the tail of the tie like a kite flyer in a high wind. He jerked and felt Hoi Sol's head smash into the door. The tie prevented the door from latching, which allowed Cody to repeat the gesture three times before his opponent had the chance to fight back.

"The tie! The tie!" came Hoi Sol's strangulated screams. "You schmuck! You'll fray the silk!"

Whack!

Cody had one hand on the door handle, a foot against the doorjamb and a fist full of tie. "Cut him loose!" he shouted to Lilac, who had disappeared into the bedroom.

She found Lick swinging in the hammock.

"What's that racket?" he asked, frightened. "Who's there?"

Lilac steadied the hammock.

"Lilac . . . and Cody," she whispered.

He swung his legs over carefully, expecting a long drop. He was only two feet off the floor. A cheap trick.

Lilac unwrapped his blanket. All he was wearing was a pillowcase and a pair of the Viking's Fruit of the Looms. She cut the nylon-reinforced wrapping tape between his legs, his elbows and his arms. He tried to pull the pillowcase off.

"Wait," said Lilac, "they've got it taped around your neck. I'll cut it if you sit still. I don't want to hurt you!"

Hoi Sol was swearing. "You backstabbin' . . ." Cody pulled: *Whap!* "Kicker . . . !" *Whap!* ". . . of crippled dogs! You made me ruin my good pants! Careful with the tie! Umph! You're a dead man when I git my hands on you!"

The bathroom captive was pulling hard to open the door. Cody suddenly released the handle. The door flew open twelve inches. Cody jerked back hard on the tie. The door's edge hit Hoi Sol on the right eyebrow with a crunching thud! "Yeow! You putz! Blood?" Hoi Sol's angry voice turned panic-stricken. "Blood? Oh, no! My new smoking jacket! Where's a towel?"

"Let's go, quick!" Cody shouted to Lilac.

Lick took the knife from Lilac, held the pillowcase up and cut the top off it like he was castrating a bull calf. The rest of the pillowcase dropped down around his neck.

She grabbed his arm and raced for the door.

"Co-de-e-e!" she screamed.

Cody slammed the door on Hoi Sol's tie and followed them out the door.

Thorhild was returning from McDonald's with an industrial-strength order of Big Macs and fries. He saw Lick and Lilac running toward the cab, though Lick was mincing in zigzag fashion on his bare feet. Lilac was urging him on. "The rodeo has already started but we still might get you back in time to ride your bull. Come on, Lick, hurry!"

The cabdriver spotted Lilac accompanied by a barebacked, bare-legged, barefooted spook in his underwear. They were headed his way. He had second thoughts about waiting. Suddenly his left-side rearview mirror was filled with the figure of a large person hurtling! On his mirror was printed the warning OBJECTS MAY APPEAR LARGER THAN LIFE. Not today, Charlie!

"Time to go," concluded the cabbie, shifting to D and stomping on the gas. Dirt and gravel kicked up behind, hitting Lilac.

Both she and Lick caught sight of Thorhild bearing down on them. "This way," she said. "Run!"

Cody ran out the door. He saw Lick and Lilac swerve away from the departing taxi and start up the side of the road. What he assumed to be "the large Viking" was in hot pursuit.

Cody heard the bathroom door open behind him and footsteps pounding across the linoleum. Cody accelerated, falling in behind Thorhild in the chase.

Hoi Sol paused in the doorway holding a towel against his right eye and under his neck in the vain attempt to protect his clothes. "Get the bull rider!" he shouted at Thorhild. "Forget the other two."

Hoi Sol reached back to close the motel door as he started for the AMC Concord. His sash caught in the doorjamb and when he stepped off the concrete step in front of the door he spun sideways. He hit the gravel on his back and rolled, scuffing his loafers, abrading his smoking jacket and ruining his day.

He climbed into the car and started it, still holding the towel to his face. He checked himself in the rearview and realized he'd forgotten his hat! He gently ran his unoccupied hand through his hair, palpating the bald spot. It was like Achilles feeling his heel. Hoi Sol's confidence ebbed slightly. He pulled out on the road.

The motel parking lot abutted an undeveloped area of thick woods. Cedar, oak brush, hickory and maple trees extended to the north along the highway. No sidewalk bordered the road but a wide gravel path meandered along between the curb and the edge of the woods.

It was along this leaf-strewn path that Lilac and Lick were kickin' up cinders as fast as they could! They were a hundred yards ahead of Thorhild.

Lilac was taller than Lick, with longer legs, but he was keeping up despite his handicap. He was barefooted and one hand clutched the elastic on the Viking's borrowed shorts.

Cody was ten yards behind Thorhild and gaining! Hoi Sol was pacing the whole bunch from the road. He was leaning out the window holding the white motel towel under his chin, shouting encouragement to his partner. "Run, Thor, get the one in your underwear! I'm gonna kill the one behind ya!"

Thorhild threw the McDonald's bag over his shoulder. Cody caught it on the fly!

He fished out a Big Mac and bounced it off the Viking's bare head! Special sauce and a dill pickle clung to his hair. Cody went over left tackle and drilled a strawberry shake just above the numbers! The Pepto-Bismol-pink sludge ran down the back of Thorhild's neck, but he remained oblivious to his assailant.

Cody darted in and out, rocketing the contents of the paper sack at the hurtling hulk like a sparrow harassing a hawk in flight!

Up ahead, Lilac and Lick had taken a fork in the path that veered down an embankment and into the woods.

Thorhild slid down the embankment. Cody reached the top just as Thorhild hit the bottom. Cody never slowed. He leaped toward the lumbering Viking, who tripped at precisely the wrong moment. Cody sailed over Thorhild's fallen body and skidded on the leaf-covered ground like a hockey puck!

Thorhild scrambled to his feet and accidently stepped on Cody's ankle as he rejoined the chase. "Sorry," he said. Cody grunted and scrambled after him.

A car door slammed out of sight, behind them! "Get the bull rider, Thor! I'm right behind ya!"

Not far up the path they could both see Lick and Lilac dropping over the other side of an eight-foot cyclone fence. Thorhild was four feet up the fence when Cody made another flying leap and got his arms around the Viking's neck. The giant never slowed his ascent.

"Look out, Cody!" shouted Lick, watching from the other side.

"Git goin'," Cody hollered. "It's you they're after!"

At the top, Thorhild hooked an arm over the wire, got a little leverage and elbowed Cody in the ribs.

Cody grunted and crashed to the ground on the top of Hoi Sol, who had just arrived and stood below trying to unfold his knife.

Hoi Sol howled. "You clumsy flatheaded bumbling clutz! Now you made me stab myself!"

Cody rolled off him and looked at the switchblade stuck in the meaty part of Hoi Sol's thigh. Blood was soaking into the Edinburgh fog-gray wool pantsleg his mother had hand-sewn just for him. Hoi Sol paused a moment, looking at the slacks. "They were wet anyway," he sighed.

"Yep. Sure were," agreed Cody.

Cody leaped up and scaled the fence! He dropped over and spotted the others running through the trees! He pursued! Hoi Sol pursued more slowly.

The KEEP OUT! NO TRESPASSING! sign went unseen and unheeded. That was unfortunate for the Oklahoma City Zoo.

43

Sunday Afternoon, December 12
Oklahoma City, Oklahoma

It was forty-eight degrees and sunny this fine Oklahoma Sunday afternoon. Strollers walked the wide concrete path in fall coats enjoying the zoo's ambience. It was a peaceful scene.

Imagine, if you will, a couple sitting on a bench soaking up the sun. Their two children are across the walkway feeding peanuts to their ancestors, the howlers. Pigeons coo nearby.

Suddenly there is a disturbance in the aviary! Bounding from the raptor section comes a Halloween hundred-yard dash! As the couple gape, five almost human figures fly by them!

Lilac was in the lead. With her long hair flowing and her graceful stride she looked sleek as a hood ornament. Lick was less than ten feet behind her, pounding the sidewalk with his bare feet! His punctured pillowcase was still taped around his neck and flutterin' in the slipstream. He held a handful of bunched-up elastic at his waist, which kept Thorhild's underwear modestly in place.

Lilac slowed enough for Lick to catch up. She spoke between breaths. "I don't know . . . uh, hu . . . where I'm . . . uh, hu . . . going . . . uh, hu . . . find a . . . uh, hu . . ." "No cop," puffed Lick, imagining the skeptical response their explanation would elicit.

"Ya see, Officer. I'm competing in the National Finals Rodeo. I'm one of the top fifteen professional bull riders in the country and I was kidnapped by these two gentlemen following me. Well, come to think of it, I think it's them. I've never actually seen their

faces. Anyway, the final rodeo performance is this afternoon and my friends here, Cody and Lilac, rescued me and we're on our way back to the rodeo grounds, if we can find it, that is.... Maybe you could help us catch a cab, 'cause I'm seriously running outta time, what time is it?... I'm late, I'm late...for a very important date.... See, I still have a chance to win the average, or I did before I was kidnapped, and I'd really like to ride my last bull, so that's what I'm doing here....

"No ... 'course not! I've never used drugs. I don't have time to take the test! Well, I don't know, a pillowcase, I guess. I don't know where the underwear came from ... a sumo wrestler, perhaps.... Look, Officer...

"We've ... uh, hu ... got to ... uh, hu ... find a way ... uh, hu ... outta here ..." continued Lilac. "You still ... uh, hu ... have a chance ... uh, hu ... to win it all!"

Lick looked over at Lilac as they ran side by side. The realization of what she said sunk in. His eyebrows shot up questioningly.

"That's right ... uh, hu ..." she said. "That's why ... uh, hu ... we've got ... uh, hu ... to hurry!"

The couple on the bench watched Lilac and Lick race down the broad sidewalk and disappear around the bend. They heard big slapping footsteps, jerked their heads back to the left, and watched Thorhild thunder by!

Cody followed, arms pumping furiously, knowing he must prevent this persistent Viking from knocking Lick out of the game. His friend Lick, who really had a chance to do what neither of them ever allowed themselves to think about: make history ... get in the record books ... a little bit of the "Big Time." Cody got a warm, fuzzy feeling and picked up speed. *Lick will make it,* he thought, *or I'll die trying!*

As the couple watched Cody tear off after the others, Hoi Sol limped by as if an afterthought. He presented an odd eyeful in his forest green smoking jacket, tattered bloodstained pants and thinning flyaway hair. Hoi Sol paused, cupped his hand and shouted down the empty sidewalk, "Git the bull rider!" He glanced over at the couple, who sat dumbfounded. Hoi Sol growled at them and took off in a sort of skipping gait.

The man on the bench turned to his wife. "Probably another celebrity ten-K. I heard about it on TV, I think." The wife nodded dutifully, knowing her husband was full of night soil.

Elsewhere, two security guards were communicating on their walkie-talkies. "I don't know, Harry. They were headed toward the ungulates!"

Lick had increased his lead on the Viking. He veered off the walkway and down a slope into a brush thicket. He crossed a trickling stream in high gear and climbed up the opposite slope. Another eight-foot cyclone fence blocked his path. He scaled it and started running across a big open pen of assorted lame and convalescing llama, roe buck, dik-dik, mule deer, eland, impala, bighorn and one blue gnu with a snotty nose!

I'll be durned, thought Lick. *I'm in the hospital pen!*

He looked back over his shoulder to see the Viking doubled over the top of the fence, his fingers locked in the wire. Cody and Lilac each had one of his legs and were pulling against the tide!

At the far side of the enclosure was an institutional-looking frame structure. Lick, panting heavily, entered through a loading door in the back. Several cloven-hoofed critters were in individual pens enduring various stages of illness or recovery. The building turned out to be the vet shack.

Lick was in the treatment room. Along the far wall ran a counter with bottles of medicine, boxes of pills and record sheets. Several 60-cc disposable syringes lay soaking in a blue solution. On a plywood wall behind him hung all manner of medieval treatment and restraining devices: sheep hooks, hog snares, coils of cotton rope, halters, twitches, lip chains and two nylon lariats.

Lick peeked back through the door. Somehow Thorhild and Hoi Sol had taken the lead and were running side by side across the enclosure headed for the vet shack. Lick thought he could see Cody still on top of the fence and Lilac below him.

Lick reached above his head and pulled down one of the lariats. It had farmer knots in it, but he managed to get the rope shook out and built a loop. On the far side of the wide entranceway was a fifty-five-gallon drum of propylene glycol. He threw his loop over the barrel. On the near side of the entrance was a six-inch steel post about four feet tall. It was sunk in the concrete floor. Lick flipped the standing part of the rope over the post. He let the rope slack to the ground across the entrance. Holding on to the tail of the rope, he stepped back about three body lengths from the trap. He was the bait.

Hoi Sol and Thorhild came sprinting through the door side by side. They saw Lick and never broke stride. As soon as the hunters appeared in the doorway, Lick squeezed the tail of the rope with both hands and jerked! His borrowed underwear dropped to his knees! The rope pulled taut at knee level. Hoi Sol and Thorhild hit the trip together and catapulted forward, arms outstretched, sliding into home plate! The force on the rope pulled over the fifty-five-gallon drum. It fell on the back of Hoi Sol's leg with a crunch! The plastic pump and spout broke off and the slippery, sticky contents gurgled out on Hoi Sol's pants.

"Great balls of flaming, sulfurous bat guano!" screamed Hoi Sol, resigned to buying new threads.

The Viking was single-mindedly clawing and crawling toward Lick's feet! Lick popped him on the head with the tail of the rope! Special sauce splattered! Lick pulled up his shorts and grabbed a halter off the wall!

The Viking looked up with determination in his eyes! He lunged for Lick's ankle! Just as he did, Cody broad jumped into the middle of Thorhild's back!

Hoi Sol looked up from his crocodilian position. He started to shout at his villainous cohort. "Get—" Before he could finish, Lilac cleared the barrel like an Olympic ice skater and mashed his face into a fresh pile of water buffalo droppings!

"Go! Go!" shouted Cody.

Lick went out through a door at the side of the animal hospital! He found himself in the surgery room. A door to his right opened onto a loading dock, a door to his left led down a small alley with individual animal pens bordering it. He went to his left. He passed two wildebeest and a whitetail doe with fawn. He read the treatment chart in its aluminum folder on the last pen:

NAME: Mohammed

SPECIES: Bactrian camel

COMPLAINT: Haematoma of the tail

RATION: Normal feed and water

Mohammed lay on his brisket, placidly chewing his cud. Lick opened the gate, eased up to the camel's head and buckled on the nylon halter. He took the tail of the lead rope and tied it back to the halter, making a rein. Pulling up his undies, he crawled on between the two humps.

"Giddyup, Mohammed!" Lick spurred the animal's flanks with his bare feet! Mohammed craned his neck around, belched and tried to bite Lick's knee!

"Cody!" Lick yelled. Cody appeared in the doorway. "Hold the door!" At that moment the Viking ran through it!

The sight of the furious warrior rushing down the alley finally inspired Mohammed to rock to his feet! Lick pounded on Mohammed's ribs! They trotted out the gate and sideswiped Thorhild, who lunged desperately and grabbed Mohammed's tail. Mohammed's tail had just been operated on yesterday morning. It was swollen and painful. Mohammed brayed and cow-kicked Thorhild in his progeny bank! The Viking paled and released the tail.

Lick astride Mohammed coursed through the door into the surgery room. Lilac was on the other side of the room holding the other outside door open.

Like the Ghost of Train Wrecks Past Hoi Sol staggered into the middle of the surgery room! He bolted around the table and threw himself in front of Mohammed, blocking his way. Mohammed stopped. Hoi Sol reached out his hand.

"Nice camel. . . . Good boy . . . ," whined Hoi Sol ingratiatingly. Mohammed spit a fetid lunger at Hoi Sol's pleading countenance! Then he gave forth a salivaceous razzberry, soaking Hoi Sol's wrinkled tie and shirtfront. Mohammed clamped his ruminant jaws down on Hoi Sol's outstretched fingers and shook vigorously. When the camel unceremoniously released his grip, Hoi Sol fell over backwards!

"Hang on!" yelled Cody! He touched Mohammed's rump with an electric stock prod! Camel and rider shot out the door, leaped off the loading dock and loped up the driveway!

"Harry, do you read me? One to two . . . Harry?"

"Go ahead, Joe."

"Some naked maniac is headed toward the front gate! He's on a camel!"

"I'll cut him off! Over."

Mohammed was running like Whirlaway when he reached the main entrance of the Oklahoma City Zoo!

"Stop! You can't leave here with that camel!" shouted the security guard as he watched Lawrence of Roswell, pillowcase flowing, loincloth billowing, clear the turnstile and a honeymoon couple from Tecumseh. Man and beast disappeared across the parking lot!

Lick took a left on Eastern Avenue. Mohammed had an easy rocking gait. They rode down the middle of the street in the fast lane. Mohammed had no fear of cars and ran every red light. At the intersection of Thirty-sixth and Eastern he took to the air like a steeplechaser and cleared a black 240Z. Lick and his steed made a wide turn and galloped two miles up Twenty-third Street, collecting a growing entourage along the way. When they swung into Broadway, against the traffic, the Channel 5 news team was set up and filming!

It was a mile and a half from Twenty-third Street to the Myriad Convention Center and the National Finals! The bank time & temperature sign said 3:21 P.M. It was 3:31 when they rode through the contestants' entrance and 3:40 when they pounded up the corridor that led to the arena.

Lick pulled back on the rein, to no avail! Mohammed took his head and picked up speed! Looking down to the end of the tunnel, Lick could see the arena and hear the crowd. The arena gate was closed.

"He-e-e-E-E-L-P!"

Lick could see two white eyes peering between the gate boards. The gate swung open with seconds to spare. He galloped into the arena!

A clown was doing his act in the arena with a dog and a monkey. The monkey was riding the dog around the coliseum floor. The announcer was narrating the act:

". . . And what's this?" the announcer fumbled when he saw the newcomers. He glanced at his script; no help. "A monkey on a camel?"

The camel and the dog loped side by side and both came to a halt in front of the clown. Snap Wilson, rodeo clown, looked up at the strange figure astride the camel. "Is that you, Lick?" he asked with wonder in his eyes!

"Yup."

"Where you been?"

"It's a long story. Am I too late?"

"No. No! The bull riding's next." The clown turned to the announcer and shouted, "Emerald . . . it's Lick!"

A cheer went up from the chute area. One of the pickup men rode out and Lick climbed up behind him in the saddle, simultaneously mooning sections F through M.

44

As Lick thundered down the tunnel on Mohammed, he passed his date. Kamikaze looked up, startled. Streaking from his right to his left came an odd sort of horse carrying a nearly naked white boy!

Kamikaze snorted in surprise and backed up a couple steps as the apparition raced on by.

What was that? he thought, aware that his pulse was pounding from the fright.

For a few fleeting seconds the big bull reflected on what he'd just seen. He was slightly offended that a horse had caught him off guard. In the swirling world of Kamikaze's prejudices, horses ranked beneath sheep. His logic was bovine clear: a horse's subjugation to a species as physically inept as humans only confirmed its stupidity. Plus the way horses constantly complained about everything from inadequate working conditions to poor circulation made them tiresome company.

Not to mention how dorky they looked! Goofy little single-toed hooves, big floppy lips and a head like a hornless rhino! And the specter that had just raced by him seconds ago was the dumbest-lookin' horse he had ever seen! He had ears like a pig, lips that could eat peanuts through a picket fence and he smelled like a burnt carpet!

But there was something familiar about the bare-skinned buckaroo in the big white wild rag. His scent was as unique as his mama's moo. A few of the cowboy's odiferous molecules lingered in the air. They were gathered up by inhalation and sent to the olfactory decoding section of Kamikaze's brain.

The red light of positive ID began to blink. Lick registered on the screen as: BULL RIDER . . . BUCKED OFF . . . TWICE . . . ESCAPED.

* * *

Just then Kamikaze heard the gates rattle and the next thing he knew he was being taken along with his pen mates to the arena. Standing single file with the other bulls in the narrow alley with six-foot sides, Kamikaze couldn't see much. He was aware of the scaffolding and lights on the roof of the coliseum. He could hear the big noise of the crowd. He could sense the tension. One by one the bulls worked their way into the chutes. Kamikaze stopped at chute number five.

As soon as the gate clanged behind him he smelled the bull rider that had given him the momentary distress back in the pen. Kamikaze had recovered from the embarrassment and had begun to resent the attack on his macho. The smell of that bull rider hit him like a gust off an estrus heifer!

He reacted instinctively, swinging his massive horns at the rider trying to loop the rope around his girth, banging back and forth in the tight box and bellowing!

Suddenly Kamikaze realized that he was losing his self-control. He stopped the chute fighting and stood still. He felt the bull rider lean over and feed the tail of his bull rope through the loop. Mixed with the molecules that identified him, Kamikaze smelled something else on the man . . . fear.

That's right, cowboy, telepathed Kamikaze, cool as a cucumber. *Yer dead meat.*

45

Afternoon, December 12
Oklahoma City, Oklahoma

Cody and Lilac paid the cab at the gate and hurried up one of the spectator tunnels. They stood in the portal entrance looking down at the arena floor. The bull riding had started.

"Oh, Cody, I hope he made it," said Lilac.

"Me, too, darlin'," said Cody. "If he didn't, it's too late now."

They watched Lennox Wildebang buck off one of T. Tommy Calhoot's best bulls, Velvet Whacker.

"There's Lick!" said Lilac. "By chute number five!"

Four more bull riders rode and then the announcer introduced Smokey. "And now from LeBec, California, presently leading in the World Standing and leading here at the National Finals, Smokey Brothers! He's drawn a Maid Brothers bull called Pecan Punch! Ladies and gentlemen, this ride may be for all the money!"

Lilac gripped Cody's hand. Smokey rode the full eight seconds.

"That's it," Lilac said dejectedly.

"I don't know," said Cody. "Looked like he slapped him to me!"

"A tough break," intoned the announcer. "The judges say he touched the bull with his free hand . . . an automatic disqualification. No score for Smokey Brothers." The crowd groaned.

"Our last bull rider has a chance to take the lead but he's got his work cut out for him. He has drawn a bull that has never been ridden! Number ten-twenty of Bobby Monday's string . . . a bull called Kamikaze!"

The whole coliseum grew silent as Emerald announced Lick in chute number five.

Will Yunk and Thermal Bind spoke in hushed tones in front of the Rodeo TV Network cameras.

"Ladies and gentlemen," said Thermal. "You could hear a pin drop in this huge auditorium. For some as yet unexplained reason Lick turned his last two bulls out. He arrived at the arena minutes ago on a . . . a *camel*!"

"A two-humped, double-toed, split-lipped, nonfiltered camel!" added Yunk in amazement!

"Both Lennox and Smokey failed to score today," continued Thermal, "leaving Lick the last chance at top money. He needs to ride this bull and score well. According to our statisticians, if he marks a seventy-nine or better he'll win the average. If not, he'll place third overall. . . ."

"Bare butt, stark nekkid, flag wavin', flyin' in on a fork-ed footed camel! Folks, you never seen nothin' like it!" crayoned Will Yunk, color commentator!

"However," Thermal broke in, glaring at his partner, "Lick is facing formidable odds. The bull he has drawn is the Buckin' Bull of the Year, unridden in four seasons, the one and only . . . Kamikaze!"

"Ride the sumbitch, Lick!" blurted Yunk, misplacing his professional objectivity. "Ride him till he'll pull a plow!"

* * *

Four rows up in a reserved box, two beefy characters puffed their cigars.

"Shootfahr, Jaybo. If he rides this bull it'll cost us a cool million!"

"How'd he git here anyways, Hoss?"

"On a camel, you moron!"

"Yeah, but . . ."

"Shootfahr! Wait'll I ketchup with Slyzack . . ."

* * *

Five miles away, two low-rent hoods were standing beside their rented AMC Concord. Hoi Sol threw a rock at the No Trespassing sign posted by the Oklahoma City Zoo. He was scraping at some nameless muck on his forest green silk smoking jacket with a flat stick.

"Peed on, hit by a door, stabbed with my own knife, run over by a barrel, stepped on, wallowed in wild animal droppings, bit and spit on by a camel . . . What a terrible day." Hoi Sol turned to the Viking. "You've got a pickle in your hair."

"Don't feel bad," offered Thorhild. "Could happen to anyone."

"Thanks, Thorhild. By the way, where are you from anyway?"

"Minneapolis."

"What's Thorhild mean?"

" 'Works construction.' "

* * *

Lick stood over Kamikaze in borrowed socks, borrowed boots, borrowed spurs, borrowed shirt, pants, chaps, glove and a borrowed hat. He burned borrowed rosin on the borrowed bull rope.

Kamikaze stood quietly. He felt the rope tighten around his girth and heard the cowbell jangle between his front legs. A light spot of weight settled on his back. He allowed it. More tightening and pulling of the rope followed. The loose strap around his flanks was adjusted. He switched his tail.

Lick slid up on his left hand. Kamikaze snorted. Lick dropped his legs down over each side. Kamikaze tensed.

Up in the stands, Cody fingered Lick's Copenhagen can. "Rub ol' Pinto for good luck," he said as he did it.

Lick cleared his head. The last twenty-four hours vanished. *Concentrate!* He looked at the back of Kamikaze's head. *The only way to ride you, pardner, is to be there when you make your move.*

Concentrate . . . the spiritual peace settled over the moment. Lick was ready. He nodded his head. The gate opened and the crowd roared!

Kamikaze propelled himself out of the chute . . . airborne! Before his front legs hit the ground, he whipped his tail end high in the air and landed with a thud, facing the chutes! Lick sunk his spurs into the bull's ribs! 1.000 seconds had elapsed.

Bull number 1020, king of the hill, top of the heap, tucked his head and whirled to the left, spinning so fast he looked like a roulette wheel! Lick's left spur was locked hard behind Kamikaze's elbow. Kamikaze set his hocks and skidded like a three-year-old colt at the Cutting Horse Classic! The Bucking Bull of the Year felt the cowboy's left heel slacken pressure. 3.090 seconds.

Kamikaze snapped his hindquarters straight out! His spinal column popped! It sounded like a switch engine taking slack out of a train of coal cars! He felt no pressure on either side from Lick's spurs. Kamikaze hopped forward like a deer and pulled Lick off his hand that was locked in a death grip to the bull rope. He kicked high with his hind legs! He felt the unwanted rider lift clear off his back! 4.900 seconds.

The instant the bull's feet hit the ground he felt the cowboy's seat hit his back and slide up under his hand. Two glinting steel rowels gouged at the thick skin on either side of his chest! Kamikaze bellowed in rage! 5.560 seconds.

The crowd surged to its feet hysterically cheering.

"We are witnessing a spectacular ride!" shouted Thermal Bind. The goose bumps came up from the back of Yunk's ankles and rolled in waves to the top of his scalp. "Stick it to 'im, Lick!"

The spectators watched the battle, captive to the adrenaline rush. That vicarious high physically lifted them out of their seats. A whirling, thrashing, bucking inferno churning up the arena dirt! The sight of such raw ability and naked will reduced each onlooker to his own primitive instincts. It was like watching an electrical motor operation out of control: sparks flying, the armature smelling like hot copper! Blue light! Shrill wailing! The crowd watched from the stands, secure in the fact that the action would never leave the arena floor.

Kamikaze hooked back with his two-foot horn and missed Lick's chin by an inch! Lick raked the bull again! Kamikaze spun tight to the right, pumping up and down! Lick was pounding his left heel into Kamikaze's side! Through gritted teeth Lick spat out, "Make yer move!" 6.250 seconds.

Kamikaze bucked out straight. Lick reared clear back and felt the small of his back come in contact with the broad smooth muscles of Kamikaze the cowboy killer! With silver flashing, chaps flying and knees pumping, Lick spurred the bull like a crazed bareback bronc rider!

Kamikaze ran headfirst into the arena gate beside the chutes! The crash could be heard in the cheapest seats in General Admission! Lumber and steel tore away with a sickening groan! Splinter and pieces of horn filled the air! The Bull of the Year spun back into the arena like a man-eating shark gliding into the shallow end! 7.150 seconds. Kamikaze was about to lose his cool!

46

December 12
Oklahoma City, Oklahoma

Kamikaze put every ounce of energy he had left into a last high wheeling buck. He sunfished and showed his cetacean underbelly to the announcer's stand. Lick stuck to the bull's back, his left arm supporting his whole weight! Bull and rider were parallel to the ground! The buzzer resounded in the arena: 8.000 seconds!

Lick bailed out in midair! Man and bull hit the ground simultaneously! Kamikaze was looking for Lick. Lick was looking for the exit. He raced for the chutes.

The big spotted bull charged after Lick, ignoring the bullfighting clowns bent on distracting him. Lick leaped for the top rail! Kamikaze caught him between his horns just as Lick made his jump! The force of the impact propelled Lick into one of the chute's vertical iron pipes, ten feet above the arena floor. Lick was madly scrambling over the chute gate! Kamikaze was trying to climb the gate after him! A gang of cowboys were pulling Lick over the back of the chute. He fell over the back boards headfirst.

Pandemonium reigned! The roaring and stomping crowd, including Emerald Dune, Will Yunk, Smokey Brothers and Bobby Monday, was making so much noise they woke up people in Tulsa! Once Kamikaze was safely out of the arena, the cowboys pushed Lick back out. He walked front and center and slowly took off his hat and tipped it.

All eyes were on the Winston Scoreboard. The numbers flashed. Lick had marked a ninety-seven!

Well, friends. He did it. Our hero did it. He moved the unmovable mountain. Wrote the unwritable song. Rode the unridable bull. A common man like the common man in all of us did the impossible. Do you think the crowd that watched those indescribable eight seconds didn't tear the roof off the stadium! I mean they shook the rafters and rattled the bedrock! They poured beer on each other and kissed their ex-husbands. Women fainted and cowboys cried. It was a moment in time frozen for posterity. They will tell the story of that eight-second ride the rest of their natural lives because they were there. "Yup," they'll say with a wistful smile and a faraway look, "you should'a been there."

Lick stood in the spotlight. He made no effort to collect his thoughts or memorize what was happening to him. He was capable only of absorbing the adulation of the crowd. He opened every sensate door in his body. The rapture of the crowd, their open admiration, their respect and affection rolled into his hungry soul in waves. It seeped into his marrow. It penetrated the recesses of his rusty feelings so long unused. It tore out brittle walls built over years of bitter heartache and slogging ambition. He filled to overflowing.

The clamor began to fade. Lick remained standing center stage long past his cue to depart. The crowd became quiet. Cody vaulted into the arena from the grandstand seats. He walked up to Lick, hand out, like he was approaching a spooky colt.

"You all right, Lick?"

Lick was staring at the far end of the big coliseum with unfocused eyes. Tears ran down his cheeks. Cody shivered. He put his arm around Lick. "C'mon, pardner." They walked side by side out of the arena.

* * *

Kamikaze stood in the pen with several other bulls. A big beefy brindle Braymer sidled by and cracked horns with him. Kamikaze backed up a step. They knew. Something had changed. He sensed there would be new nominations for the peckin' order soon.

He saw two cowboys stop and look through the boards at him.

One of them registered immediately! *Bull rider . . . bucked off . . . twice . . . rode . . . once . . . escaped . . . two out of three.*

Kamikaze gave a quick glance at the brindle bull, pawed the ground twice and charged the fence! Cody and Lick fell back as dirt pelted them! Kamikaze stood staring unblinkingly at Lick. He could smell that the fear was still there.

Big shot! He bored his brain waves into Lick. *With fences and ropes and clowns and spurs and horses. But you and I know you won't set foot in here. Brave rabbit. Go back to your hole and tell your stories. Maybe you will look strong in the company of cottontails.*

He swung back from the fence and walked toward the feed bunk. The brindle bull stepped back. Not far enough. Kamikaze swung a horn into his shoulder. Brindle backed clear to the corner of the pen!

Kamikaze looked over his shoulder toward Lick, who stayed back a safe distance from the fence. The other bulls stood watching quietly.

He swung his massive head around, awaiting any challenge. Seeing none, Kamikaze walked to the hayrack.

* * *

Lick's victory was not without cost. He had separated his collarbone from his shoulder when Kamikaze slam-dunked him into the pipes above the bucking chute. The ambulance delivered him to the hospital.

Lick returned to the party in progress, arm in a sling, with the stern admonition from the doctor not to eat or drink anything after 6:00 P.M. His surgery was scheduled the following morning at 8:00 A.M. Lick got knee walkin', blood pukin', commode huggin' drunk!

He spent the night with a woman who wanted to show him her tattoo. He passed out before he got it uncovered!

Cody and Lilac partied until midnight and retired to room 1225. They crawled under the covers, sharing each other's warmth.

"Do you think Lick will ever change?" she asked Cody.

"Whattya mean?"

"Get married and settle down?"

"Stranger things have happened."

"Gosh, that was disgusting the way he drank tequila out of that girl's shoe." She laughed.

"Yeah, disgusting!" Cody agreed. He started laughing, too.

"I can't imagine any woman putting up with him for long. I'm glad you're not like that!"

" 'Settle down' is the key phrase here. He's not ready. Till a person's ready to settle down, they'd make a sorry mate. But Lilac, don't ever worry 'bout ol' Lickity. Worryin' about him is like worryin' about the weather.

"He may never amount to much by some folks' standards, but he's the kind of man who'll be there for ya when the chips are down. Wherever the ragged ol' coyote winds up, he'll always have me to help him, if I can."

"You love him, don't you?" she asked.

"Lilac, there's only one person outside my family that I love more than him. That's you."

Silence slid between them, separating their thoughts. Finally Lilac spoke.

"Cody, would you propose to me again?"

Cody sat up. "What! When?"

"Now."

"Lilac, would you marry me?"

"Cowboy . . . this is your lucky day!"

47

So there you have it. A simple story of two cowboys chasin' a dream. I added a little violence in the form of action, a little intrigue in the form of plot and a little sex in the form of love. That's all part of writin' a book.

But it should be easy to tell that I am a real rodeo fan. As a past participant and as an appreciative spectator. But mostly I enjoy rodeo and the real-life cowboy life-style that it imitates because of the people and the animals who live in it.

When it's all said and done this book is about two of those people and how they take care of each other.

Friend is a word . . .

that I don't throw around
Though it's used and abused, I still like the sound.
I save it for people who've done right by me
And I know I can count on if ever need be.

Some of my friends drive big limousines
Own ranches and banks and visit with queens.
And some of my friends are up to their neck
In overdue notes and can't write a check.

They're singers or ropers or writers of prose
And others, God bless 'em, can't blow their own nose!
I guess bein' friends don't have nothin' to do
With talent or money or knowin' who's who.

It's a comf'terbul feelin' when you don't have to care
'Bout choosin' your words or bein' quite fair
'Cause friends'll just listen and let go on by
Those words you don't mean and not bat an eye.

It makes a friend happy to see your success.
They're proud of yer good side and forgive all the rest
And that ain't so easy, all of the time
Sometimes I get crazy and seem to go blind!

Yer friends just might have to take you on home
Or remind you sometime that you're not alone.
Or ever so gently pull you back to the ground
When you think you can fly with no one around.

A hug or a shake, whichever seems right
Is the high point of givin', I'll tell ya tonight,
All worldly riches and tributes of men
Can't hold a candle to the worth of a friend.

JUNIOR

Now, Junior is tough and can't git enough
of lively confrontations
And bein' his friend, I'm asked to defend
his slight miscalculations.

Among his mistakes, too often he makes
none of his business . . . his.
So I counsel restraint 'cause sometimes he ain't
as tough as he thinks *he is!*

Like the time he cut loose in a bar called the Moose
in Dillon on rodeo night.
I stayed on his tail in hopes to prevail
and maybe prevent us a fight

But Junior's headstrong and it didn't take long
'til he got in a debate
Involving a chair and big hunks of hair
and startin' to obligate

His friends, I could see, which only was me!
A fact I couldn't ignore,
So takin' his arm to lead him from harm
I drug my pal to the door.

No one disagreed and I thought that we'd
made our escape free and clear
But he turned to the crowd and said good and loud,
"Who is the toughest guy here!"

Not the smartest remark in a place this dark,
ol' Junior had gone too far!
No one said a word but I knew they heard
'cause all heads turned to the bar

And there in the hole like a power pole
stood the pressure for all his peers.
"Ugly for Hire" and he wore a truck tire
that came down over his ears!

He had on some chaps with big rubber straps
but over his arms instead!
And sported a pattern like the planet Saturn
his eyebrows went clear round his head!

His good eye glared while his nostrils flared
like a winded Lippizan
Which lent him the air of a wounded bear
whose pointer'd been stepped upon!

A Crescent wrench swung from where it hung
on a log chain wrapped round his neck,
Along with a claw, a circular saw
and parts from a Harley wreck!

With his Sumo girt he needed no shirt.
Hell, he had no place to tuck it!
And wonders don't cease, he wore a codpiece
made from a backhoe bucket!

He was Fantasyland, the Marlboro Man
and heartburn all rolled into one!
From where I was lookin' our goose was cookin',
our cowboys days were done!

Then he spoke from the hole like a thunder roll
that came from under the sea,
He swallered his snuff . . . said, "If yer huntin' tough,
I reckon that'ud be me."

I heard a pin drop. The clock even stopped!
Silence . . . 'cept for me heavin'.
But Junior, instead, just pointed and said,
"You! Take over, we're leavin'!"